A LIFE LESS
Beautiful

ELLE BROOKS

A Life Less Beautiful
Copyright © 2017 by Elle Brooks

A Life Less Beautiful \ Elle Brooks – 1st ed.
ISBN-13: 978-0-9929888-9-0

"Accept the things to which fate binds you, and love the people with whom fate brings you together, but do so with all your heart."

— MARCUS AURELIUS

PROLOGUE

PRESENT DAY

My chest feels so tight it hurts. It would be a cruel twist of fate to drop dead of a heart attack at this point, but I absolutely believe it could happen. All of this would be for nothing, and Christ, that scares me. My hands are trembling so hard I need to place the pen back down onto the nightstand and take a long deep breath.

You can do this—you have to.

I press the heel of my hands into my eyes. I don't want to cry, so I push hard, so hard that for a moment it hurts more than the ache in my chest. I doubt what I'm about to do will take the sting out of the tears I'm trying to make disappear or loosen the vice wrapped around my heart. I can hope, though. The pen is an unexpected deadweight in my grip when I pick it up and press it to the paper once more.

This is it.

The beginning of the end...

Dear Harlow,

Being in love with you hurts. It's the sweetest form of torture, but it's torture all the same. You consume my every thought, every moment, and every breath. I can't recall a time when I didn't love you. What did I even think about before you took over my mind? What do you suppose I had done with my hands before they were able to pull you close? When I close my eyes, it's your face imprinted on my eyelids, and it's your voice I hear, even in silence. I'm an ordinary man, but I love you with a brilliance beyond anyone's understanding. It scares me.

I realized today, or maybe I've always known, I can't live without you, Harlow. I sustain myself with your affections, and that's why it needs to be you who must live without me. You'll hate me at first; I can accept that because I know that when enough time has passed, you'll realize it had to be this way. I can't see any other path, I've exhausted all avenues, and when I weigh the pros and cons, the answer is glaringly obvious: I have to be the one to do this for you.

You've had my heart since I was ten years old—you have it still. I gave it freely without any agenda, only a fierce hope that you'd one day give me yours in return, and you did. I don't pretend to know why, but you did. I can't even begin to express how terrified it made me feel—and how powerful—that you loved me back. I know the extent of the love I've given you, but it worries me that I'll never truly know what **you** received— does that even make sense? I'm wracking my brain, trying to figure out if I told you enough what you mean to me, what you've always meant to me even when we were apart, because you deserve to be reminded every day.

Every.

Single.

Day.

And more than that, you deserve to be shown. I hope you saw it, I hope you felt it, but above anything else, I pray you never forget it.

Goodbye for now. I love you.

Ellis

I drop the pen and fold the letter, stuffing it deep into the envelope as quickly as possible— the weight of what I've written makes my throat burn.

I don't want to do this, but I have no choice.

My head feels too heavy for my neck to support; I rake my fingers wearily through my hair, lean back on the cheap plastic motel chair and let out a frustrated blood-curdling scream. It bounces around the room, echoing off one grubby laminate surface to another. Streams of light tear through the shadows as the ceiling pendant swings from the occupants next door banging loudly on the paper-thin walls. The din of their television rises as I hear it being turned up—no doubt to drown me out. I could be murdering someone in here for all they know, and they ignore it, annoyed by the interruption in whatever drivel they're watching. Pay-per-view porn, if this motel is anything to go by.

I have to laugh a little—not because any of this is funny, it's not. But the irony of the situation causes a strangled moan, half disguised as maniacal laughter, to hiccup out of my mouth. I am about to murder someone in this motel room.

Me.

"Wherever you go,
go with all your heart."

— CONFUCIUS

CHAPTER

ONE

Love Hurts

Harlow

I lean over the edge of the balcony and peer down at the garden below. I'd take a moment to enjoy the cool Wilmington wind against my flushed face if I could breathe. For a solid minute my vision swims as I struggle to suck in enough air to keep from passing out. The sound of my pulse rushing in my ears begins to ebb as everything starts to calm and I thank my lucky stars. Soft strains of music slowly drift free and steal the silence I rushed up here to find, as the patio doors beneath me open. I can hear fractured snippets of people regaling fond stories of Mrs. Adkins. I move slowly backward into the shadows and watch as *he* steps out onto the deck, running his hands through his hair. I should take the opportunity to leave while he's out here, but I can't seem to make my legs work.

I watch as he links his hands behind his neck and stares out at the sky. My heart rate begins to accelerate again when I remember idly how I used to love running my hands through his messy blonde locks. He looks exactly the same and yet somehow completely different. The natural, infectious energy that used to surround him has disappeared, but I guess prison will do that to you. The boy I last laid eyes on has long disappeared, but the man that's taken his place bears all the resemblances to my first love.

I wish I'd known he was going to be here—I could have avoided him. I'm not ready to see him, and as he stands looking out into the night, I can't pull my eyes away. I've practiced every day for ten years what I would do in this situation. I'd ask him why he didn't come clean. Why he lied. Why he shut me out and ruined what was left of my already broken heart. I was positive I'd be able to deliver it spurred on by anger alone. I was wrong. I assumed I'd be furious, but now that it's actually happening I'm not.

The floorboard creaks when I jerk as a cold shiver races to the base of my spine. I quickly step behind the curtain, worried he might have heard me jump, but when I peer out he hasn't moved a muscle. My body temperature suddenly feels as though it's dipped to ten below zero and I'm trembling, despite the mild night. He's so still it doesn't look like he's breathing. I can't see his face; I should at least thank the universe for that small mercy. I shiver violently again and fold my arms tightly under my chest, trying to get a hold of myself. The sight of him has knocked out the little air I'd managed to suck in clear from my lungs, and my body's decided to betray me yet again. I shouldn't be surprised; it's nothing new. I'm trembling uncontrollably now, and I try to relax and take some deep breaths like I'm supposed to. I've seen people shake violently with anger before, but I know that's not what this is. This isn't rage or hatred—it's an acute realization.

I've missed him. I've missed the one person in this world I should hate.

1990

You're not supposed to find your soul mate until you're a respectable adult. Or at least until you're done with college hook-ups, and are ready to settle down and choose a partner based on compatibility and a mutual appreciation for the same things in life. Not based on how hot they look in a hockey uniform, and certainly not when you're still a pre-pubescent ten-year-old.

Little girls should be obsessing about ponies, jumping rope and prancing around the house in fairy wings, plastered inch-deep in glittery makeup and wearing their mother's heels. Much to my parent's dismay, I was far too preoccupied with trying to keep up with my brothers to act like your average ten-year-old. I didn't play with dolls, and I despised anything even remotely girly.

I grew up in a house filled with so much testosterone it's a wonder I didn't choke to death on it. With two older brothers, our three-year age gap had me idolizing the twins from the moment I could walk. Jared and Jake were superheroes in my mind. Wherever they were, and whatever they were doing, that's where I wanted to be. My mom mourned the daughter she hoped I would be. All ideas of shopping trips and makeovers were quashed at an early age when all I wanted to do was play paint-ball, roughhouse, and climb trees.

There wasn't a single photograph in our home where I wasn't sporting some injury, be it scraped knees or a broken arm. If my brothers could do it, well then, I could too. That was my motto growing up. The boys loved how much I idolized them, and in real big brother form, used it to their advantage. I was ba-sically their slave: when they said jump, I'd ask how high. I didn't mind; honestly, I didn't—not in the slightest. I'd do any-thing they asked if it meant they'd let me join them. As soon as they worked that out, their twosome became a trio.

I didn't really have any girlfriends; I wasn't quite sure how to properly relate. Two girls my age lived on our street: Molly and Sarah. We were in the same grade at school, and while they were nice enough, we didn't play together. They had no desire to make skateboard ramps and throw themselves off the rope swing over Mr. Anderson's pond. I had zero interest in painting my nails, or whatever it was they did to occupy their time. All my friends were boys older than me who were friends with Jared and Jake first.

Except one.

Ellis Hughes and I were the exact same age; our birthdays were on the same day. He'd moved in next door with his folks after Mrs. Anderson died, and Mr. Anderson had to go to an old persons' home. I'd always liked Mr. Anderson; he'd let us play in his backyard for as long as I could remember, and he was the one who helped my brothers build the rope swing out back, along with my dad. Mrs. Anderson would watch us like hawks whenever we'd play there, often saying we'd be the death of her, swinging out from the big knotted old oak that hung over their pond. We were all good swimmers, but she'd insist that if there weren't an adult to watch over us, then we weren't to go near the water. We honored her rules—most of the time.

Ellis was my first real friend rather than a buddy by association. He dismissed me at first sight, of course. He wanted to make friends with my brothers until I shot him in the knee with Jared's BB gun. That got his attention. I was grounded for two weeks and not allowed to leave my room from the moment the school bus dropped me home. It was the longest fortnight of my life.

Jake had ratted me out to my mom the second I'd pulled the trigger. It wasn't premeditated, and I certainly wasn't aiming to shoot Ellis. The boys and I had been taking turns shooting cans from the back fence when he'd rounded the corner, asking if he could join in. It was the first time I'd really gotten a good look at the new kid that had moved in next door. I'd seen the back of him as he'd been walking towards his house talking to Jake. I had tried to say hello, but he'd only given me a half glance, immediately dismissing me as he carried on walking after my big brother.

I swung around to see who the unfamiliar voice belonged to. The sun was glinting off his golden-blond hair, and he was beautiful. I'd never thought a boy beautiful before, and it caught me off guard. The BB gun was still in my hand, my finger gently squeezing the trigger. I wasn't thinking about what I was doing, my mind was too preoccupied with Ellis standing twenty feet away looking directly at me. Staring at him felt like trying to look at the sun. I shuddered, his gaze had made my tummy feel funny, and then BANG!

His even regard morphed instantly into a furious scowl before the pain registered and his eyes scrunched up tight. He dropped to the floor hugging his knee to his chest and screaming, "YOU SHOT ME!"

My brain took a little while to catch up with the events I was witnessing. I dropped the BB gun on the grass in front of me like a hot coal. Realizing I was the one who'd shot him sent my pulse skyrocketing, and I quickly looked around frantically, waiting for someone to signal what we should do. Jared busted out laughing, I burst into a fit of panicked tears, and Jake ran to the kitchen door shouting at the top of his lungs to my mom that I'd shot the next-door neighbor.

It wasn't all as bad as it sounds. As it happened, I hadn't even broken his skin, just caused an angry purple welt to appear.

"Harlow Marie Stevens, what on God's green earth have you done?" The shrill sound of Mom's flustered voice reached me from the back stoop. She raced past me, her eyes fixed on the strikingly attractive boy writhing in pain by the fence. After Mom had tended to him, she marched me around to his house by the collar of my shirt. My mother—Dianne Stevens—was a tall, lithe woman with delicate features and a kind face, but when she was mad it always amazed me that she didn't Hulk out, turning green and growing an extra ten feet. She was terrifying.

"Harlow is here to apologize to you," she began as Ellis's mom opened their front door. Ellis didn't say a word; he slipped in quietly behind his mom with what I was starting to suspect was an exaggerated limp. She was an equally stunning blonde and was proving to be an excellent human shield between her son and me. It was easy to see where his good looks were spawned. Ellis and his mom looked like an airbrushed advertisement for good healthy American living, and I was genuinely surprised I didn't hear a ping when Mrs. Hughes opened the door and flashed us her pearly whites.

From the two minutes I'd known him, I was sure Ellis hated me already. And for reasons I didn't quite understand, it bothered me a whole lot more than I cared to admit. My face burned with the heat of his eyes searing a hole into my cheeks as he studied me astutely. I was doing my absolute best to not look him in the eye. I was embarrassed, and I knew my face was blotchy from crying, I most likely resembled a panda bear.

It took a lot to make me cry, mainly because I knew that once I started, there was no hiding it. My eyes would be red, and my lids swollen and puffy for at least an hour. I was supposed to be one of the boys, and they almost never cried—especially not in front of strangers. They'd have a field day teasing me once I got home. I was normally much better at dampening down my emotions; growing up with two older brothers it was kind of necessary—you should never show weakness. I learned that lesson young.

Ellis's mom looked slightly mortified that the sweet little girl with strawberry blonde pigtails from next door had shot her only son, and mildly relieved once I'd clarified it was only a BB gun. From the way her eyes swelled to the size of saucers I could tell she saw me as the shotgun-wielding hillbilly I most likely resembled. I was wearing my blue and purple plaid shirt, and grass-stained shorts, which did little to cover my muddy knees. I'd pulled my old red rain boots on in haste when Mom began to drag me over here. As first impressions go, I probably wasn't making a good one.

Still, Mrs. Hughes seemed to appreciate my apology, and even invited our family around for dinner to get to know us. It was most definitely not the reaction I'd expected on the hundred-meter walk over there. That walk had felt more like a mile, my stomach twisting in guilt-ridden knots with each hurried step. My mom promised they'd set a date and said she'd bring a pie before hurrying me off their porch and ordering me home. I'm not sure if it was the circumstances or my appearance that embarrassed her more, but she chattered on about "a fine way to make a first impression with our new neighbors" all the way home. When I glanced back to the Hughes' porch I caught sight of Ellis watching us leave, a small smile playing at the corner of his mouth. I assumed it was because he could hear me being scolded; it wouldn't be until much later that I'd find out that wasn't the case.

That was the day I met my best friend, and it was many more years before I realized it was also the day I had stumbled upon my soul mate. Some people describe finding love akin to being shot through the heart with Cupid's arrow. Ellis Hughes was shot in the knee by a skinny almost eleven-year-old wielding a BB gun—but I'd decided it was pretty much the same thing. Falling in love is *supposed* to hurt; otherwise, it wouldn't be called falling.

"Love sought is good, but given unsought, is better."

— William Shakespeare

CHAPTER TWO

Welcome to Crazy Town

Ellis

She's here. I know because there's a definite shift in the mood of the room as my foot falls over the threshold. I knew it was wrong of me to come, but I couldn't make myself stay away. I want to see her, even if it's only for a minute. I've convinced myself I'll be able to leave after that. All I need is closure; I won't approach her or attempt to talk to her. I just want to see that she's happy—that I made the right decision to let go. Maybe then I can.

"As I live and breathe, Ellis Hughes. I didn't expect to see you here, son."

"Hello Mr. Adkins, I'm so sorry for your loss," I answer the old man. "I was always very fond of Mrs. Adkins, I don't think the town will feel the same without her cheery face behind the counter at the general store."

"Well, that's nice of you to say, Ellis. I happen to know Jeannie was fond of you too. She was very upset, when…well, you know. She was so sure she'd be dusting off her hat one day, ready to watch you marry Harlow."

I swallow hard, because once upon a time that was my fate. Apparently, a decade isn't long enough for the pain in my chest to subside when hearing her name. I haven't responded, I realize, and sufficient time's elapsed with me standing here like a mute for it to be considered awkward. Floods of memories are washing over me, playing through my mind on a torturous bittersweet loop—I'm completely paralyzed.

"Well, excuse me, Ellis. I have to do the rounds and make sure I've talked with everyone. Jeannie will no doubt haunt me if I don't," Mr. Adkins says, letting out a sad laugh and patting me on the shoulder, pulling me back into the present. He steps around me to accept the next person passing over his front stoop and I shake my shoulders out and make my way further into the room.

Half of the town is crammed into the downstairs of the Adkins' house. There are people huddled in every nook and corner chatting idly as they sip their drinks and reminisce about Mrs. Adkins' life. I make my way through to the kitchen to get myself a drink. God knows I need one. People greet me as I pass; their expressions confirm I'm the last person they expected to see. Nobody mentions whether or not Harlow is here, but I don't miss the way they acknowledge me and then immediately scan the room as if looking for her. I glance at the stairs leading upstairs from the kitchen just in time to see a slim pair of milky, smooth legs under a thin black skirt in a pair of beat-up chucks disappear skyward.

My skin literally prickles in recognition. I haven't even seen her face, but my body has gone into an adrenaline overdrive. I'm pretty sure I can hear my own pulse, and I want so badly to race up the stairs after her but I don't. Obviously, I don't. No matter what else I am I'm not an asshole. I have no right to ambush her at a friend's wake. Against every instinct within me to follow her, I turn on my heel and march out of the patio doors to get some much-needed air. I haven't even seen her fully, but it doesn't stop the ache in my chest or the guilt in my stomach from unfurling. Memories I've spent years burying are resurfacing faster than I can blink them away. One glimpse is all it's taken. One glimpse and I feel like I'm about to pass out.

1990

My knee ached more than I let on as I sulked at the kitchen table, moving mashed potatoes from one side of my plate to the other. I'd have to remember to tell Logan about being shot. He didn't need to know it was a BB gun, or by a girl. It would sound way cooler if I left those parts out. I would write him a letter as soon as I was allowed to leave the table unless the new phone was working. Mom had said a line was being installed, but I wasn't sure if it had yet.

I'd been out exploring the neighborhood, trying to gage what was what, when the crazy girl next door tried to kill me. I noticed Jared and Jake in their backyard, shooting at old cans. It looked like fun. Logan had a BB gun, and I knew I was a good shot. I figured they'd like me when they saw how accurate I was.

Logan's grandpa had a farm back in Montana, and he'd taught us how to shoot straight—well, me anyway. Logan couldn't hit a fifty-foot standing target if it were two feet in front of him. Didn't stop him from practicing, of course. He'd been my best friend for as long as I could remember, and our mothers had been friends since they were little girls, too. We spent almost every holiday with the Smith family. My mom seemed as miserable about leaving them behind for Dad's new job as I was.

I didn't see Harlow at first; the twins shielded her. Jake had said hello to me a couple of times and told me he was an identical twin, but he failed to mention he had a kid sister that looked about my age. It was only when I called out, and she turned and pointed the gun right at me that I noticed her. She was definitely their sister; much smaller than her brothers, but the likeness was unmistakable, if not a little creepy—like maybe their parents cloned them?

I'd been frozen to the spot, waiting for her to lower the gun; everyone knows you don't point a loaded weapon at someone, right? I wondered for a moment why she was staring at me funny. Her eyes were scrunched up as though I'd asked her a really hard question, and she was having trouble figuring out the answer. She was kind of pretty, I suppose. She wasn't dressed particularly nicely, and her hair reminded me of the straw Logan's grandpa kept in the barn for the horses. It was tied up with pieces jutting out in all directions.

I decided in that split second I'd try making friends with her. Something about her seemed familiar, either her pale skin with its smattering of freckles, or the fact that she'd forced me to think of my best friend.

Then she shot me.

Did I mention she was crazy?

"If you're finished playing with your food, empty your plate and hand it over please, Ellis," Mom ordered.

I quickly pushed my chair back and hurried over to the trash, scraping away the remnants of my dinner. I had zero appetite when my mom had called me to the table. My tummy felt queasy, and the welt on my knee was throbbing. "It's probably just the shock," Mom had said. "You'll feel better once you've eaten."

I hadn't felt better. I felt the same as I had when I'd been looking over at Harlow as she apologized at the door. She cried the moment I'd fallen over in pain. I don't know if it was because she realized she was about to get into trouble, or because she genuinely didn't mean to shoot me. Either way, as she stood on my porch wringing her hands together talking to my mom, I couldn't take my eyes off her. I felt sick that I'd made her cry. Her eyes were red, and her cheeks had turned splotchy. That's twisted, right? She was the one who was supposed to feel guilty, not me.

"Mom, can I call Logan?" I asked.

She took the empty plate from my hands and placed it in the sink.

"Go ahead, I meant to call Kathryn and give her the new number. Let me have the phone when you're done with him, though. I want to speak to his mama."

I was in the hall looking for the telephone before she even finished speaking.

I yelled back, "Yeah," but had no clue what I'd agreed to. I heard her mumble something else but was too distracted; I just wanted to talk to my best friend.

Stretching my injured knee out in front of me, I pulled my other to my chin and settled on the third step of the staircase, cradling the telephone to my ear. It was just like I used to do at home, except that wasn't my home anymore—this was The Cape in Wilmington, North Carolina.

I missed Montana; it was different here, and even the air smelled strange—like salt. The sound of seagulls had woken me every morning, and as soon as my hearing tuned into their cries I couldn't ignore them, no matter how hard I tried—or how badly I wanted to stay asleep.

The churning in my stomach intensified when I thought of what Dad had promised me: it would be an adventure, and I'd love living so close to the beach. I'd been down to the pier a couple of times on my bike. The water was wild and harsh, not at all what I'd expected. The pier and harbor were dotted with bait shops, cafés and those tourist-type shacks that my mom loved— the ones that sold postcards, sea glass wind chimes, and shell necklaces. Everyone seemed to wear polos and khaki shorts. I didn't fit in. I looked like a tourist, and I didn't like it—it felt weird.

Maybe it had been homesickness that got me all worked up. When Logan finally answered I started to relax and feel like myself again. Normal.

"So, your next-door-neighbor shot you—but you're okay?" he scoffed in disbelief at my version of accounts.

"That's what I said, isn't it?"

"And you didn't need to go to the hospital?"

I could tell my story was falling apart at the seams; he'd always been the type to badger me until he had all the details.

"No, it was a BB gun pellet. Didn't break the skin. I'm tough," I told him. The line went quiet for a beat, and then Logan's laughter boomed from the receiver so loud I needed to move it away from my ear.

"Dude, I thought you meant you were shot! Like for real!"

"It *was* real, jackass. It still hurts, she got me good."

"Wait, what?"

The second he paused I realized my mistake. "I said it still hurts."

I hoped he'd drop it, but Logan wasn't the type to drop anything.

"I heard that, but the other part. Did you get shot by a *girl*?"

18

The smile in his voice was unmistakable. I could picture the wide goofy grin on his fair, freckled face, his red eyebrows rising up to meet his hairline.

"Yeah, but—"

"Man, this just keeps getting better. It's gone from you being almost killed in a shootout in your neighbor's yard, to you being capped in the knee with a BB gun by a girl! Ha, this is so awesome!"

"Yeah, yeah laugh it up. I shouldn't have even told you," I said, grinning. There's no way I wouldn't have spoken to him about it. He probably knew all there was to know about me better than I knew myself.

"Was she an older chick? Because that would at least make it sound badass."

I laughed out loud at that, and gave the sore spot on my knee a rub. I wished the conversation were face-to-face; it had only been a week since the move, and I missed Logan and his sense of humor.

"I think we're about the same age. She doesn't look too girly, though. She wasn't dressed anything like how your sister does. Oh, and she has older brothers—twins. They seem cool."

"Too bad she's not pretty. It makes for a better story when the people are good looking," he said matter-of-factly, and it made my skin prickle.

"I never said she wasn't pretty," I told him defensively.

"But you said—"

"I said she wasn't dressed girly. Harlow's pretty all right, but completely mental, too—you can't just go around shooting people!"

He began to laugh again, and Mom interrupted, telling me to wind it up and pass her the phone.

"Got to go, Logan. My mom wants to speak to yours. I'll catch you later?"

"Sure. Bye, Ellis."

I passed my mom the phone and headed up the remaining stairs to my room. I limped a little, not because it hurt, but because I knew my mom had been watching and I liked to milk situations. If I kept it up, ice cream could be in the cards.

Back home in Montana I had a view of the mountains from my bedroom window. My view from the Wilmington house looked out over the Stevens' property. It was almost identical to ours, only their house was painted light blue and ours was white-washed.

I'd been staring at the empty window across from my own when Harlow appeared. I needed to narrow my eyes and strain so I could see a little better as I watched her move back and forth, in and out of view. I waited for a while before I saw her suddenly standing right there, staring back at me. It was awkward, but kind of a good awkward. She looked confused that I was watching her and didn't have the decency to at least look away once she caught me.

"Hi," I mouthed, raising my hand in a small wave. Her eyes looked as though they'd narrowed to slits, and I could just about see her back straighten. Before I could even drop my hand, she stuck out her tongue and pulled her curtains closed, leaving me standing open-mouthed like an idiot.

I remember being confused as all hell, wondering why she was mad at me.

I dropped down onto my bed and folded my arms behind my head deciding I was right about her.

She was crazy.

The stubborn window interactions with Harlow carried on throughout the week. I wasn't sure why she'd taken such a dislike to me, but it was pretty evident that for whatever reason, I wasn't her favorite person. I found myself spending an inordinate amount of time in my room, hoping to catch a glimpse of her and wondering if today were the day she'd finally relent and wave back.

Up to that point I'd been on the receiving end of two complete dismissals, two instances of her sticking her tongue out at me, and an especially memorable moment when I actually thought she was about to concede and return my wave. That was until she flashed me the sourest smile I'd ever witnessed, flipped me the bird and drew her curtains.

It seemed the more I waved at her, the angrier she became. I should have ignored her rudeness, but it bugged me that she appeared so unwilling to try and be friends. We were neighbors and by the next week we'd be classmates too. I'd already forgiven her for her lousy shot. The bruise on my knee didn't hurt for very long, a couple of days at most; the only evidence of the event was a faded yellowing mark. Mom always said that I took after my father in that I was, and guess I still am, a people pleaser. I like to be liked, and the fact that Harlow seemed to loathe me without reason was beyond maddening to me.

I'd seen her brothers by the pier the day before when I finally got tired of staring at the same four walls in my bedroom. I had jumped on my bike and ended up buying a waffle cone stuffed with mint ice cream from the quirky-looking wooden shack by the water. I noticed Jared and Jake inside eating burgers with two other guys, and I leaned my bike against the weathered post boasting a huge metal sign reading "Bait House Tackle & Tavern" that moaned and creaked in the steady breeze.

I fished out the remains of my allowance from the depths of my cargo shorts pocket. I'd worn them to fit in and not look like such an outsider, although I'd foregone the obligatory polo everyone seemed to wear for a faded O'Neil hoody. The kids in town had a preppy vibe about them and being from Big Sky, my skater-boy clothes screamed, "he's not from around here."

I couldn't tell the twins apart, and the one I thought was Jake called me over to their table. I hesitated for a moment. I wanted to go over there but wondered if they had the same problem with me that their sister seemingly had. I couldn't consciously remember anything that I could have done to offend them.

"How's the leg?" Jake asked around a mouthful of fries.

Jared smiled and then leaned into the other two guys sitting at the table.

"Ellis here's the guy Peewee nailed with the BB gun," he said laughing.

I snickered to myself, betting she just loved that name. "It's good now, thanks. All forgotten," I answered. I didn't want them to think I was holding some sort of grudge against their little sister.

"Oh, it's not forgotten in our house," Jake guffawed. "Harlow's still grounded for another couple of days, and damn do we all know about it. She's moping around the house like a bear with a sore head."

I winced. I genuinely felt sorry that she was still being punished. "Is that why she's in such a bad mood?" I asked.

The twins' heads snapped in unison back to me.

"How would you know if she's in a bad—?" Jared asked suspiciously.

Jake interrupted him. "Has she been sneaking out?"

I could feel the heat rise in my cheeks, knowing I'd have to admit that I'd been watching her through my bedroom window. Even though I knew it was innocent, I was still aware of how bad it would sound to her older brothers.

"She flipped me off through the window," I offered, hoping they wouldn't want me to elaborate further.

The slightly chubby black-haired guy sitting to my right had snorted into his soda, causing it to fizz up in his face as the table erupted with laughter.

"Nice, Blake," the other boy with them had grinned.

"You should come hang out with us later," Jake offered. "We're gonna go home and watch horror movies all afternoon."

And just like that, my mood lifted. I'd been invited into their home, the same home that Harlow was holed up in and wasn't allowed to leave. She'd have no choice but to acknowledge me. That was my in.

"A woman knows the face
of the man she loves
as a sailor knows
the open sea."

— Honore de Balzac

CHAPTER

THREE

Murky Waters

Harlow

I could leave now. Hold my head high, walk down the stairs and straight out of this house. I've paid my respects, shown my face. Nobody would think it impertinent—I doubt they'd say anything even if they did. The way Ellis's white shirt is stretched taught over his shoulders is clouding my judgment about the *sensible* thing to do in this situation. I'm ashamed to be checking him out, even if it is only from the back. Internal struggles aside—I kind of hate that he looks so good. His navy suit pants fall perfectly from his narrow hips, and it pisses me off. Where does he get off looking like an extra from a GQ shoot at a damn wake?

I rushed upstairs the second I'd heard his voice. I knew it immediately, like somehow he'd been whispering to me in my sleep, subconsciously making sure I'd never lose the memory of his timbre. I didn't wait for confirmation that my mind wasn't playing tricks—I bolted. Now I'm paying the price. Like every ditsy female character in all of the horror films we used to watch as kids, I ran upstairs to escape danger. It's ironic that Ellis and I used to laugh and shout at my mom's TV that the dumb busty blonde should run for the door, not the stairs. It never crossed my mind that one day I'd do the same—or that I'd be running from him.

1990

"Why'd you bring *him* here?" I'd asked. Trying to inflict a hissing tone while whispering was surprisingly challenging and useless, it seemed, because Jake didn't pick up on the irritation in my voice—or he did and chose to ignore it.

"He's come to watch a movie with us," he answered, patting my head as he maneuvered himself around me and into the family room.

Older brothers can be both a blessing and a curse. On the one hand, you know they'll always have your back when it matters; on the other, they like to torture you.

Ellis was standing in the doorway watching me. He was pretty perceptive, picking up on my mood—unlike my moronic brother—and he had the audacity to look like he was enjoying it. Jared called out from the kitchen, and Jake thrust the movie at me before patting me on the head again, even though he knew how much I hated it. I didn't like feeling belittled, and every time he did it I wanted to scream, but my brothers thrived on getting a rise out of me. If I showed him how much I actually hated being patted like an obedient pet, they'd do it twice as often.

"Set it up, Peewee. I'll go see what he's shouting at," he said, passing me on his way out of the room.

Ellis moved out of the doorway to let him by and then strolled up beside me as I knelt waiting for the VCR to buzz to life.

"Have I done something to upset you?"

His breath tickled my ear as he leaned in close, waiting for my reply. I couldn't turn my head to look at him; he was too close, and it made my tummy want to flip. Have you ever noticed that if you get too close to a cat, their hair stands on end? That's the effect Ellis was having on me.

"You know what you did," I hissed, and he took a welcome step backward.

"Um, no, actually I don't. I called round to see your brothers, and you shot me. I don't think I've missed anything, so I don't get how I'm supposed to know what it is I've done. You're gonna need to be more precise."

He tucked his hands loosely into the front of his hoodie as he shifted from side to side. I noticed he wasn't smiling anymore; he looked a little confused, worried even.

"You were laughing at me," I relented. "I was upset and trying to apologize, and you were standing on your porch, smirking at me while my mom was scolding me, I don't—"

"No, I wasn't!" he shouted over me with a hefty amount of indignation.

"Sure you were. I saw the way you were watching me as we left. And the smug little waves you keep doing every time I look out my window. It's not nice to tease someone when they're grounded. Especially when it's all over a mistake. I didn't try to shoot you, ya know! Although, now I kinda wish I had."

I shoved the cassette into the VCR and stood, finally turning to face him properly. He was gaping at me like I was some kind of crazy person. It bugged me. The couch groaned as I threw myself down and then scurried as far over to the corner as I could.

"Movie's in, guys!" I shouted to my brothers.

"I wasn't laughing at you, I swear," he murmured.

I looked up from the television to see Ellis moving to come sit by me.

"I was pissed that you shot me for about two minutes before I realized it'd made you cry," he said with a shrug. "I actually feel kinda sorry for you."

I didn't know how to respond. I couldn't tell if he was lying. It didn't seem like he was, but then I didn't know anything about him. I'd always been pretty easygoing—I liked making new friends, and I'd never been as cold toward someone as I was acting towards Ellis. My parents raised us better than I was behaving and I swallowed the realization like a bitter pill. Ellis was new in town, and all I'd done up to this point was be mean.

"What's with all the smirking then?" I bit out, angry with myself more than him.

"I don't understand. I'm not trying to... It's, it's just my face!"

When Ellis Hughes grinned, he was magnetic; he pulled you in with an invisible force. I was powerless not to mirror it. "Well, you should maybe work on that."

"Work on my face? How am I supposed to do that?" he asked.

When I didn't answer, he sat back, making himself comfy. I liked boundaries, but he didn't seem to respect personal space at all. He positioned himself only inches away from me, even though there were five other seats he could have chosen—each with more room.

"Tell you what, Peewee—"

"Don't call me that!" I cautioned.

"Fine, sorry. Tell you what, Harlow," he said widening his eyes as he exaggerated my name. "Why don't we start over? I'll pretend that you didn't almost kill me, and maybe you can try and act like you don't hate me already."

"I—"

"Hi, I'm Ellis Hughes, and I just moved in next door. I'm from Montana, I don't know anyone here, and I could use a friend."

He held his hand out for me to shake and was smiling so wide it almost looked menacing. I swatted it away before my brothers walked in.

"You're weird," I told him. "But I guess we can start over. I'm Harlow Stevens, and I've lived in this house my whole life. I'll be eleven on July 4th, and I'm in 5th grade. Jared and Jake are three years older than me, and they won't think twice about kicking your ass if I ask them to."

"Wow, okay. Please don't ask them to. The 4th is my birthday too, how awesome is that? We're the exact same age, I guess that means we might be in the same class at school—I start Monday."

"Harlow, you let the movie start!" Jared interrupted, barreling into the room and dropping down opposite us, depositing a huge bowl of popcorn on the coffee table.

"I've got it," Jake told him, dropping two sodas between Ellis and me, snatching up the remote and pressing to rewind.

"What are we watching, anyway?" asked Ellis.

"*IT*," Jake replied. "Horrors are Harlow's favorite."

The sofa bounced as Ellis bolted forwards. "What!" We all watched his eyes widen, bugging right out of his head. Ellis turned, giving me a skeptical look. "How is this is your favorite movie? Don't your parents mind you watching it?"

The twins busted out laughing at the panic in Ellis's voice.

"They don't mind. I watch what the boys watch. Why? You're not scared, are ya?" I teased.

He looked over at the twins and then squared his shoulders and leaned back. "Course not."

"Good." I smiled. "Jake, press play."

I have to admit the film wasn't on for very long before it began weirding me out. I don't think I've ever been able to look at a clown without shuddering since. However, I did better than Ellis. He watched most of the film from behind one of my mom's scatter cushions. Even Jake looked a little freaked out, although he'd rather die than admit that he'd been scared.

Jared disappeared, and I assumed he went to go refill the popcorn, but he'd been gone way longer than it took to walk to the kitchen. I was trying not to squirm as I watched the demented Pennywise terrify some poor boy when I noticed a flash of color pass behind me. Then all hell broke loose at the sight of the clown screaming from behind the sofa. Jake shrieked, scaring the living hell out of Ellis and me, and we jumped from our seats in a frenzy. The clown grabbed my arm and Ellis yanked me free, pushing me behind him before punching the frizzy green-haired fiend in the throat. Only it wasn't a murdering, psychopathic, killer clown that he'd hit. It was my idiot brother—now gasping for breath and slumped over the coffee table, wheezing.

A few flustered seconds went by before we realized what had just happened and cracked up with laughter. Jared didn't seem to be smiling, but it served the moron right for trying to frighten us. Jake couldn't stop chuckling that Ellis had throat-punched him, and I'd been too busy trying to not hyperventilate to do anything other than watch the scene unfold.

"You alright?" Ellis finally asked me. The soda that was resting beside him had spilled all over his pants.

"Better than Jared."

My brother was still rubbing at his neck and coughing as though he were about to spit up a lung.

"Thank you for saving me," I told him as I smiled sheepishly. I may not have been in any real danger, but it would be a lie if I said I wasn't at least a little impressed that Ellis had tried to protect me.

And just like that, we became best friends.

Weeks turned into months and months into years. Each year that passed our friendship grew stronger.

"They're as thick as thieves," I'd hear my mom tell her friend Jade as they'd sit sipping coffee at the kitchen table. Ellis was my saving grace; as the twins neared the end of high school, they spent more and more time hanging out with girls their own age rather than entertaining their little sis. If I hadn't had Ellis's friendship, the day they both left for college would have been beyond devastating. Not having them around the house had felt as though I'd lost a limb, but I could always count on Ellis to soften the blow.

Until the summer of 1994, that is—that's when things began to change.

The pond water felt like acid in my eyes, mixing with the mascara I'd stolen from my mother's room. Each time I blinked it burned to holy hell, and of course, that only made me blink more. It was an unforgiving and torturous cycle I couldn't seem to break. Treading water while trying to rub your eyes is surprisingly more complicated than you would first imagine, like rubbing your tummy while patting your head. Not impossible by any means, just strangely confusing.

A welcomed second of respite gave me a momentary glimpse of my hands—streaked watery black with the stupid mascara. I panicked, thinking *if my hands look this grubby I shudder to think what my face looks like.* I took a deep breath and let the cold water rush over my head as I held still, letting myself sink. The instant I was completely submerged, I began frantically rubbing my eyes, hoping to wash away the evidence of my insecurity.

This was all Molly Parker's fault. I was sure of it as I'd broken through the surface again, taking a huge gulp of air. In reality, it wasn't her fault at all, but it made me feel a little better apportioning at least some of the blame on her. If anything, she was actually completely innocent, and my predicament was my own doing.

Admitting that stung almost as much as my eyes had. Molly, with her stupidly shiny glossed lips and long lashes. She'd mocked me unknowingly with her perfectly poker-straight hair and a distinct lack of any freckles. Who did she think she was, being all perfect like that? I'd never paid her much attention; appearances were something that I'd never given any mind to until I overheard Elliott and Ellis talking about her.

Elliott Roberts was in our homeroom at school, and friends with Ellis. They were in a few classes together, and although he would sometimes hang out with us, I hardly knew him. We'd been skating in the board park when I happened upon Elliott describing what he thought of Molly, and for reasons I didn't want to admit to myself, instead of rolling on by, I hovered behind them listening for Ellis's response. What he thought of me had never been an issue, but unexpectedly, what he thought of another girl had me more than a little curious.

My stomach tightened as I held my breath waiting, straining to hear what they were saying.

"She's pretty, I guess," Ellis said.

Elliott scoffed, "You *guess?* Ellis, she's the best-looking girl in our year—look at her."

"I am," he shrugged.

"Check out her eyes; it's like she undresses you when she's looking at you, the way they're all smoky and stuff."

He fake shuddered in delight, and my head had immediately whipped over to where Molly was standing, talking with a group of girls. It moved right on back to the boys when Elliott added, "And look at her boobs, they're huge."

He was right with that: for a fourteen-year-old, Molly looked much older than her years. Everything about her was more advanced. She was taller than most other girls our age and had hips that swayed when she walked. I quickly scanned my own chest, realizing that I looked every bit the fourteen-year-old that I was.

"Yeah," Ellis agreed, smiling. His voice had been laced with appreciation, and it made the blood boil in my veins, and my back stiffen.

The idiot actually sighed, and that did it. The shock of him checking out a girl's boobs made my shoulders sag, and my foot slipped off my board. If I'd been loitering at the bottom of the ramp eavesdropping, it wouldn't have been an issue. My foot would have found purchase on the concrete, and I'd have had enough time to straighten my features, act a little less affected by what I'd just heard. But, I wasn't at the bottom of the ramp—I was at the top.

My foot slipped, and all that greeted it was air; standing so close to the edge was not a well-thought-out plan. My body lurched sideways, the board flipped, and suddenly I was weightless.

Films will sometimes slow down a fight or crash sequence, letting you take in all the elements around what's happening, elements you'd no doubt have missed in real time. Falling backward was like that. It was as though someone had pressed "slow"

on a remote, letting me take in what was happening in fine, ago-
nizingly embarrassing high-definition detail.

I gasped. Ellis and Elliott's heads turned sluggishly, their
smiles slipping as their mouths formed O's, their eyes widening.
The crash of my board echoed against the ramp, the sun shone in
my eyes, and Ellis moved forward shouting my name. Once my
butt hit the smooth, curved ramp surface life flicked the "fast"
button. The skate park became a blur of blue sky streaked with
gray concrete and blonde wood, as I pin-wheeled my way to the
bottom.

I came to a stop with a painful thud.

When I was sure I could open my eyes without tears escaping, I took a deep breath and looked up. The whistles, cheers,
and sounds of laughter from the guys mixed together and hung
heavy in the air while someone shouted, "Did you see Stevens
wipe out? Epic!"

I rolled to my side, trying to catch my breath as Ellis skid-
ded down onto his knees beside me, moving my shoulder back to
see my face.

"Damn, are you alright?" His eyes darted from left to right
as he scanned my whole body, head to toe, and then back up
again.

I groaned out a "Yeah," before sitting up gingerly. Physically, I'd been a little winded and was sure I'd have some pretty
impressive bruises by the next day; nevertheless, I was okay.
Emotionally? I felt like I was dying of both embarrassment from
what I'd overheard, and humiliation from taking a fall while sta-
tionary. I was certain my cheeks were colored with an uncon-
cealed, mortified heat.

"Seriously, you didn't fall so good…you sure you're alright?"

I wanted to cry, and I didn't think it was from the fall. He
was staring right at me, his hair falling into his eyes and I had to
look away to lie.

"Totally fine, just embarrassed," I squeaked, standing up and dusting off my butt. I was not fine, not even close. But he looked pleased with my answer, the concern in his eyes shifting to humor and a small smile tugged at the corner of his mouth.

"Harlow, you fall like a girl," he laughed and raised his fist for me to bump.

I didn't leave him hanging; in fact, I punched my fist into his with way more aggression than necessary. Not that he noticed.

"I *am* a girl!" I huffed, and it was probably the first time in my life that I'd actually acknowledged it. I looked over to Molly and then bent to collect my board with a strange feeling of jealousy uncurling in my veins.

The next morning I pulled on my jean shorts, spent twice as long brushing through my crazy hair before tying it back in the sleekest ponytail I could manage, and raided my mom's dresser. I painted a ton of black mascara onto my blonde lashes and then applied a slick of soft pink lip gloss, then scrubbed it from my lips when Jake walked past the room and gave me a wide-eyed gawp that had me second guessing what I was doing. I'd left the mascara on, though, and I secretly quite liked how it framed my eyes and made them look twice as big. That was a stupid mistake.

"What's wrong with your face?" Jared laughed as he swam over to me and out of the drop zone. Ellis took a leap; the branches moaned as the rope swung high above us, and he fell into the spot Jared vacated. I looked back to my brother, whose eyes were narrowed and peering diligently at my own.

"Are you wearing makeup, little sis?" he smiled, teasingly.

"Does it look bad?" I asked swiping my fingers under my lids. No matter how much I wiped, they came away covered in black—I didn't get it.

"Why the hell are you wearing makeup to swim in the pond? There's only us and... Wait, are you trying to impress someone?" He beamed at me, and then I was embarrassed on top of being partially blind.

"Don't be stupid!" I shrieked. "There's only you two morons," I quipped, tipping my head in Jake's direction, "and Ellis. I was just trying it out."

"Riiight," he said. "You're way too young to be wearing that stuff, and you don't even need it."

I missed my brothers like crazy while they were at college. Sure, they'd only moved an hour away and came back most weekends for Mom to do their laundry, but it wasn't the same without them at home. I had Ellis, but increasingly I hadn't wanted to tell him the things that were going on with me. I didn't have a problem confiding in the twins, but Ellis was different suddenly.

He'd grown much taller than me, and he wasn't the skinny ten-year-old I'd first met. His chest and shoulders were getting much bigger. When he walked out in his swim shorts, I didn't know where to look—he had abs! How had I not known that he had abs? And when his eyes flicked fleetingly to my chest in my bikini, my whole body set on fire.

It was all I could do to run and leap in the pond as fast as I could. He'd never looked at my boobs before; or if he had, it certainly wasn't with any kind of appreciation. I told myself I was silly; he was my best friend, and he fancied Molly. I was probably just imagining things.

The late afternoon sun was glinting off the surface of the water, and between the glare and my makeup fail it was becoming increasingly hard to see.

"What are you guys talking about?" Ellis asked swimming towards us. The water made his gold hair look almost brown; only he could look good doused in murky pond water.

"My sister wearing makeup to swim," Jared answered him. Jake swam up from behind and before I had a chance to move, my head was being pushed under the water. I broke the surface a moment later spluttering and ready to wage war on him.

"It's a good look for her, don't you think, guys? You can see less of her face when it's covered in that black gunk," Jake sniggered.

I watched in amusement as Ellis cupped his hands and thrust a giant surge of water over his head. Jared seized the opportunity to lurch forward and dunk him, saving me the hassle.

"Don't listen to him, Harlow," Jared huffed, trying to hold Jake's head under as he flailed his arms out wildly, splashing us all in the process.

"He's right, you don't need makeup, H, and I like being able to see your face." Ellis reached out and wiped under my eyes, catching me off guard. It was an innocent gesture; he'd touched my face and hair a million times before, but this time felt weird. It was different.

"Are you two having a moment?" Jake tormented me with the question as he escaped his assault. Jared quickly halted Ellis's attempts at dunking my brother further, pinning him with what I assumed was a warning glare.

I'd never witnessed Ellis move so fast; the sudden jerk of his retreat caused a significant ripple to race across the pond.

"Don't be stupid, it's your little sister!" he said with a shudder that hammered the point. He was most positively repulsed by the thought of my brothers thinking he liked me. Jake's laughter broke the tension, and Ellis's words broke my heart.

"A kiss is a lovely trick
designed by nature
to stop speech when words
become superfluous."

— INGRID BERGMAN

CHAPTER

FOUR

First and Last Kisses

Ellis

I can feel her watching me. I was only outside for a few seconds before the sensation slid over me. I bit down hard on my bottom lip to stop myself from saying her name, and the metallic tang of blood swamped my mouth. If this is going to happen, it needs to be on her terms, and no matter how much I want to turn around right now, I can't let myself. I don't think I can survive the rejection I know I deserve. At least this way, even if she chooses not to say a word, I know she's here and she's okay. It'll have to be enough.

I've spent a long time not having any privacy, constantly being watched. When I was released from prison, I burrowed down in my apartment for a whole week without leaving, just to enjoy the solitude. I'd forgotten what it was like to not have to share your every waking moment with another person. You know what the funny thing was after that first week back in the real world? I missed the knowledge that I wasn't alone. I realized I didn't like that it was just me, because up until that point it never really had been. I went from a kid living with his parents to a teenager living with his girlfriend to a convict living with a cellmate. That right there was fifty shades of screwed up.

"Why are you here?"

My heart stalls in my chest, and an uncomfortable knot begins to form at the back of my throat, making it hard to swallow. Her words are clipped, but they're not harsh or upset. She sounds completely indifferent. I hadn't expected that. I thought maybe if she did ever speak to me again, there'd be a fire in her voice; it would sound gravely or elevated—or at the very least betray some form of emotion. I'm not sure what to do with the realization that it now sounds dead. I reel back from the wave of guilt threatening to drown me.

"I wanted to pay my respects," I answer hoarsely. I let my arms drop from my neck and quickly push my fists deep into my pockets. As body language goes, I'm probably sending out all the wrong signals to try and make her feel comfortable with my presence. I still haven't turned around, and now I don't know if I can. I've taken so much from this girl already; she sounds flat, and if I've stolen the light from behind her eyes I don't ever want to know.

"That's what flowers are for. You could have had them delivered and saved yourself a trip." Still not the slightest inflection, I notice.

"Harlow, I—"

I don't finish because she interrupts me.

"I swear to you, Ellis, if you say sorry to me right now, Mrs. Adkins' isn't the only wake that'll happen today. I don't want your apologies, I want your reasons."

There's a wobble as she says the last word, like she's trying not to cry, and my resolve shatters to a million regrets landing heavily at my feet. I turn slowly, looking up towards her voice and suddenly I'm a fourteen-year-old boy, watching the best thing in in my life slip through my fingers all over again. She's barely changed at all. The years have been kind to her. The last time I saw her face we were still kids. I figured I knew it all back then, had my life—and hers—all mapped out. It's funny how things can change so drastically in the blink of an eye. I'd planned on marrying Harlow Stevens from the very first time we kissed. There was never a part of me that doubted for a second that we were meant to be together.

She takes a step closer to the rail on the balcony and her hair whips across her face in the wind. It's shorter than she used to wear it. Her straw blonde hair was always a wild mess with a life of its own when we were growing up. Now it sits on her shoulders, tussled but sleek. She looks more put together and conservative than I've ever seen her. She always dressed for comfort back then. T-shirts and cut-offs were her signature, but I guess that wouldn't be appropriate for the occasion that's afforded me a chance to see her again. She's wearing a simple black slip dress, although I noticed earlier she's still a fan of sneakers.

I swallow around the lump lodged in my throat, searching for something to say to her. The truth is I don't want to talk. I want to scale the drainpipe and climb up onto that balcony, pull her into my arms and beg for forgiveness. Standing so near to her, and not being able to touch her makes me miss her more than I ever did in jail. The physical barrier of being locked away was easier to rationalize than this. Standing ten feet away and not being able to hold her is a new and debilitating torture.

"You look good," I tell her, hoping to stop her from retreating. "How are you?" As stupid fucking questions go, this one hits the mark on every level. We're at a wake, and the last time that we saw each other was the day I was sentenced for killing her father. The words are out now though, so I shift uncomfortably from one foot to the other and clamp my jaw shut tight.

"Go home, Ellis."

She drops her arms to her side and turns to walk away.

"Harlow, stop!" I sound desperate, but I am, so I don't give a shit. "Please, don't go. Let's talk!" I call out.

She pauses by the curtains, and before I can talk myself out of it I'm climbing over the deck's fence and clambering up the drainpipe toward her. My dress shoes are next to useless against the cladding, and it's only luck that I make it high enough to reach and grab hold of the railings. I pull myself over onto the balcony, stumbling as I land, and quickly smooth down my pants as I take a deep breath. The climb was harder than I'd anticipated and I've broken a sweat, but that could just be the nerves. I straighten and take a step toward her. She takes two back, looking at me as though I scare the living crap out of her, and I don't think I've ever truly experienced pain until this moment.

"What the hell are you doing?" she asks. This time her voice isn't flat, it's straight up horrified.

"I'm not about to hurt you," I choke out. "I'd never."

"You'd never hurt me? Are you serious right now? Ellis, you've been hurting me for the last ten years. Every single day."

I was wrong. *This* is pain. My chest aches so bad I rub the heel of my palm over it to try and extricate some of the discomfort. Breathing hurts. Looking at her hurts. Knowing I did this intensifies the feeling to an incomprehensible magnitude, and I know I can't ever make it right. I can't take away the pain, just like I can't undo the past. God knows I've prayed that I could. I wake up every day and go through the motions, knowing that my world will always be a little darker because she's not part of it.

She shifts, and when I build up enough courage to look her in the eye, I see a lone fat tear drop across her cheek. If there's one thing I know about Harlow, it's that she hates to cry. Another tear follows and before I can gather my wits, she launches herself forward and begins hitting me. Her fists are balled tightly, pounding into my chest as she screams, "Why?"

I deserve every bit of hatred she can expel. I don't attempt to block her hits, and I let her rain every ounce of her frustration on me. She pushes and thumps as hard as she can, and I take it.

"Why didn't you tell anyone? WHY! Why did you leave me?" She sobs as her fight begins to tire. "You left him, and then you left me! I hate you, Ellis." She can barely breathe through her exertion, and I'm scared that she's going to have a panic attack and pass out. "I hate you so much."

I grab her wrists, and pull her tightly to my chest, swiftly pinning her in a bear hug as she whispers to herself how much she abhors me. Her words cut through me like knives slicing at my heart, but having her in my arms is worth every single slash. She finally gives in to her grief and then her tears really start falling. The shaking that wracks through her body is almost my undoing. She's balled up with her arms trapped between our torsos and I rub her back, letting her loathe me as I stand quietly loving her.

If I had a shred of decency I wouldn't have come today. I'm a selfish man for even entertaining the idea.

Harlow's sobbing has slowed; just the odd random hiccup and tremble reverberate against me as she leans into my stance. I don't stop rubbing her back, and now that she's calmer it feels too intimate, too much. There's a seed of hope, it's the tiniest speck, but it's there wanting to take root deep inside of me. Maybe we could talk after all. Maybe she could learn to forgive me. Maybe I'm a hopeless optimist. Without conscious thought, I place a soft kiss on top of her head, and she rears back like I've just shot her.

Her eyes are red and swollen, her face is stained with the evidence of her misery, and her lips are parted just enough for her breath to warm my neck. I shiver, remembering the taste of them, and part mine to ask if she's okay. Her hand is hot and unforgiving as it makes contact with my cheek, and her slap catches me off-guard. Her posture screams that I disgust her, but her eyes tell me something different. They're angry and sad, but there's still a light behind them.

"You don't get to do that anymore," she says dejectedly. "You don't get to kiss it all away."

"I know," I whisper. "But it doesn't mean that I don't want to, Harlow."

She'll never know the lengths I'd go to earn her kisses again. I close my eyes and let the memory of our first kiss soothe the pain of knowing this may have been our last.

"Love is of all passions the strongest, for it attacks simultaneously the head, the heart and the senses."

— LAO TZU

CHAPTER FIVE

Two's Company, Three's Just Embarrassing

Ellis

1994

Just when I started to feel like I was figuring life out, it decided to kick my ass. I'd spent so long trying to convince myself of my own lies that by the time I finally accepted that the feelings I had for my best friend were less than platonic, I'd missed my chance.

The "right time" to come clean to Harlow had come and gone while I was busy drowning in indecision. My resolution to tell her that I was pretty sure I might love her hadn't come easy.

The prospect of scaring her away and destroying our friendship terrified me almost as much as the thought of her never knowing how I felt about her.

Even at fourteen years old I was convinced that's what it was—love. Misread words and misheard names all manifested as Harlow; she was everywhere I looked, always. The stirring feeling I'd get in the pit of my stomach, and other places, wasn't entirely unpleasant. Whenever we were together, the rush of blood that would make my head swim if she grabbed my hand, or laughed at something I'd said—all of it was my drug, and I needed to feed my addiction.

I was caught between a rock and a hard place. It wasn't that I necessarily wanted to be more than friends right there and then. I wasn't stupid, I knew we were young, probably too young to fall in love. I just wanted her to know that I didn't see anyone other than her. It was only ever her.

The twins didn't exactly help. I'd been friends with Harlow all of one week before we had "the talk"—and by talk, I mean the boys pinned me down and explained in graphic detail what they'd do to me if I made a move on their little sister. It was easier to ignore once they moved away to college, but the threat still lingered in the back of my mind, even if I was half convinced that it was empty. Probably just one of those things big brothers did out of some weird primal protective instinct.

Even so, I valued my kneecaps ever since Harlow had tried shooting one out. I kept a close but subtle distance, biding my time. It didn't occur to me that my time would eventually elapse. I hadn't even noticed I wasn't the only runner in the race.

I'd walked to the Stevens' house on an ordinary Saturday evening, just like I always did. But this time was going to be different: I'd psyched myself up, ready to profess my feelings, and eager to put myself out of my own misery and take a chance. The weight of lugging around my secret crush was already lifting, and although I couldn't stop my hands from shaking, I wasn't nearly as nervous as I thought I would be when I knocked on her door.

The sinking feeling I got when her mom said Harlow was out on a date still gives me a chill. I stood on the doorstep, frozen in a state of disbelief and absolute agony. How had I missed the signs that she was ready to date? I chastised myself, wondering why she was out with someone other than me. Mrs. Stevens said she'd gone to the movies, and I must have done a pretty shitty job of hiding the pain splintering across my chest because she patted me on the shoulder and gave me a look so full of pity I couldn't stand to meet her eyes for a second longer. I turned and ran.

I made it to the pier before I let myself stop to take a ragged breath. The burning in my lungs was a welcomed distraction, if fleeting. Dusk in the harbor was my favorite time. When it was clear you could see the exact moment day turned to night, and watch the show of the stars beginning to make their appearance. It was a sight that never failed to awe me.

As I stood, hands on knees trying to catch my breath and willing the pounding in my chest to stop, jealousy began to unfurl itself, washing over me in a flood of anxiety and bitterness. Who was she with? Did she like him? Would he try to kiss her? Would she let him? I was irrationally mad at her, and even more so at myself. How could I have been so blinkered?

I listened for a while to the tide lapping against the docks and the boats creaking, their ropes straining as water pushed and pulled them from their moors. It wasn't a loud enough distraction, and trying to focus on anything other than Harlow felt impossible.

The Cape was a beautiful neighborhood. When we first moved, I'd been sure that I'd never feel at home. I was desperate to go back to Montana. Harlow soon changed that. I was from Big Sky; I spent my spare time in one of two places, snowboarding on the slopes of Little Couloir, or at Logan's grandpa's farm.

A small waterside tourist town held no appeal for me—I couldn't sail or surf and had little desire to do either. Everyone in town knew each other's business, and I wasn't sure I liked the thought of strangers knowing anything about me. It always grated on me when I went into a store with my dad, and he would look at the clerk's name badge, and then address them like he'd known them for years. It was a phony interaction. I liked to stick to sir and ma'am; if we progressed to using names it was because we'd made an effort to talk and become friends. If people in this town were going to talk about me, they'd better get to know me first.

After a rocky start, Harlow made it a one-girl crusade to win me over to her hometown, and she managed it in next to no time. I was dragged around day after day, getting introduced to every single store owner in town, with Harlow expertly presenting each of us with a small but thoughtful piece of trivia.

"Mrs. Adkins, this is Ellis Hughes. Ellis, Mrs. Adkins has run the general store here since my daddy was a boy, and there isn't a single thing she can't source if you bribe her with some of my Mom's pie. Mrs. Adkins, Ellis just moved into the Andersons' property. His daddy's a Red Sox fan, just like Mr. Adkins."

Within the space of a month, I was on first-name basis with almost everyone in town.

The wind carried the sound of a couple chatting animatedly as they strolled along the waterfront, hand-in-hand. They looked over, and the woman smiled. I could feel the heat rush to my cheeks in embarrassment. It wasn't like they could possibly know what was running through my mind, or that I was pretty close to tears. I stood taller and pushed the hair out of my eyes, trying to pull myself together.

I started walking in the opposite direction of the couple, stuffing my hands deep into the pockets of my hoodie. I wondered if Harlow and her "date" would be in the old picture house already, or if they had gone to eat first. If it were me, I'd have taken her out to dinner first. At least then we'd have been able to talk to one another. Taking a chick to the movies pretty much guarantees that you don't need to do much talking.

The more I thought about what might happen when the lights went down, the faster my pulse raced, and my stomach hurt. Would her date try and put his arm around her? What if they went to sit in the back row? I screwed my eyes up tight and shook away my last thought. Harlow wouldn't make out with someone on a first date. I'd bet my life I would have known what she wanted to go and see if she were at the movies with me. The theater only had three screens. Before I'd even processed what I was about to do or say, I was running again—this time in the direction of the picture house.

She was mine, and I needed to make sure that she knew it.

"One ticket for *The Crow* please, Mr. Ryan."

The second I noticed the billboard, I was pretty damn confident she'd pushed to watch this one.

"Sorry, Ellis, this one's rated R. Unless you have the Stevens boys with you, I can't let you in on your own."

My heart sank; I couldn't get in because everyone in the damn town knew me. I paused for a second wondering if I should just wait out in the foyer for her, or buy a ticket for a different movie and try to sneak in.

"Has Harlow already gone in?" I asked testing my luck.

"Oh, yeah. As a matter of fact, she has, with Kate and Jim Sanderson's two boys."

I needed to keep my anger in check. She was here with Cory Sanderson, which in itself made me want to crush him into dust, but they'd obviously come with his older brother Troy, a complete douchebag. He was Jared and Jake's age, but unlike the twins, he wasn't a nice person. Sure, he was a stand-up guy in front of anyone who mattered, but I'd heard plenty in the boys' locker rooms at hockey about what he got up to in his spare time. The fact that he was inside with Harlow, even if he was just playing chaperone, made me want to tear at my own skin.

"I'm late. They were supposed to wait for me, but I guess they figured I wasn't coming and decided to go ahead without me. Can you let me in to go meet up with them?"

Mr. Ryan looked skeptical, but he pushed my ticket under the glass and took my money. If it weren't for the booth, I'd have hugged him.

"Thanks, sir."

I made my way through to screen two, trying not to make a sound as I slipped into an empty seat at the back and began searching for Harlow in the darkness. It wasn't hard; it was pretty empty, there were only about thirty people in the place. They'd chosen seats slap bang in the middle of the theater, and I could just make out Cory sitting on her right side, and then Troy, by himself, all the way at the end of the row.

I hadn't given a thought about what I would do if I actually found them, and once I was sitting in the back of a darkened theater watching them, the pounding in my chest intensified. Hearing she was out on a date hurt. Seeing her on a date was paralyzing. I watched in morbid captivation as he leaned in closer to her; I bit down on my cheek until I tasted blood when he whispered something and she threw her head back, laughing. When his arm stretched out boldly and hung across the back of her seat, I was on my feet and marching in their direction.

"Hey! I thought it was you guys. Mind if I sit here?" I dropped down beside Cory, not waiting for confirmation. "Oh, hey Harlow," I leaned over and smiled before sitting back. She looked like she'd just seen a ghost. Good. She didn't say hi in response. Instead, she stuffed her mouth full of popcorn and sunk lower into her seat.

I figured I could play this two ways: one, focus on Harlow and try my best to convince her to ditch Cory and come home with me. Or, two, ignore her, so Cory didn't feel threatened and try to up his game, then steal his attention until she was pissed at him for ignoring her.

I decided to go with option two.

"Dude, this is the film Brandon Lee died filming, right?" I said trying to keep my voice low enough for only Cory to hear.

"Yeah, he was shot for real."

"How messed up is that? I bet it took ages for everyone on set to realize he wasn't acting."

Cory's arm dropped from the back of Harlow's chair as he angled himself toward me. It was the first time since I'd walked in on them that my pulse wasn't drumming wildly in my ears. I'd shifted his focus, and now I had to hold it long enough for Harlow to get pissed with him.

He started giving me a rendition of his conspiracy theories on Lee's death. I was starting to feel confident that maybe I could pull this off. Sitting back in my seat, I half listened to Cory. The guy was a dumb ass; he was sitting next to the most amazing girl I'd ever met, ignoring her to talk to me.

He didn't deserve to date her.

"What's your deal, Ellis? What the hell was all that about?"

I watched as Troy's car pulled away from the curb, Cory hanging out the window shouting that he'd see me at hockey practice. I'm not even sure he said goodbye to Harlow.

"What?" I looked back at her and shrugged. The flimsy yellow sundress she wore was billowing around her legs in the breeze. I let my eyes fall from the dress to the beat-up pair of sneakers she mainly lived in, then back up to meet her stare.

It was hard to breathe.

Her hair was braided loosely over one shoulder, and I hadn't missed the way her hands were fisted like she was about to slug me. I didn't care. I took a step toward her instead of back.

"You just hijacked my date," she fumed. "Why were you even there?"

"It was a date?"

She didn't buy my innocent doe-eyed act. I'd never seen her look so angry with me—her face was almost purple.

"Don't play dumb, it doesn't suit you!"

"Why were you out on a date with Cory Sanderson, Harlow?" I didn't like the way the sentence fell from my lips. Even I could hear the hurt in my voice.

Her head dropped, and her fists loosened.

"He asked me if I wanted to go to the movies to watch *The Crow*. You know I've been dying to see it. I said yes."

It was my turn to drop my eyes. I kicked at the pavement with the toe of my shoe, watching scuff marks appear. "I'd have taken you."

She took a step away from me, creating more distance. I hated it.

"I didn't like seeing you with him," I admitted; still not brave enough to look up. I could handle her being angry with me, but I wasn't sure I could stomach any more rejection tonight—my emotions were already frayed.

"Jeez, you sound like the twins. I don't need another brother, Ellis! It was my first date, and you showed up and took over. I don't think Cory realized I was even in the car when he dropped us off."

She sounded genuinely upset, and my stomach rolled. "I'm not trying to be your brother, Harlow. Trust me, that's the last thing I ever want to make you think."

"Well, then you need to stop acting that way. You embarrassed me tonight. How do you think it felt being ignored, huh? It was the first time anyone's ever asked me out. You're supposed to always remember your first date, and you just ruined it!"

"You shouldn't have even been out with him!" I seethed, the frustration of the night finally taking its toll.

"WHY!"

I snapped my head up, and it collided with the glare she was willing me dead with. I swallowed hard. "Because."

"Because what?" she threw back.

"Because it should have been with me."

The front door creaked open, and Mr. Stevens stepped out onto the porch.

"What's all the commotion?" he asked, eyeing us both wearily.

Harlow looked between us then shouted back to her dad.

"It's nothing… I'm coming in."

My heart sank to the floor. Nothing? She called my admission nothing. I didn't give her a chance to stick the knife in any further. I turned and made my way to my house as quickly as I could. My feelings for her weren't *nothing*; they were most definitely something, if only to me.

I made it to my lawn before I felt her grab my arm, pulling me back. "Wait."

I shook myself from her grasp and turned around to face her. Her arms were crossed over her chest protectively; she didn't look angry with me anymore, just confused.

"You don't like me, Ellis," she whispered lightly.

Suddenly I was the one confused. I couldn't fathom how she'd ever think that. "Are you mad? Of course, I like you." God, I wish she only realized how much.

"No, I mean like, like. Why would you want to take me on a date? I'm Jared and Jake's little sister. I'm just me."

My palms were sticky; I wiped them across the leg of my jeans and took a deep breath, moving closer. My head and heart had waged war on each other, and my heart finally won out. The gleam of the porch light lit her from behind; she looked as though she were glowing.

"That's precisely the reason, Harlow—because, you're you." I closed the remaining few inches and kissed my best friend. Not on the forehead or the cheek like I'd done probably a million and one times before—but on her lips. I'd imagined kissing them for almost as long as I'd known her, and it's fair to say that I obviously had a poor imagination. The fantasies I had about her while I lay alone in my room didn't even come close to the real thing. There wasn't a single spot on my body that didn't feel that kiss. It was soft and chaste, and all too fleeting. She moved back, her eyes completely dilated and fixed on mine. I'd taken us both by surprise, but I couldn't be sorry because her lips against mine felt like magic.

It was everything.

"The course of true love never did run smooth."

— William Shakespeare

CHAPTER

SIX

Just Like in the Movies

Harlow

There's a certain comfort that comes from familiarity. Me trying to beat the shit out of Ellis was neither comforting nor familiar, but his reaction was. The way he'd pulled me tightly to his chest and enveloped me in his strong arms was how I'd longed to be held every night since he'd left me.

I should have carried on walking back inside. It would have been the smart thing to do, but hearing the panic in his voice when he thought I was leaving had stopped me in my tracks. I hadn't expected him to climb up after me and it threw me. In fact, it did more than that—it completely infuriated me. Trying to engage in any type of conversation with him was a stupid idea. Doing so in such a volatile mood was downright senseless. I had no warning that he'd be showing up, and my emotions weren't ready to be tested so brutally. I made a mental note to call Logan and ask if he'd known Ellis was coming.

Letting Ellis console me was a fatal mistake, especially given that he was the very reason I'd broken down in the first place. Still, as much as I hate him he's the only person who's ever known exactly what I need with just one glance. Was I really exuding how badly I needed to be held so blatantly? I hadn't even recognized it until I found myself tucked into his chest as he rubbed my back and made me forget myself for a moment. His kiss broke the spell. I'm not sure how long I'd have let myself soak up the memorable scent of his skin and take refuge against the warmth of his chest. I'm ashamed and disgusted with myself, not for letting it happen, but for enjoying it. It was wrong.

His kiss, though... Damn him. Damn him to hell for kissing me. Damn him for chasing me down and not letting me leave. Damn him for holding me as I crumbled. Damn him for making me remember what it should feel like to be kissed.

1994

We didn't say anything for a long while. We just stared at one another, trying to process what had just happened. One minute I'd been ready to tear my own arm off so I'd have something to hit him with for turning up on my first date. The next, I was thrown so far off guard that I couldn't even form a cohesive thought.

He kissed me. Ellis Hughes had actually kissed me.

It wasn't a dream; I was one hundred percent awake, and he freaking kissed me.

His mouth was softer than I'd ever imagined it would be. His kiss was like burying my face in a warm comfy pillow, and his breath tasted like the cinnamon gum he always chewed. Cinnamon was going to be my new favorite thing. I was going to run and buy gum so I wouldn't forget the taste, I decided. Right after I remembered how to make my legs work. They turned to Jell-O the second he'd stepped forward, and I realized what he was about to do.

Ellis was staring at me; his mouth was moving and I knew he was forming words, words that I should have been able to decipher but couldn't. The only thing I could hear was my mind shouting: *He kissed you! He kissed you! He* kissed you! And the frantic beating of my heart answering: *I know! I know! I know!*

He reduced me to a pile of raging hormones with a single brush of his lips. I was happy, angry, amazed, confused and every other emotion I'd ever experienced all at once. Ellis's mouth was still moving, his eyes clouding with concern before me as I watched him.

"Harlow, I'm sorry. I didn't mean to upset you, I just... I don't know. I'm so, so sorry."

The momentary high I was suspended in disappeared like a sinking ship. The warmth that had flooded my skin turned cold and sent a sobering cold wave of insecurity racing down my spine.

"Why are you sorry? Is it because you kissed me?" I asked. "Don't be, Ellis. Don't apologize unless you wish that you hadn't, and you want to take it back. I'm not sorry you did it."

He smiled. It wasn't a shy or unsure smile either; it was full and bright and dazzling. It was the smile he reserved and used solely for me.

"I don't ever want to take it back," he said, reaching out and taking hold of my right hand. He threaded his fingers loosely between my own. "Can I do it again?"

My pulse took off like a racehorse, and I wondered if he could feel it throbbing through the tips of my fingers. I was so sure he was apologizing because he'd made a mistake and the instant relief of knowing that wasn't the case was jarring. My nerves were in tatters. I couldn't believe he wanted to kiss me again.

"Not until you take me out on a real first date."

"Well, technically that was our first date," he grimaced.

"Nope, it was three friends at a movie—four, if you count our ride. It doesn't count if there're more than two people there."

He squeezed my fingers lightly and laughed. "So, I still get to be your first date?"

A rush of warmth flooded my chest. "Yeah," I replied, biting at the corner of my lip. "And if it's good, you'll get my second first kiss." I pulled back my hand and turned, quickly hurrying across his lawn and back over to my house.

"It'll be better than good!" he shouted as I reached the steps of the porch and threw him a cursory wave.

"Night, Ellis!" I stepped across to my door and out of his line of sight, leaning against the cold wood and letting myself sigh. It didn't feel true; it was too perfect to be real life. I closed my eyes absorbing all that had happened. It felt like something straight out of a cheesy '80s film. I pressed my fingers to my lips, tracing over them with a ridiculously wide smile.

It was the best worst first date in the history of worst first dates.

After spending the night trying but failing miserably to fall asleep, I was sure I'd be somewhat of a write-off the next day. You know those people that can function on only a couple of hours' sleep and still seem cheery and unaffected? Yeah, that wasn't me—not even close. I've always needed a full eight hours of sleep to be able to perform even the most basic tasks. The consequence of falling short on my sleep quota is that my usually sunny disposition turns to thunder and hail. It's not like I try to be mean, it's just out of my control. By now my parents and brothers are used to the tirades of a tired Harlow, but Ellis had yet to witness it.

I'd woken the day after our kiss, and instead of being filled with excitement and butterflies, it felt as though my head had been filled with rocks. My throat hurt something fierce when I tried to swallow, and there wasn't a single solitary spot on my entire body that didn't ache. I practically rolled from my bed and headed sleep-blind down the stairs to the kitchen in search of my mom. I needed all the drugs she had, and quick.

"I'm dying," I announced dropping into a chair at the table as she waited on the coffee pot to brew.

"So dramatic, Harlow. Good morning to you too, sweetheart."

I lifted my face from where I'd planted it on the tabletop. The cool surface felt good pressed against my skin.

"No, really, Mom. I need medicine—all the drugs. And an ice pack for my head. Oh, and maybe a hot water bottle for my back. Everywhere hurts."

"You do know it's Sunday?" she asked, eyeing me suspiciously. "There's no school to try get out of today."

It wasn't like I ever tried to not go to school; like I said, I just wasn't a morning person. I've actually always loved school.

"I'm not joking, Mom," I groaned.

She took my temperature very scientifically, using the back of her hand.

"You do feel a little on the hot side," she confirmed dropping down beside me. "Have you eaten anything funny?"

"No," I whimpered, placing my head back onto the table. "I was all right last night, but then I woke up feeling like this. I think maybe I have the flu."

My dad walked into the kitchen and gave my mom a kiss on the cheek before leaning over and ruffling my hair in his usual greeting. I don't think I'd ever wanted to kill a member of my own family until that very moment.

"Mike, no!" Mom scolded. "She's not well."

Her warning was too late. He'd already nuggied me, and I let out a strangled cry of distress, causing him to step back.

"Sorry, kiddo. I didn't realize."

I couldn't have responded even if I'd wanted to, my head was swimming, and I was doing my best to ignore the nausea.

Mom instructed him to call the doctor's office while she took me back to my room and helped me dress.

I had a feeling that she quite enjoyed playing dress-up with me. I was too exhausted to put up a fight when she pulled out of my closet a pale pink sundress she'd bought me (that I'd never worn) and a pair of gold flat sandals. My mother was the epitome of a "girly girl," and I couldn't have been more opposite. I didn't bother to object and grab my jeans and sneakers, which pleased her to no end. I was dressed nicer to go to the doctor's office than I had been to go out on my date. I did, however, draw the line when she attempted to fix my hair. The comb felt more like a gardening fork being pushed into my scalp. I swatted her away, not bothering to finish brushing it. I didn't care if it looked bad; it would coordinate perfectly with my mood.

"Mono?" Mom looked at Dr. Peterson like he'd be speaking Chinese.

"Yes, mono," he replied.

Her head slowly turned in my direction; you could practically see the suspicion bloom behind her narrowing eyes. I swallowed uncomfortably; she was definitely thinking the same thing I was. How had I contracted a kissing infection?

"Sorry, Doctor, but I'm confused," I rasped. "I've kissed one boy, just one time—last night, in fact. How can I have a kissing disease from that one time?"

"Cory?" Mom asked surprised, her brows lifting to meet her impossibly neat blonde hairline.

"Ellis," I whispered. Talking hurt, but not as much as the thought of Ellis passing on a kissing disease.

Dr. Peterson replied, breaking the uncomfortable exchange I'd gotten myself into.

"Here's how mono works," he said, looking from Mom to me. "It's usually transmitted through saliva or mucus—hence the reason people refer to it as a kissing disease. However, the kissing or close contact that transmits the disease doesn't happen right before you get sick. It takes thirty to fifty days from the time of exposure to begin to display symptoms. Coincidently, it's not only kissing that can transmit it."

I let out a relieved sigh, and Dr. Peterson smiled, sitting back into his desk chair.

"So what does?" Mom asked moving forward, poised for an explanation that better appeased her.

"Well, Mrs. Stevens, drinking from the same glass as an infected person, or even just being close when that person coughs or sneezes. Some people can carry the virus in their system without ever having symptoms and pass it on unknowingly."

A further ten-minute interrogation of Doctor Peterson had transpired before we climbed into our car and Mom's questioning swiftly turned on me. I'd used the restroom in the doctors' office, knowing I needed a few minutes to process what was happening before Mom pounced. It took almost the entire car ride home to convince her that Ellis and I hadn't been fooling around in secret, and were still only friends.

Even as I spoke the words I was unsure of the truth behind them. I didn't really know what Ellis and I were—it may have only been one kiss, but it had changed everything for me. The problem was, I didn't know if I was reading too much into it or not. What would happen the next time I saw him? Would he act differently? Would he try and kiss me hello? Were we supposed to hold hands now, or did we simply carry on as normal? The anxiety of trying to analyze what came next was almost as nauseating as the mono.

I assumed that since I'd most likely contracted the disease a month ago, Ellis would be sick too, or at least be displaying a few symptoms. It wasn't the case. We'd been home for all of thirty seconds when Ellis knocked at the door. I was still slumped on the steps trying to unbuckle my shoes. The little gold fasteners may as well have been tiny combination padlocks because I couldn't muster enough coordination to open them, and being bent over was making my head spin. I could see Ellis's silhouette in the glass door pane and shouted with as much exertion as I could manage for him to come in.

Mom had disappeared somewhere out back, and the fifteen steps it would have taken to reach the door and answer it would have been my last, I was sure of it. The second Ellis noticed me sitting on the steps, his smile faltered and he quickly closed the distance between us, kneeling in front of me.

I'd never cared about how I looked or what people thought of me, but the second Ellis's eyes scanned me over, I wished to God I'd been strong enough to let my mom rake a comb through my hair. I was clammy and hot, I couldn't have smelled great, and he kneeled down way too close for me to do anything other than surrender to the fact that there was no hiding.

"You look sick, what's wrong?" he asked.

I stopped fiddling with the fastener on my shoe, and let out a disgruntled moan, flopping back defeated.

"Mono, according to the doctor."

Instead of moving away, he leaned forward and began gently taking off my sandals. I had a sudden urge to cry and swallowed roughly before thanking him. "I kind of thought that maybe you'd have it too, but you look fine. Are you feeling okay?"

"Better than you by the look of it," he smiled sympathetically. "I'm good, but I guess if you've got it, then I'm probably gonna get it too, right?"

"Probably," I sighed. "I'd tell you to stay away, but according to my doctor, I was more than likely contagious a month ago."

He placed my sandals neatly at the foot of the stairs and moved around to sit by me. His whole left side was pressed up against my right, and I let myself lean into him a little.

"You know, for someone who's sick you look lovely today."

Ellis and I had never had the type of relationship where we complimented each other on how we looked; it just wasn't us, but I basked in the comforting warm-heartedness his words blanketed me with. My hair was plastered to my forehead, and my chest was glistening with sweat, but he still thought I was pretty.

"Thanks." I nudged him. "My mom took advantage and decided to play dress-up with me."

"I guessed that," he sniggered. "I can't remember that last time I saw you in anything other than your sneakers."

I stretched out my tired legs and wriggled my toes. "They're practical and comfy," I told him.

"Hey, no judgment here." He smiled, flexing out his own legs and pointing down to his beat-up blue Chucks. "You want me to help you up to your room?"

"She's fine, Ellis," Mom interrupted as she walked into the hall carrying a glass of water and the bottle of Tylenol the doctor had advised. I was hoping for a magic set of pills and what I was prescribed may as well have been candy for all the good a couple of Tylenol would do me.

"I'd prefer it if you were downstairs," she said, trying to engage in some sort of silent conversation with me. "You can go sit in the family room," she added, passing me the water and pills. Ellis threw me a strange look as Mom walked back toward the kitchen.

"She knows we kissed," I said, attempting to answer the "what's with her" look on his face. Ellis Hughes didn't have much of a poker face. You could read what he was thinking by looking at him ninety percent of the time. His eyes widened, and I swear he began to blush.

"She saw?" he whispered.

"I told her. I think she thought I may have caught mono from kissing Cory."

"Right... Wait, does that mean she now thinks you caught it from me?"

I shrugged because honestly, I didn't know what she was thinking. She'd never acted weird about Ellis's and my friendship before. If anything, she'd always given me the impression she assumed we'd end up dating, like it was just a given.

"Do you think I gave you mono?" he asked.

"Honesty?"

His eyes were burning into my own, waiting for me to answer. "Always."

"Okay, When the doctor first said I had it, I was sort of angry because I thought it was just a kissing thing, and you're the only person that I've ever actually kissed," I confessed, and didn't miss the way his lips lifted slightly at one corner. "I thought that maybe it was your fault for about two minutes until he explained how you catch it, and how long the incubation period is. Then I guess I decided I didn't mind if it was you or not. Thinking about it logically, it was more than likely one of the twins that passed it on. I've overheard them talking about their hook ups; seems like college is more about sex than study."

He laughed and nudged gently into my arm, although he may as well have backed into me with his dad's car, the way my body responded.

"Film in the family room?" he asked.

"Sounds like a plan."

"Sounds like a date," he winked, pulling me up from the stairs. He leaned forward and placed a quick kiss on my forehead before leading me out of the hall. It was a good thing he had a hold of my hand because even though seconds before my body had felt like it weighed a thousand pounds, his kiss made me feel like I might float away.

"The way to love anything is to realize that it may be lost."

—GILBERT K. CHESTERTON

CHAPTER

SEVEN

Questions and Answers

Ellis

"Ellis, you need to go. Just leave me alone, please."

There's an even balance of pissed off and pleading in her tone that makes me comply, even though everything in my body is telling me to ignore her. If her voice wasn't enough of a clue that she meant it, the death glare she's pinning me with drives the point home. I take my hand from the top of her car door and stand helplessly as Harlow moves around to climb in. We no doubt have an audience, since me calling after her as I chased her out of Mr. Adkins' house wasn't what you'd call in-conspicuous. Frustration is clawing at my skin with searing white hot talons; I'm so angry with myself for kissing her that I want to shout and scream and kick the shit out of something—anything—so very badly I might just combust. The car door begins to close, and I lurch forward catching the handle to stop it.

"We still need to talk. It doesn't need to be today, but I have to see you again," I rush. "I'll meet you anywhere you like, just name a time and a place, Harlow."

I should be embarrassed about the level of desperation that's pouring out of me, but for her, I'm not above begging. I'll drop to my knees if I have to.

Her shoulders sag as she shifts, sitting deeper in her seat. Her hand makes a slapping noise as it falls from the door handle before gripping the Mercedes steering wheel with enough force to pull it off and throw at me. The muscles in her slender forearms strain and stretch as she pushes her head back into her seat so hard it's like she's trying to disappear into it. It's blatantly evident that I'm stressing her out.

"Fine." Her nostrils are flared and her answer is curt, making me second-guess if I heard her correctly.

"Fine?" I echo, wondering if she'll correct me. I feel like I won that argument way too quickly, and she's lulling me into a false sense of victory.

"Get in. I'm heading to my mom's; you can say your piece and then we're done."

"Your mom's?"

"Yes, Ellis, my mom's. Are you getting in or not?"

"Can we not go someplace else? Anywhere else?" I ask in a croaky voice. She lets out a small huff as she shakes her head at me and pulls the door closed.

Fuck.

"Wait! I'm coming," I yell as I run around the front of her car and pull open the passenger door. I throw myself into the seat and land with a thud before she can change her mind and drive away without me.

Of all the places in this town to go and talk she chooses the one that I have nightmares about on a regular basis. The Stevens house used to be my favorite place on earth—that was, until it became the setting for the demise of our relationship. My parents moved from next-door six months after I was sent to prison. My mom couldn't handle the risk of facing Dianne every day. She moved back to Montana as soon as her divorce to my dad came through. He didn't want to live next door to where his wife had ended their marriage, and his son had ended another man's life. He bought an apartment near his office and lived there for a couple of years before meeting Miranda and moving in with her. They married the following year. I've only met her twice.

Harlow puts the car in drive and peels out of the Adkins' driveway, spraying her shiny red Mercedes with gravel and dirt. I quickly buckle my seatbelt and push my hands through my hair, wondering how I got myself into this situation. I really should have planned this out better.

"Harlow, I really want to talk with you, but I don't think it's a good idea to do it in front of your mom. It's not fair of me to just show up; it'll upset her."

Her head whips around to face me so fast I'm genuinely surprised she hasn't broken her neck. "You don't want to upset her?" she laughs without any humor and then stares blankly at me for a beat before sliding her eyes back to the road. "So, it's fine to ambush me out of the blue, but you don't want to do it to my mom?" she seethes.

Her knuckles whiten as she twists them around the steering wheel and I sigh. She has every right to be angry; my comment was thoughtless, but it doesn't make it any less true. The last thing I need is to confront Dianne Stevens like this. I'm a mess and she deserves answers, just as Harlow does, but I don't think I'm strong enough to face them both in one night. We pull up to a stop sign, and I whisper yet another apology.

"I'm sorry. I didn't come here to upset you, I just…"

"My mom's not at the house," she interrupts. I turn in my seat to look at her and God she's still as beautiful as ever—even after crying. I close my eyes for a second and exhale. "Where—"

"She's in Cleveland visiting Jared and the boys," she interrupts again. "It's Cooper's first birthday tomorrow."

I'm assuming Cooper is Jared's son. I swallow realizing that I know nothing about any of their lives anymore. I used to be a part of them, but now I'm just the monster who robbed them of their father. Harlow senses that I have no clue who Cooper is, and she almost looks as though she's about to explain when the car behind us beeps. I want to turn and flip them the bird, but I suppress the urge. Her mouth clamps shut, and her eyes narrow as she scrunches her brows. She shakes away whatever she was going to say and pulls back out into traffic, headlining to the place I used to call home.

Her keys hit the bowl hard enough to chip it as she tosses them in and makes her way down the hallway. Maybe I'm just hyper-aware of my surroundings but the sound echoes through the house like a bomb tearing through it. I'm rooted to the spot while she mindlessly toes her sneakers off in the dark, unaware that I'm no longer following behind her. Everything feels familiar but different. I can't bring myself to step any further inside. It seems all wrong. I take a deep breath, attempting to coax myself out of the sorry state I've plummeted to since climbing into her car. But it only makes everything a million times worse: a waft of furniture polish and lemon air freshener pulls me back in time. I'd forgotten what home smelled like.

"You coming in?" I hear before she flicks the lights on and I'm on my ass before I know what's happened. Not figuratively. Literally.

"Ellis! Hell, are you alright?" Harlow asks hurrying over to where I'm sitting on their faded doormat that reads, "Home Sweet Home" in a faded black script.

I look around and notice the pictures hanging where they always were. Except now instead of Harlow and the twins' faces grinning back at me, there are pictures of Dianne holding a little girl and an even smaller boy I don't recognize. There are pictures of Jared and a woman I'm assuming is his wife. There's a photo of Jake and two little boys holding hands. Then I see a family portrait. The twins flank Harlow and Dianne, and the children are all in front, perched on their mother's knees. It looks off until I realize why. It's missing Mike.

"I think I'm gonna throw up," I murmur, scrambling to my feet and retreating out onto the porch.

"You want me to get you a glass of water?" Harlow asks as I dry heave over the side of her fence.

I lift a thumb up to signal please without having to turn around. My stomach continues to roll, but I think I'm okay after a minute. That is, until I lift my gaze from the flowerbeds and it collides with my old bedroom window. That sets off a whole new wave of nausea, and I empty what little is left in my stomach as Harlow's bare feet stop in line with my own.

I grab the glass she pushes in front of me and take a gulp before straightening my stance. She doesn't look at me. She doesn't attempt to rub my back or ply me with any comforting words, and I'm grateful for the silence. It's the first time this evening it isn't awkward as hell. I take another sip of my water, studying my old bedroom window. I spent roughly half my adolescence peering through it hoping to catch a glimpse of my girl.

I must let out a huff because it cues Harlow.

"The family that lives there now have a son called Max," she offers. "That was his room until he left for college last year." She's pointing out toward my old room, and I nod not knowing where she's going with this. "I was here with my mom the day they moved in and was collecting something from my room. Probably a book or something, I don't remember. I got that feeling you get when you know someone's watching you. You understand me?" she asks, finally turning to catch my eye. I nod, and a small smile pulls at the corner of her mouth, but it looks sad.

"Anyway, I looked up and froze. I couldn't move a muscle. Max was standing in your old window, looking straight into my room. He must have been around nine or ten years old. I was stunned because here was this kid that looked just like you did—gold hair, angelic face, the works. He waved at me, and I thought I was having some sort of breakdown. This kid was your complete double. I rushed over to my window and pulled the curtains closed and didn't leave my room for the whole day. My mom had come to find me when I hadn't returned downstairs after maybe an hour, and I was laid out on my bed shaking and crying."

I place my glass down at my feet and take a step forward. The look on her face as she remembers this makes my chest hurt, and I want so badly to pull her into my arms. I lift my hand slowly toward the one she has resting on the fence, and she senses my intention to touch her and pulls it back.

It's only one small movement, but she may as well have stabbed me for how much it hurts.

"I thought I was losing my mind, Ellis. My mom had to walk over and introduce herself to the new neighbors to confirm that they did actually have a little boy, because I was convinced it was the ten-year-old version of you I was seeing. That was seven months after you'd gone. My mom put me in therapy a week later. Not because I couldn't handle the grief of losing my dad, Ellis," her voice strains, breaking my heart a little more, "but because I couldn't handle losing you."

I don't register that I'm about to cry until it's too late. Her face becomes a blur, and I have to blink to bring it back into focus. What can I ever say to her to make things right? There's nothing in this world that can erase what I've put her through, and we both know it.

I pinch the bridge of my nose, leaning forward slightly and taking a shaky breath. "I don't know what to say to you," I admit, not making eye contact.

"Why did you reject my visitation requests?" she asks guardedly.

I think back to the first time I received one. I was sitting in that goddamn blue cell on a paper-thin mattress, staring at the little piece of card handed to me by the warden. I remember wondering why in hell she'd want to see me. I was responsible for tearing her family to shreds. My cellmate Ryan was laid on his bunk humming out of tune as he leered over an old, faded, dirty magazine. I looked around at my surroundings, and they were awful. Chipped paint, cold concrete floors, a dented stainless steel toilet and a basin in the corner of the room with no privacy. My face was full of scruff; I'd lost a few pounds from not being able to stomach the shitty food, and I was terrified. The last thing I wanted was for her to see me like that. I couldn't even look at myself in the mirror. I denied the visitation request because I was too ashamed to look her in the eye—kind of like how I feel right now.

I keep my eyes trained on the middle distance, trying to avoid her as I admit my cowardice out loud. It's not as cathartic as I'd hoped. She doesn't say anything for a long while; instead, she rests her arms on the fence rail and mirrors my posture, staring out into the darkness.

"I can understand that you'd be scared in that situation," she says with a lilt of empathy in her quiet voice. "But, you owed me a chance to speak with you. I lost everything within the space of a few weeks, and you just cut me off. I deserved closure at least."

"I know that, Harlow. Jesus, do I know that. But I didn't have a clue what was happening. One minute you were being admitted into the hospital, and the next I was being hauled into the back of a cruiser and charged with..."

The words die on my lips. I've had plenty of time to repeat them over and over in my head, but somehow speaking them aloud to her feels like an impossible feat.

"Killing my dad," she finishes.

I flinch at the words falling from her mouth. They flow out like poison, thick and deadly, suffocating me with their truth and slaying me with their curtness.

A set of headlights breaks the tension as a car pulls into my old drive. The crunch of gravel drowns out the cicadas, and Harlow stands back from the rail, smoothing down her dress.

"Evening," the tall silhouette of a stranger shouts, exiting his car and waving over to us.

"Evening," Harlow hollers back before turning to me. "Let's carry this discussion inside." It's more of an order than a request. She walks into the house not waiting for a response, not looking to see if I follow, not exposing the wounds I know we've just ripped open.

"To love at all is to be vulnerable. Love anything and your heart will be wrung and possibly broken."

—C.S. LEWIS

CHAPTER

EIGHT

The Right Kind of Wrong

Harlow

'm emptying my overnight bag onto the kitchen table when Ellis walks in and takes a seat. I gather up my toiletries and pajamas, stuffing them back into the leather carryall, leaving my pillbox out. I think for a second about going to my room to take my meds, but it's not like he hasn't seen me do this before. I move to the sink and pour myself a tall glass of water.

Ellis sits quietly observant as I pull open the container and take the six pills out: a combination of ACE inhibitors, beta-adrenergic blockers, and diuretics. The clinical trial I agreed to has shown some success in other patients with parallel conditions to my own, and at this point I'll try anything. I take so many pills it wouldn't surprise me to hear a rattle when I walk. I swallow the pills one by one and Ellis watches me with such burning intensity that I need to look away.

"Still need to take them one at a time, huh?" he ponders out loud.

"Yep." I let the p pop sarcastically as I finish taking my medication. I've never been one of those people who can throw a couple of pills back and swallow them without choking. Taking my contraceptive used to make me gag like I'd swallowed a brick, and they weren't even a quarter of the size of my current tablets.

I take my time assessing Ellis over the rim of my glass, here in my mother's kitchen. It's a sight that used to be so common-place, and yet tonight it feels completely alien. He's leaning against the counter, obscuring his lower half, but his broad chest and long, muscular arms are in full view. Tonight would feel so much easier if he didn't look so damn good. I hate it. He'd held me as I cried into his chest, and the shoulder of his white shirt has the remnants of my mascara smudged into the fabric. I let my eyes wander over the expanse of his shoulders, trying but failing not to imagine them in the flesh. I lift my gaze a little to his collar and note the way his throat bobs under my scrutiny. By the time my eyes meet his my glass is completely empty, and I'm drinking nothing but air. Crinkles appear ever so slightly at the corner of his eyes, letting me know I possess all the subtlety of a hand grenade.

I turn around from the counter and place my glass in the sink, taking a deep shaky breath to remind myself that I'm not supposed to feel anything other than contempt for this man.

The coroner's report said Daddy had died of a contrecoup brain injury. The night of the incident I'd been admitted to the hospital; I'd fainted, my blood pressure was through the roof and Ellis couldn't reach my parents. My mom had gone out of town with her girlfriends to watch some theater performance, and my dad was planning on staying home. Ellis decided that he'd make the hour drive back to The Cape from Duke and let my father know I was being kept for overnight observations. From what I remembered he'd called from my bedside at the hospital and left a message for his parents, asking them to get back to him. His dad traveled some for work, but his mom Emma should have been home.

I don't know all the details of what happened when Ellis made it to my house that night. Only that he walked in on his mom and my dad. They'd argued, and Ellis threw a punch. Just one. A knee jerk reaction, and completely out of his usual laid-back character. One snap decision to throw his fist in anger had changed the course of our lives forever.

A "one-punch-killer" the media had called him.

My father had apparently fallen over backward on impact. He hit the back of his head against the stairway and fractured his skull. The coroner explained to us that the collision on the hard ground had caused my dad's brain to ricochet into the opposite wall of his skull—his forehead—causing a brain hemorrhage. He didn't die instantly. Ellis had stuck around, shouting and arguing with his mom for a few minutes. When Emma realized that my dad wasn't getting up she called an ambulance. Ellis walked away thinking he'd knocked my father out for a few minutes. He had no idea that while he was driving back to Duke *my* dad lay dying in *his* mother's arms.

"You've never explained why you didn't tell me about our parents' affair," I announce, stepping away from the sink and taking a seat opposite him, never breaking eye contact. The countertop makes for an efficient and appreciated barrier between the two of us.

I know about the affair. Ellis's mom had the decency to explain her actions to my mom. Not that it helped at the time, but looking back, at least she allowed my mother some closure. I'll never forgive her, but I'm not delusional enough to place the blame solely on her shoulders. My father wasn't an innocent party to all that happened, but it's difficult to lay blame on someone who can't defend his actions.

"What did you expect me to say?" he challenges.

"You came back to the hospital and failed to tell me that you'd caught them cheating, or that you'd gotten into a fight!" My voice is tight as I try desperately to keep my cool.

"I couldn't do it. I wish I could have, Harlow, but I couldn't. I was so scared that if I told you what I'd walked in on, you wouldn't survive it...that *we* wouldn't survive it. At first I was scared to say anything because I was worried about your health, but then I realized what it would do to our relationship. It was your dad and my mom—what normal couple could ever get past that? I hadn't even wrapped my own head around it."

The sincerity in his voice puts a chink in my armor, but it doesn't deter me from arguing his logic.

"You had no right to keep it from me!" I throw back at him. "He died, and I was devastated. I didn't think I could ever be more upset, and you still stayed quiet. You should have told me what happened. I had to sit in a hospital room and listen to my mom, distraught and traumatized, tell me my father had died, and twenty-four hours later you let me watch the police arrest you at my bedside for killing him! How the hell did you think that would have been better than coming clean in the first place?"

My blood boils beneath my skin. I'm agitated and annoyed and upset and every other emotion all at once. My toes curl as I bang the heel of my hand down on the countertop, rattling the fruit bowl and mug tree, making him flinch.

"I didn't know he'd died until you did," he implores. "I switched my phone off when my mom started blowing it up with texts and calls. I thought she was trying to call me to smooth things over. Persuade me not to say anything—I don't know. The moment we found out he'd died I shut down. I knew it was my fault instantly when your mom walked into the room and told you. I didn't need any explanation—I can't explain how—I just knew. You were both in shock. Hell, I was in shock. Keeping it from you wasn't even on my radar at that point. I watched you break down, and all I wanted to do was protect you. Make it better."

"Not telling me didn't make it better." My throat burns as I push the words out. They sound much weaker than I'd intended, my sadness diluting their inflection.

"By the time I realized I needed to say something, it was too late," he acknowledges.

I let my head drop to soak in what he's telling me and about jump out of my skin when the telephone rings. I use the interruption to gather myself and take a few calming breaths. Ellis rests his head in his hands before running them through his hair wearily and says, "You'd better get that."

I slide from the stool and walk across the kitchen, aware of his gaze burning holes into my back as I answer the call.

"Hi, Mrs. Birch. No, I'm okay thank you. Yes, yes it was a shock. I'm all right, though. I'll see you tomorrow, no doubt. Bye, bye."

I place the phone back on its deck and return to Ellis. He doesn't pretend not to stare as I pad along the wooden floor, each step making a faint creak under my weight.

"Mrs. Birch saw us leave and wanted to check in with me," I tell him. "No doubt the whole town will be talking about us now." I'm surprised it's taken this long for anyone to call. I would have bet real money that I'd have had more than one call by now.

"I'm sorry about that. I didn't intend on making a scene." He sounds miserable.

"You know how this place is, you can't blame people for talking. After all, you're kind of newsworthy." It was an off the cuff remark, not meant to offend but Ellis's brows pull together rapidly, causing a deep crease to form between them. I've obviously touched a nerve because he runs a finger around his shirt collar to loosen it. The movement must not help because a moment later he pulls at it again and this time he undoes the top two buttons. The V it creates isn't deep enough for me to see if his chest is still as smooth as it used to be, and I wonder if the years have brought a smattering of golden hair. It bothers me how much I want to know.

I'm tired, that's all it is. The day is catching up with me and causing my brain to fog. That's surely why I'm having inappropriate thoughts when I look at him. Even telling myself this, I don't fully believe it, but the alternative is too painful to process, let alone accept. I let out a yawn, far more exaggerated and louder than I'd anticipated, and not ladylike in anyone's estimations. I was already a little weary from having to say goodbye to a beloved friend. Mrs. Adkins was like the crazy old aunt most people have. The one everyone insists you call "aunt" even though she's no relation whatsoever. I've known her my whole life and her death, although not a shock, still lay heavily in my heart. I can't help but wonder how Mr. Adkins will cope without her.

"You look tired, Harlow," Ellis comments. "How's everything?" He moves his hands up and down pointing at me in a gesture signaling he means my health.

"Oh, you know. I'm still just about breathing," I tell him offhandedly, and try to dismiss the concern that settles like a veil over his face. "I'm part of a clinical trial," I admit.

He nods, staring at me like he wants to know more. *Sorry, buster*, I think to myself. *You lost all rights to know what's going on in my life the moment you decided to shut me out of yours when I needed you most.*

His face looks stricken with panic when I say, "Maybe we should call it a night." He's more than likely worried I won't want to talk to him again. Honestly, I'm still undecided.

"I thought you'd have more questions…" he mutters.

"I do. I'm just not sure I can stomach any more answers to-night."

"Oh," is his response. "I don't suppose you have a number for a cab, do you? My car's back at the Adkins house."

"No, the only cab company left in town stops taking fares past ten. Can you not call an Ubër?" I suggest.

"A what?"

"A cab, an Ubër," I say, repeating myself.

"I have no clue what an Ubër is, Harlow." His confused grin looks genuine, and I can't help but smile.

"How the heck haven't you heard of Ubër?" I muse and watch his face fall, his lips setting in a hard flat line.

"Well, I haven't had much need for taking a cab these last few years," he declares sheepishly, and I instantly feel guilty for not working that out.

"Sleep in one of the twin's rooms," I offer without engaging my brain before opening my stupid fat mouth. I almost gasp when I realize what I've just done. I'm genuinely confused as to why I didn't give it a second thought until the words had already fallen from my lips. And if the stunned expression that's just slid over him is anything to go by, he's as shocked as I am.

What the hell, Harlow? Take it back, tell him you made a mistake, you can't offer him a place to stay, my brain screams.

I shift my weight from one foot to the other, waiting for his response.

Don't panic. He'll say no. Obviously, he wouldn't agree to stay the night. Would he?

"Okay," is all he replies.

Well, shit.

I let out something between a squeak and a noise resembling the word "fine" all in one strangled breath.

I busy myself around the house locking doors and drawing curtains. My shoulders are tense and I'm not sure if it's the strain of a long day taking its toll, or that I'm waiting for the feeling of dread and unease to surface. By the time I'm saying goodnight to Ellis on the landing, a pang of something hits hard in my chest. I walk into my bedroom and climb onto my bed wondering why this situation—as messed up as it is—feels right.

"Love is composed of a single soul inhabiting two bodies."

— ARISTOTLE

CHAPTER

NINE

Safety First

Ellis

What the hell am I doing? I chide, quickly closing the door and leaning against it. Once upon a time this door led to Jake's bedroom, but when I flick on the light switch I see I'm standing in what looks like a room full of crafting stuff. There's a bed pushed up beneath the window, but positioned against every wall are cupboards and cabinets overflowing with quilting fabric and spools of thread. A sewing machine occupies a little station in the corner and looks as though it's seen better days, with a pile of what looks like baby clothes resting precariously next to it. Curiosity gets the better of me, and I move over to take a better look. There are boys and girls clothes in different sizes, all apparently used and a little faded. Some have been cut into squares and are stacked by the machine in a small pile. I thumb through them, wondering who they belong to because some look really dated. There's a small, framed picture above the machine of Harlow, Jarod and Jake. It's candid, none of them are even looking at the camera, too busy playing *all pile on*. Harlow's perched on top of her brothers looking smug and I don't think I'd fully realized until this moment how much I've missed the twins. They were like my older brothers too.

The pipes begin to moan and rattle in the walls and I drop the fabric, realizing Harlow must be about to take a shower. I don't intentionally try and think about her naked in the next room but the moment the thought enters my head I can't seem to push it away. Being here was a stupid mistake. I can't stay knowing she's right next door and I can't go to her. It was a reckless decision; I should have just walked back into town to collect my car. The instant I hear her shower door slide open I let out an involuntary groan, picturing her stepping in under the water. Now I know I've royally screwed myself over. Thoughts of her undressed dance behind my eyelids when I shut them tight, and I unwillingly remember the sensation of wanting her so badly that first time. The ache spreads across my torso quickly and begins pooling, hot and heavy, deep in my gut. Red flags go up and now I'm sure it's definitely not safe to stay.

1996

It was almost a whole year before Harlow showed signs of fully recovering from mono. I, like everyone else around her, had expected her to bounce back within a couple of weeks, but it didn't happen. She went back to see her doctor numerous times with little in the way of an explanation. I never did catch it, even though we were practically glued at the hip. Sure, the main effects of the disease had subsided, but she never really seemed to recover her energy. She was always tired and lethargic—a complete contrast to the Harlow I'd first met.

Sixteen-year-old Harlow may have had less vigor when it came to taking our boards out to the skate park or swimming in the pond out back, but when it came to making out, my girl had stamina. From that first hurried kiss on my lawn two years ago, we'd perfected our technique. Each and every time we kissed I was astounded at how much more I wanted to do it again. At some point she'd gotten me hooked, and I became addicted to her. Harlow was my drug of choice and one I couldn't imagine I'd ever want, or even be able, to give up.

My parents weren't surprised when we told them we were dating. My dad felt the need to give me a man-to-man discussion on how to treat a girl, along with a watered-down, panicked attempt at the birds and the bees. My dad's always been as cool as a cucumber—you couldn't rattle him no matter how hard you tried. Except, of course, unless you asked him to talk about sex and relationships with his then fourteen-year-old son. It was like one of those ridiculously old Sex-Ed videos they used to make kids watch at school, only far less informative.

Being the model child that I was, I decided to have a little fun with him. He'd managed to babble on long enough to ask me if I'd ever used a condom. To say he looked uncomfortable at that point in the conversation was a massive understatement. He was clutching his glass of Jack like his life depended on it.

"Sure, I've used them a couple of times," I told him, trying to keep a check on the laughter I was struggling to not blurt out.

His face crumpled. "Right, ah, hmm. Was it on your own? Or, you know…with a girl?" he spluttered.

"Don't worry, Dad, it was a solo mission. Got to say, though, I don't like them much."

"No guy does," he retorted instinctively, before deciding it was the wrong thing to say. "But it's important to use them," he added. His shoulders relaxed a little, and he pinched the bridge of his nose shaking his head. A few seconds passed as he regained his composure and then gave me a questioning stare, his eyes narrowed in confusion.

"Why don't you like them?" It was evident he didn't want the answer, but feeling duty-bound to have this talk, he'd asked anyway.

"They're too small, they kind of hurt," I replied nonchalantly. I watched as the side of his mouth lifted in a smirk, and I had to bite down on the inside of my cheek.

"Too small?"

"Yeah, do you not think so?"

"Well son, it's a problem I bet every man wishes he had," he laughed. "But, they're pretty stretchy. I can't say that I've ever had a problem with them," he admitted looking somewhat embarrassed. "Are you sure you're putting them on right?"

I wanted to laugh so badly, but winding him up was too much fun, so I kept going.

"Sure," I shrugged. "Rolling it on is fine, it's a snug fit. It's tucking my balls in that's uncomfortable."

Looking back, I could have timed it better. Dad had just taken a sip of his whiskey and promptly spat it out straight into my face. Whiskey burns like a bitch on your eyeballs. I'm not sure if it was his reaction that had my eyes watering as I broke out in laughter or the sour mash melting my irises, but damn it was worth it.

"Are you messing with me?" he asked looking alarmed.

"Of course!" I replied, wiping my eyes.

"Jesus, kid!" He pushed my shoulder and shook his head before breaking down and laughing with me.

Dating Harlow didn't really feel like dating at all. We still hung out as much as we ever had, and laughed and played stupid pranks on one another. The only notable difference was being able to kiss her anytime I wanted, and at sixteen years old, that was a lot. I felt like I was living my life with a perpetual hard-on. I'd spent a lot of time getting acquainted with my hand, just to be able to function. Aside from the odd not-so-accidental boob graze, we kept everything pretty much PG. I wanted to take things further, what guy wouldn't? I wasn't an asshole, though, and just because I couldn't look at her for more than fifteen seconds without picturing us naked didn't mean that she couldn't. There was an invisible boundary we pressed against every time we made out. Call me a romantic, or a goddamn wimp, but I needed her to be the one to push through it. I wanted her to need me as much as I needed her. If it meant that I had to wait, it was a small price to pay.

Harlow was insanely pretty, and the best part was she didn't even know it. Other girls at our school seemed hyper-aware of the guys around them checking them out, but not Harlow. She was completely oblivious. She stood out for all the right reasons: her face was always fresh and make-up free, or at least it looked that way. Her hair was always wild and unkempt. She practically lived in shorts, and I thanked the Lord every day for it because her legs were amazing. She was literally the beautiful girl next door, and my raging hormones couldn't take her proximity. I couldn't get enough.

"How do I tell Harlow I want to take things to the next level?" I asked Logan, cupping my hand over the receiver and whispering like it was some deadly top-secret, sensitive information that nobody was allowed to hear.

"Define next level," he asked through a yawn.

I'd decided to call him for advice, given that my other three options weren't really options at all. I could have asked my dad, but asking your father for tips on how to put the moves on your girl just seemed plain wrong and creepy. I could have asked Elliott, but in doing so, I'd negate the need for his advice because that boy has a loud mouth. The whole town would know my intentions within seconds of me asking him for his opinion. He had an uncanny knack for distributing gossip faster than a bullet can leave a gun. Harlow would kill me if she ever thought I'd talked to him about us, which left me with my final option.

The twins.

They were the closest things to brothers I had, and we had a great relationship, but not so great that I could ask them for advice on how to initiate a build up to sex with their little sister. After all, I didn't have a death wish, and I'd grown quite fond of both my kneecaps. That only left Logan—my oldest friend, confidante, and the one person I could guarantee would never let me live the question down.

"Don't be a dick. You know what I'm asking. Don't make me spell it out, Lo."

"Well, how far have you been with her? I can't help you if I don't even have a starting point."

"Jesus, I'm beginning to regret this already. It feels awkward telling you what I do with my girlfriend."

"Stop being such a damn girl. Has your mom been buying that creepy bread with the extra estrogen in it or something?"

"What?" I asked, utterly perplexed at his question.

"You, my friend, are turning into a pussy. I figured you must have been eating the same shit that my mom does. She's going through menopause, or at least I think she is, that's what my dad keeps saying. She found some weird store that sells food packed with female hormones. I'm not even joking, I don't dare eat at home anymore. I'm probably gonna start growing boobs."

"What the hell, Logan?" I said through my laughter. "I have no clue what you're even talking about anymore."

"Look, you're the one calling for my expert knowledge," he uttered. "What base are you at?"

"I don't know. I guess I'm rounding third?"

"Nice! I'm virtually high-fiving you right now, bro. If she's already blowing you, why do you need to know how to take things further?

"She's not blowing me yet, Christ."

"You just said you were rounding third. Ellis, do you even know your bases? Or has she just not returned the favor yet?"

I considered his question and promptly decided that I was an asshole. I could practically see him raising a brow and grinning like a moron.

The only person I needed to speak to about Harlow and me was Harlow; I just didn't want her to feel any pressure.

"You know what? It doesn't matter. I'll figure it out," I answered, looking out of the window toward her house.

"Dude, it's midnight, and you woke me up to have some internal battle with yourself that I really didn't need to be part of. You've been together forever; if you wanna have sex with her, just wine 'n dine her and pull out the big guns. Drop the L word, and you're golden—now, can I go back to bed? I was in the middle of a pretty awesome dream about the new guidance counselor at school. Man, she's smoking hot," he said before letting out a low whistle. "I need to come up with some issues that I can get her to help me with."

I couldn't help but laugh; Logan talks the talk, but that's pretty much it.

"That fact that you're having wet dreams about your school guidance counselor is probably issue enough."

"Fuck off, Ellis."

"Miss you too, Lo."

"Night."

I dropped the receiver down and went to bed wondering how in the hell I'd broach the subject of going further with Harlow. What we had was solid and good. The last thing I wanted was to push for something that she might not be ready for and ruin everything in the process.

I didn't get much sleep that night, or any other night for the next two weeks while I built up the courage to talk to her.

"Am I missing something here, Ellis?" she asked as I led her through the garden, past the pond and out onto the jetty at the back of my house. The sky was just turning from a warm orange dusk to a blanket of darkness. The sound of the cicadas and crickets was more pronounced out here by the long grass flanking the water's edge.

"Nope, I just wanted to talk with you," I answered, leading her out across the creaky wooden walkway.

"So what's all this?" She gestured to the mason jars I'd stolen from my mom's pantry and filled with tea lights. I was almost sure they'd have all blown out, given the time it had taken me to get Harlow down here. They were nearly all still alight, though, casting flecks of gold that danced across the ripples in the creek. It had worked out better than I'd imagined.

"It looks so beautiful," she smiled, twirling around and soaking up the sight.

"Not as pretty as you," I laughed.

"That was lame."

"I know. I don't even have a good comeback from that," I told her. I captured her waist and pulled her close to me, flattening her back to my chest and resting my head on one shoulder so that our checks were grazing.

"So, I've been thinking," I began.

"Wow, you should maybe sit down," she teased so I squeezed her a little and pinched at her side, making her giggle.

"I'm serious. I've been thinking a lot about us lately, and I wanted to talk some things through with you."

Her eyes instantly lost the humor that shone in them seconds before, and her smile flattened.

"It's nothing bad." I was quick to reassure her.

"Okay then…what is it?"

I took a deep breath and steeled myself, ready to admit to her that I wanted her—in every possible way you could ever want another person. It's funny how you build a moment up so big in your head that it becomes damn scary. Suddenly standing with her pressed against me, I couldn't quite figure why I'd ever been nervous as all.

"If I loved you less, I might be able to talk about it more."

—JANE AUSTEN

CHAPTER

TEN

Crossing a Line

Harlow

The thing about grief is that it manifests and affects people in different ways. It doesn't even have to be death that elicits the grieving process, just loss. When my father died, I mourned him in the way you might expect a daughter to mourn a parent. I was acutely aware of his infidelity, but the emotion and anger it caused were soon squashed under the crippling weight of the sadness, knowing I'd never get to see him again. I understood the grief I was feeling, it made sense to me. What confused me was the way I could never grieve Ellis; I had no outlet for that particular sorrow. I couldn't let my mother watch me pine for the person that took her husband. I couldn't talk to my brothers about how much I missed the man that had stolen their dad, so I internalized—I shut down. Once it was clear that Ellis had no intention of speaking with me, or ever letting me visit, I locked my melancholy and heartache up and buried it deep inside me. I refused to talk about missing him with my therapists, and slowly over the course of the years, I tricked myself into believing I didn't miss him.

I hoped that standing under this scorching stream of water would wash some sense back into me but it hasn't. Taking a shower usually clears my mind but it's failing tonight. Knowing Ellis is right next-door has clear blown the locks off the chest where I'd packed my feelings for him. His being here has left me completely exposed, too sensitive, and too raw. The heat of the water isn't enough to chase away the chill bumps that cover my body whenever I think about him, how much I hate him for leaving me, and how badly I want him to stay. How badly I want him, period.

I don't need to ponder the notion that there's a relationship between sex and grief. It's a well-documented opinion, even if it's a little taboo. In much the same way that people turn to or from food or alcohol, sex is merely another appetite at your conscience's disposal to either be suppressed or magnified. It seems that in a cruel twist of fate, the latter is proving true for me.

It's not surprising if I really think about it. I'd fallen for Ellis the same way a person falls from a height. Once you've slipped over the edge it's over and you're gone, tumbling powerlessly, knowing that the only thing left to do is pray you survive the fall. Plenty of movies feature estranged couples stricken and overcome with lust when they reunite. It's a typical reaction—or at least that's what I'm letting myself believe. Wanting Ellis, even after all this time, is my body's way of responding to the sudden flood of anguish that's hit me.

I turn into the spray and let the water cover my face. *I'm not a bad person for missing his touch*, I tell myself as I let my mind drift. I'm only human.

1998

My mother has always maintained that patience is a virtue, and the best things in life are worth waiting for. I have to give her credit; although I like to think of myself as a well-balanced individual, patience is one quality I've struggled to practice my whole life. I like moving forward, I've never been the girl who takes things slow. But when it came to Ellis, I'm grateful that for once I listened to my mom.

The first time Ellis broached the subject of sex, I could quite easily have agreed to take that step with him, and it would have been the wrong time. I was constantly battling my conscience in a lust and hormone-fueled fog. I'd wake up one morning and be absolutely convinced that I wanted to have sex with him. It would be all I could think about. But, then there were days where I'd obsess over taking the next step to the point of inducing a panic attack. What would my parents think of me if they found out? What if I became that one dreaded statistic—the teenage girl who ends up pregnant even though she's on the pill?

I was in love with my boyfriend and couldn't imagine wanting anyone more, but it wasn't enough to quiet my fears. We weren't ready in any sense of the word. Our relationship, though strong, was far too immature. We spent many nights sitting out on the jetty behind his house talking about what we wanted from each other. When it came down to it, we agreed that it wasn't just a need to fulfill a physical urge that was driving the conversation—we wanted to feel a deeper connection. It would have been more than easy to fall into bed with each other; things with

Ellis were always easy and natural, but sex has a way of complicating situations.

I remember the day Jared came home from college looking like he'd seen a ghost. He broke down in front of my mom the second she asked if he was okay. I don't think I'd ever seen Jared cry out of sheer turmoil until that night. A former one-night stand had shown up at his dorm claiming she was pregnant, and that the baby was his. I remember the look of disappointment on my mom's face and the utter helplessness on my brother's. Three weeks later, the girl contacted him and told him it was a false alarm, but I'm pretty sure the stress alone of the whole debacle had aged him ten years overnight.

Ellis and I had made a vow to abstain from sex until we were both confident that we were ready, but decided that if sex was our end goal, we could have fun exploring everything else that came before it. I never realized that talking about it would turn us into insatiable animals. Once we both knew that it was eventually going to happen, the anticipation, along with our sexual tension, skyrocketed. What began as fooling around and exploring each other's bodies became so much more. Touches turned to caresses; kisses became embraces and lust evolved into love. We eventually decided that we were ready, and it was a day neither of us will forget.

It started off like any other Saturday. Mom and Dad were packing up the car to drive to their favorite old Inn at Sea Breeze. They'd been going every year since they began dating, and usually, my brothers were drafted back home to make sure I didn't burn the place down. This was the first time I'd been allowed to stay by myself. Honestly, I don't see why one tiny kitchen fire when I was thirteen had been held over my head for five years.

"Morning, beautiful," Ellis crooned as he stepped onto our porch and caught hold of my belt loop, pulling me into him for a hug. His six-two frame dwarfed my five-five as he dipped his head to kiss the top of mine. He was wearing cargo shorts and his faded red hoodie that had been through the wash so many times it was almost coral-colored. He rocked back and forth on his heels looking like the cat that got the cream, making it far too obvious that he was excited to see my parents leaving.

"Morning, buttercup," Dad deadpanned as he carried Mom's bag to the trunk of the car, doing his best to ignore our PDA. Dad and Ellis had a great relationship, given that they were both maddeningly infatuated with the Wilmington Wild-cats—our school's hockey team. Dad was a former assistant coach, and Ellis was our school's starting center. If they started talking plays or stats, I knew to make other plans because they'd go at it for hours.

"Two whole nights," he whispered into my ear, sending a shiver down to the base of my spine. "I get you for two whole nights."

"Shush!" I admonished in a whisper-shout. Having your father suspect what was likely going to happen between you and your boyfriend was one thing, having him overhear that his suspicions were founded was not something I wanted to occur.

"Morning, Ellis." My mom brushed passed us on the porch carrying a blue striped beach umbrella that had definitely seen better days. She off-handed it to my dad at the car before skipping back up the steps and giving me a kiss on the cheek.

"You have the number of the Inn—it's stuck to the refrigerator, and there's plenty of food in the cupboards. Oh, and for heaven's sake, Harlow, make sure you have Ellis close by if you attempt any cooking on the stove. I'm sure you guys will stay out of trouble while we're gone," she said looking at Ellis's hands still resting on my waist.

"Relax, Mrs. Stevens, I'll take good care of her."

The double meaning of Ellis's words wasn't lost on me, and by the look on my mom's face, she hadn't missed it either.

"They're eighteen!" my dad called from the car. "Leave them be, Dianne, we need to get on the road. Oh and Ellis…"

"Yes sir?" he called back.

"I know where you live." I'm sure Dad's facial expression was his attempt to look menacing, but it looked more like he was experiencing stomach cramps. Mom shook her head at him and rolled her eyes.

"Okay, we're off. I'll call later."

Ellis and I watched as my mom climbed into the car and my parents each waved a hand out of their windows as they descended from our drive.

"So, should we just get naked now or wait a little while?" Ellis teased.

"I'm good, thanks. But, if you want to sit naked while Molly and I study for our English Lit final next week, feel free."

His groan was kind of adorable. "Are you serious? She's coming over?"

"Yeah, but only for a couple of hours, max. She's acing that class, so I'm not going to turn away her offer to help me study. Besides, we have a whole weekend together. Two hours won't kill you."

His pout told me that maybe he thought it would.

Molly and I had become friends over the past two years since we shared most of our classes. We still had relatively little in common, but I think that's what made our friendship work. We were chalk and cheese—had differing opinions on everything from music to fashion to politics. Not that I had the first clue about anything political, but Molly did. Behind her bubblegum pink lip gloss and teeny, tiny midriff exposing t-shirted exterior—she was ridiculously smart. When Molly first started coming over, I thought my mom would about burst with happiness.

"It's not normal to have no female friends," she'd said once while we were at the mall. She was looking over at a group of

girls sitting at a table in the coffeehouse we'd stopped at. I'd insisted that she buy me caffeine if she were going to drag me
around any more stores. "I never had lots of girlfriends, but a
select four or five. We did everything together," she carried on.
"Shopped, hung out. You always spend your time with Ellis and
his friends. I never see you talking to any girls."

"They're not only Ellis's friends," I'd replied, "they're my
friends too, and we all like the same things and have fun. So
what if they're guys?"

She'd huffed and dropped the subject, sipping on her latte
instead. I looked over at the group of girls that had caught her
attention; they didn't seem to be doing anything that I didn't do
with the boys. They were talking animatedly and laughing, just
like I did with my friends, and I didn't feel like I was missing out
on anything. Even if my Mom seemed to think I was.

"I'll take more pizza."

Ellis's scowl was etched across his ridiculously handsome
face. I'd never seen his clear blues look so stormy. Molly had
reached across the kitchen table, snatching up the last slice of
pepperoni, and Ellis used the distraction to give me the "why is
she still here" glare. A couple of hours had turned into all morning and most of the afternoon.

"Molly, what time are you heading home? Harlow and I
have plans."

His attempt at subtlety left little to be desired. Molly looked
over at me sheepishly.

"I guess we did get carried away. Let me finish up." She
gestured to her pizza and soda. "I'll get going in five."

I kicked Ellis's shin under the table.

"No hurry," I told her. I half wanted to invite her to stay, just to get back at Ellis for his rudeness.

"So, what do you have planned?" she asked.

"It's a surprise," Ellis answered, winking, and I could literally feel the blush crawl up my neck and heat my face.

"Oh…well, have fun," she fumbled, loading the textbooks she'd brought with her into her backpack at an insane speed. I walked her out, feeling like she knew all too well the surprise he had planned.

Molly barely made it down the porch steps before turning and flashing me a megawatt smirk. "I expect details," was all she said as she walked across the grass, making her way home.

My neighborhood was the kind of place where nobody bothered to lock their doors, and everybody seemed to know everything that was going on almost as soon as it happened. I stepped back into the house, locked the front door and drew the curtain across the window. I didn't need anyone popping in to check on me and catch me with my pants down—metaphorically or literally.

"Finally!" Ellis appeared at the entrance to the family room. His grin was crooked, and his eyes hooded as he looked me over unashamedly. His tall frame filled the door as he leaned casually against the mount, crossing his bare feet at the ankle. What was it about a guy with bare feet? It should have grossed me out, but instead, it did the opposite. It's like the strange voodoo trickery men do by wearing a dress shirt and rolling the sleeves up, instantly making them appear ten times hotter.

I padded over to him, lifting on my tiptoes and tilting my head, waiting for him to bend down so I could kiss him. I intended it to be a peck, a quick, chaste apology for spending almost the entire day ignoring him while I studied. Molly and I had been on a roll and effectively left poor Ellis to fend for himself. He disappeared for a couple of hours mid-morning; no doubt the boredom had gotten too much for him.

His answering kiss wasn't fleeting, though, nor was it chaste. It was a deep, passionate toe-curling kiss. The type you see in romance films that cause the girl to pop her leg, fairytale-princess style, and sigh. I wanted to melt against him as his mouth moved over mine, his teeth grazing my bottom lip. I couldn't pop either leg because suddenly they didn't even feel like my own.

"Wow, what was that for?" I asked pulling back to take a much-needed breath.

"I missed you."

"I've been right here all day, how can you have missed me?" I asked incredulously.

His blue eyes sparkled as he scooped me up from the floor like I weighed nothing at all. I may have a small frame and the kind of figure that could have me mistaken for a twelve-year-old boy in the right lighting—but weightless I was not. I wound my legs around his waist as he linked his hands beneath my butt, resting me on his tight narrow hips. He liked to pick me up to kiss me; it saved on the kinks in his neck from having to bend.

"I haven't really spoken to you all day, and you were sitting there with a pencil stuck in your hair, chewing on another while reading. It was unreasonably arousing." He wiggled his brows, and I laughed. "All I've wanted to do all day is get you on your own, so I could do this."

I didn't have time to ask what "this" was. His mouth was hot against my neck, dragging slow, damp kisses down and across my collarbone, sending a swarm of butterflies wild in my stomach. It's not as though Ellis and I hadn't explored each other's bodies before. There had been two years of exploration and conquering firsts. This time was different. This time held the promise of sex, and even though I was madly in love with my boyfriend, trusted him implicitly and wanted more than anything to take this final step—nerves still overtook me.

"You're trembling?" he whispered.

I looked at Ellis's face, the familiarity of his bright blue eyes, framed by impossibly long dark golden lashes—they were soft and adoring. He looked comfortable and confident like we weren't about to cross a line that could never be stepped back over. I couldn't help being a little envious of his seemingly natural state.

"Aren't you nervous?" I asked, letting a little of my usual bravado slip.

"Of what? Being alone with you? Harlow, we've been alone a million and one times before now. There's really nothing to be nervous about. I'm not going to suddenly pounce on you or make you do anything you don't want to do just because we get to spend the night together."

His smile was evident in the soft tone he was using with me.

"Okay, but let's be real, Ellis—we're about to lose our virginity tonight, and you know it," I blurted. "You don't look even the slightest bit apprehensive."

He removed one of my arms from around his neck, still resting me on his hip. I watched curiously as he placed my palm flat against his chest, and over his heart.

"Does that answer how unaffected you seem to think I am?" he asked.

I held my breath for a second, registering the way his heart was swiftly fluttering beneath my palm like a hummingbird's wings. That's all the reassurance that I didn't know I needed. I instantly felt a little of my tension dissolve.

"I can't speak for you," he confessed, "but I don't feel like I'm about to lose anything. It can't be defined as a loss when it seems so much like all I stand to do is gain another piece of you."

I didn't know at that moment whether I wanted to laugh, cry, or kiss the heck out of Ellis Hughes for being sickeningly perfect.

I went with the kiss.

My stomach tightened in anticipation as he shifted his stance and began to carry me up the stairs toward my room, never once breaking the kiss our lips were locked in. He lowered me onto the bed and slid on top of me, framing my face between his forearms. Every part of my body was suddenly very aware of the fact he'd laid me down on my bed. Excitement and nerves caused a shiver to race across my body. The look of pure reverence in his eyes mirrored what I'm sure he must have been able to see on my own.

"I want to give you everything, be with you always, you know that, right? You know how much I love you?" he asked, leaning in to kiss the tip of my nose.

I nodded, emotion clogging my throat. My pulse was racing frantically as I waited for him to touch me. I'd never craved it so much, and yet I was trembling as though it were something new, not something I'd already experienced.

His hands found the button on my shorts, popping it open with adept fingers. I watched him as he carefully removed my shorts, pulling them all the way down my legs, and then running his fingertips back up over my thighs. My body was on fire. We'd been in this position before, but knowing where it was leading this time had my blood coursing like lava through my veins.

I wanted him on a whole new level that I never realized existed. The sexual tension between us was palpable, and I was almost at breaking point.

"I'm so in love with you," I whispered as he pressed his body back down over me and his lips found mine. I moaned as his tongue slipped into my mouth, and I pulled him as hard against me as I could. Our kiss was only interrupted when I scrambled to remove his shirt up over his head, and he did the same with mine.

My body tightened in anticipation as I realized he'd managed to remove the remainder of his clothes while I was appar-

ently caught up in a kissing-induced haze. My head was screaming that this was really happening, and I closed my eyes, trying
to contain the elation building. I felt his weight lift from me, then
heard the telltale sound of a foil packet being torn. His palms
spread over my stomach, causing my eyes to snap to his face. I
watched as he bit the corner of his lip and dragged his fingers
lower over my abdomen. His breath hitched as he hooked my
underwear and removed them.

"You're sure?" he whispered against my neck, burying his
face into the crook of my shoulder.

I slid my hands up his back and around over his shoulders,
making my way up to cradle his face, loving the warmth and
weight of him on top of me.

"Positive," I smiled.

"I love you," he whispered fixing his hand under my thigh
and lifting it to rest against his hip. "So damn much."

He pushed into me without warning, not giving me time to
worry about the logistics of what was supposed to fit where. The
sound of his breath catching was drowned out by my startled cry
of his name.

His body pushed deeper before he paused perfectly still.
"I'm sorry if that hurt," he panted, trembling, as he remained
poised above me. He dipped his head to kiss my forehead. "Are
you okay?"

Tears pooled at the corners of my eyes, and I needed to
blink rapidly to clear them away. I nodded. "It's fine, I'm fine." I
breathed shakily.

"You're crying, Harlow. Baby, we can stop," he whispered,
as worry rapidly clouded his demeanor.

"No, honestly, I don't want to. I'm okay."

His face softened, a lingering sense of hesitance still there. I
rocked into him, the movement so slight I wondered if he'd miss
it. His lips parted with his intake of breath and the way his eyelids almost fell closed confirmed that he hadn't.

"Tell me what you want me to do. If you want me to stop I will. I'd never…"

"Ellis, keep going."

I smiled as he cradled my face and began to kiss me, slow and steady at first, matching the rhythm of his hips, only stopping when he moved his mouth to my ear to tell me how incredible what I was doing was, or how much he loved me. It didn't take long for our bodies to fall into synchronization. Our kisses deepened, soft caresses became hurried and breathless along with our tempo.

Our movements turned into an insane war of crashing lips, and wandering hands, hard deep thrusts, and gentle strokes. I could feel his heartbeat thundering against his smooth, hard chest each time he leaned over me. I didn't know if I wanted him to speed up, slow down, or mix up the two, but when his hand slid down between our slick hot bodies, it was game over for me. There were too many sensations to handle, and I was dizzy as my body gave into Ellis's touch.

I'd thought about what our first time would be like a lot over our relationship, wondering how it would play out, where we'd be, if I'd enjoy it, if he would. I never considered that I'd feel even closer to him just by making love—but it happened. I didn't contemplate for a second that instead of closing my eyes, I'd watch him in the exact way he was watching me. Feeling so in the moment that I wished I'd be able to memorize every touch he pressed into my skin, every little movement, and each meticulous detail of our lovemaking.

My body lay heavily on the mattress as I tried to control my breathing and calm the erratic drum beat in my chest. My limbs felt tired and cumbersome. I'm no stranger to romance novels and movies, so I figured I'd only need a minute before we were ready for round two.

The whole fiction-versus-reality thing didn't work out for me. I was still out of breath a full five minutes later, and fighting against my too heavy eyelids that wanted so desperately to close. I conceded that I was no romance heroine, made my peace with it, and nestled down deep onto Ellis's chest, knowing that at that precise moment in time, I was right where I belonged.

"The heart has its reasons of which reason knows nothing."

— BLAISE PASCAL

CHAPTER

ELEVEN

Missing a Beat

Ellis

Sleep doesn't come easily to me, not as an adult anyway. I used to close my eyes and drift into a deep, peaceful slumber knowing Harlow was lying beside me and our whole life was ahead of us. Ever since being locked up I rarely sleep a full two hours without waking up in a cold sweat. Sometimes I'm able to remember my nightmares, but other times I'm jolted awake in a panic and have no real cognitive recognition as to why.

Prison will do that to a guy—make everything they've ever taken for granted, even sleep, into something to fear. You'd have to be an idiot to think that the experience is anything less than torturous, but what you don't realize is that it's the little things that get to you the most. Sure, you have some of your own belongings while you're inside, but they provide little to no comfort. When I was first locked up, I used to try to drown out all the noises before I could fall asleep. There'd be constant banging, shouting, and even smells that kept me awake. I soon realized that the external noises were easier to fall asleep to than the quiet.

Silence was scarier than the noise because it left room for your own imagination. It's amazing what your mind can conjure up to torment you.

Surprisingly, it hadn't taken me long to fall asleep tonight. Rehashing the past was mentally exhausting, but I'd fully primed myself for not being able to rest for even a wink. Here I am, though, at 3:23 am if the clock on the windowsill is correct. I apparently misjudged how drained I was, and now I'm feeling more rested than I probably have the right to. The last thing I remember is undressing and climbing under the comforter that smelled like Harlow and being ridiculously turned on by that. The bed groans and the floor creaks as I shift from my back and roll onto my side to find a comfier position. The sound reminds me of the rickety bed Harlow and I bought at Duke. Anyone within a ten-block radius could hear the springs squeak whenever we attempted to get it on.

I'm smiling at the memory and the heat it causes to slide over my body, but it's short-lived because I hear what sounds like sobbing coming from the landing outside the door. The warmth quickly turns to an icy chill as I toss the sheets aside and swing my legs out of bed, letting them hit the floor with a thud. I'm at the door in three long strides in nothing but my underwear, and out onto the landing before I can register what the hell I'm even doing. The hall's dark and still, there's no indication that Harlow was even out here. Her bedroom door is firmly closed and I'm about to turn and go back to bed, convinced I'd imagined the noise, when a light flicks on from somewhere downstairs and filters up the stairwell from below. I don't hesitate for a second as I rush the stairs, and when I hear another sob, I jump the bottom three, rounding into the kitchen as quickly as I can.

She's bent at the fridge, the door obscuring most of her from my view, but when she straightens and closes it, she turns around and lets out an almighty shriek, hurling the milk carton she's taken out straight at my head. Sleep has apparently left my reflexes sluggish; I duck but not quite quickly enough. The carton connects with my forehead and implodes on impact, dousing me in ice-cold milk and prompting an involuntary yelp of my own.

"Jesus, that's cold!" I screech as my body spasms like a fish pulled from the water. I tilt at the waist in a futile attempt to stop the milk running the full length of my body but it's useless, I'm covered. The shock of the cold gives way to an acute ache across my forehead, and I rub the spot where the carton connected.

Her eyes are trained on my abs, now coated in a slick gloss of white liquid, as she takes a second to register what the hell is happening. I can almost see the cogs turning as she works out the view in front of her. I'm swiping milk from my lashes, and her features are turning from wide-eyed and startled to something resembling humor. I'm standing in a puddle, wearing a soggy pair of boxers, a shocked expression, and nothing else.

Then something magical happens.

What sounds like a mixture of a bark and a snort escapes her, filling the silence between us. It lifts the heavily-charged energy that's been following us around and replaces it with something altogether lighter. That's all it takes. She's gone. Full-blown hysterical laughter bubbles from her wide-stretched lips as she desperately grabs hold of the countertop, bending and gasping for air through her giggling fit. Her hair falls across her face and she clutches at her side, laughing uncontrollably.

It sounds amazing. If throwing shit at me is all it takes to make her laugh like this, she can empty the full goddamn fridge and pelt me with its contents all night long.

"You're soaked," she hisses through her teeth, trying to rein herself in and failing miserably. "I didn't mean to throw it at you...you scared me and I just...I reacted."

The thing with laughter is that it's ridiculously infectious, like when you see someone yawn, try as you might, you can't help but yawn yourself. I begin laughing at how incapacitated her own laughter has rendered her, and it only adds fuel to her flames. Tears gather at the corners of her eyes, and for the first time this evening it's the good kind—the kind I have absolutely no problem causing. The more she laughs, the more it makes me laugh, and the more I laugh it causes her to continue on even harder. It feels incredible.

"You've been working on that pitching arm I see," I joke, rubbing my head again.

"Nah, just a lucky shot," she retorts. "I think it's gonna bruise," she confesses and scrunches up her nose like she may actually feel a little guilty.

I couldn't give a toss if there were blood pouring from my head right now, it would be a small price to pay for the last three minutes. I can feel my smile widen as she takes a step closer, squinting at my forehead. She's standing barefoot in the puddle of milk that surrounds me and lifts onto her tiptoes, reaching out to touch the spot she's looking at. The movement raises her chest up closer to mine, and the oversized gray t-shirt she's wearing slides dangerously high up her thighs.

Suddenly this whole situation isn't half as humorous anymore. Her teeth sink into her bottom lip, and the faintest of sighs escapes. It's just loud enough for me to notice as she runs the tip of her index finger across my temple and I about lose my mind. I have zero clue about how to react or what to do with my hands as I freeze in place. My heart is screaming for me to wrap them around her waist and pull her in, but my head is telling me to stop being an irrational prick and take a step back for both our sakes.

"Well, there's no lump at least," she coos.

I attempt to flash her an easy smile that's anything but. "Good."

My voice comes out lower than I'd anticipated and doesn't sound like my own. I'm pretty sure I've stopped breathing, too. Harlow's face is hovering in front of me, and I have to wonder if she knows what she's doing. If she's purposefully trying to torture me right now. I watch as her top teeth slowly drag against her bottom lip and the groan it brings out in me can't be helped. Every single nerve ending in my body spontaneously combusts, and the need I have for her is unbearable. I close my eyes because if I have to look at her for even a nano-second longer, I can't be held accountable for my actions, it just wouldn't be fair.

"Ellis?"

My name's a whisper, and I screw my eyes up even tighter so I don't accidently look down at her mouth. It's painful. Physically painful to be this close to her and hear her whisper my name like she wants me. I don't respond, but it's not because I don't want to, it's because I physically can't. I'm fighting a magnetic force so irresistible that I begin trembling as I force myself not to move and stand my ground.

"Ellis," she says again, only this time I feel the word breathed over my mouth and my eyes fly open instinctively just in time to watch hers close.

She leans forward.

I stop breathing.

And then she kisses me.

It takes a moment to register that her lips are pressed against mine by her own will and as soon as it does the gloves are off. I respond with a desperation that should embarrass me, but I couldn't slow myself if my life depended on it. My pulse is wild and out of control, thrumming heavily under my skin as her lips fall into a perfect tempo with mine and I can feel the flush of her skin radiating against me. There's too much longing, and way too much love for me to even attempt to disguise, so I give in and don't.

One of my hands finds the small of her back, pulling her closer still as I slide the other beneath her hair to cradle her head. Her arms slip behind my neck, and her tongue traces the seam of my lips, then everything else ceases to exist. There's no painful past, and no repercussions to fear for the future, just us. In this moment she's just a girl and I'm just a guy, loving each other the only way we know how—passionately—the way we're meant to.

1998

Nothing about Harlow was predictable. She kept me on my toes and lit a light inside of me that only shone when she was around. Without her, I felt like I was left fumbling in the dark. I was in far too deep, and I'd known it from our very first kiss. She was effortless, it took no exertion or strength to love her, and when I was with her she made everything brighter. So, when I watched helplessly as she collapsed out of the blue, my world spiraled into an unfathomable darkness.

"Let's go out, I'm bored." Two hours of reading a math textbook on a Saturday was never my idea of fun, and I'd have been lying if I said that I'd been able to concentrate with my girl-friend perched at the end of my bed. I had a million and one thoughts about how to cure my boredom, but every one of them was tainted by the fact that my parents were sitting downstairs. I'm not opposed to fooling around in public; the thrill of maybe getting caught is an adrenaline rush like no other. Sadly, when it's your parents that stand to catch you, the game loses its appeal. There's nothing quite like the thought of your own mother to calm your libido down to subzero temperatures.

"What do you have in mind?" she'd answered, eagerly closing up her book and scooting closer to me.

"Anything but this, I feel like we've been cooped up in here all day."

"Ellis, it's not even lunchtime." She rolled her eyes and stood up from the bed, stretching like a lazy house cat. The hem of her t-shirt flashed the creamy taught skin of her stomach, and I quickly grabbed her waist, pulling her onto my lap as she let out a startled squeal.

"Don't do that!" she laughed. "You almost gave me a freaking heart attack."

"Always so dramatic, Peewee." She hated the nickname, but I kind of loved the response it initiated.

"DO NOT CALL ME THAT!" she spluttered, trying to twist and nip me. It wasn't hard to hold her back, she was tiny after all, but man, was she fierce when she wanted to be. She could also Chinese burn your arm like a bitch. I guess that's what growing up with siblings teaches you. You don't need size or even a lot of strength to inflict pain.

"Okay, okay! I'm sorry. You're not gonna play dirty, right? If I let go of your arms, please don't make me regret it."

"Fine, but the next time you call me that, I'm revoking all sexual activity—for a week."

"What! How is that a justifiable trade-off?" I scoffed. Her answering scowl told me she wasn't joking.

"Okay, you win. I'm sorry, Harlow. I will not call you Peewee anymore. Scout's honor."

"You forget that I know you've never been a scout, jack-ass."

"Now, now. Less of the name calling or I'll revoke all sexual activity for a week," I mocked. I guess I never did know when to quit because she moved like a ninja and nipple twisted me to the point of actual tears.

I shouted to my dad that we'd decided to head out to the skate park. It was a bright, warm day and far too beautiful to be spent inside. Harlow grabbed her board, and we made our way into town, coasting idly along the quiet winding roads.

"Race you to the park!" she shouted after she'd already passed me.

"You little cheat!"

I frantically began kick-pushing to pick up speed. "You better skate faster than that, H, you're not exactly making this a very hard race. It would be more of a challenge to let you win!" I teased. I was gaining on her fast, but she was still a little way ahead of me.

I watched as she began to slow and then came to an abrupt stop, kicking the tail of her board and catching it under her arm.

"What's up, why'd you stop?" I asked rolling to a halt beside her. "Are you really so worried about losing that you decided to quit?" I tutted.

Her chest was heaving as though she'd run a marathon, not skated two hundred feet. She let her board drop at her side and put her hand up while bending at the waist trying to steady her breathing.

"Harlow, you okay, babe?" I asked rubbing her back.

"I can't—"

Heave.

"Catch—"

Heave.

"My breath."

Heave.

I lost the playful tone in my voice immediately. Her head was glistening with sweat, and she looked pale, at least a few shades lighter than normal.

"Sit down, baby, and rest your head between your knees. Take slow, deep breaths." I had no idea if it would help or not, but that's what my coach told us to do whenever we'd been running drills on the ice all morning, and the rookies looked ready to pass out.

"Does that help?"

She looked up at me, panicked. "I think I'm—"

I jumped back as she vomited onto the sidewalk, her whole body trembling while being wracked with her retching.

"Shit—you're okay, Harlow, I'm here," I told her, quickly trying to gather her hair away from her face. I was racking my brain trying to recall if we'd eaten anything that could have disagreed with her, but in truth, she had a stronger stomach than me—I'd never known anything to make her vomit. She can drink more liquor than a sailor (we'd stolen plenty from her brothers) and still wake up the next day and eat a breakfast burrito. I couldn't think of any logical reason why she would get ill so quickly except one.

"Harlow, you're not pregnant are you?" The question left my lips as soon as it had entered my head, and I had no time to try and disguise the panic in my voice. If the flare of her nostrils were anything to go by, I'd hazard a guess that she didn't appreciate the terrified tone.

"No, why would you think that?" she panted, tilting her head to glare at me.

"I don't know, just the random sickness, I guess."

"I'm more concerned with not being able to breathe," she gasped.

"Shit, I need to get you home."

I searched my pant pockets, but all I turned out was my wallet, a packet of gum and a handful of lint. I hadn't picked up my cell when we'd left the house. We were still a little way off from the skate park, and we were closer to the pier than we were to home.

"You think you can make it to the Bait House? I can call us a cab, or get my dad to come get us."

She nodded but looked less than confident. Her skin was cold and clammy as I slid my arms beneath hers to help her stand.

We walked tentatively down to the pier, stopping a couple of times for her to dry heave. She looked terrible, more so every time I risked a glance in her direction, and it was beginning to worry the hell out of me.

"Ellis," she whispered as her legs gave from under her just meters away from the Bait House entrance. Her eyes had rolled to the back of her head, and my heart dropped to the floor.

"Harlow!"

She didn't respond as I held her body limp against my own.

"Harlow!"

I scooped her legs up and flew through the doors of the Bait House screaming for someone to help me.

I vaguely recall Sal, the owner, dialing 9-1-1 and shouting out questions to me that I didn't have answers for as I laid her down. I'd never felt so useless. One of the kitchen staff that knew first-aid rushed around the counter to help me.

"She's stopped breathing," I cried, staring down at the eerie stillness of her chest. I hovered over her, gripping my hair, tears streaming down my face, praying she'd be okay while the guy from the kitchen looked for her pulse, then began CPR. I could only watch in shock, feeling like I was seeing it unfold in horrifically slow motion. A lady ran in with a portable defibrillator from her boat, pushing me aside and sliding to her knees. She began opening up the box and reading out the instructions loudly to the guy still giving Harlow compressions.

I was terrified, and it dawned on me that if Harlow could hear us, or were even aware of what was going on, she'd be terrified too. I dropped down beside her, grabbing her hand and lacing our fingers together while I did my best to even out my voice, whispering reassurances to her. I kept repeating that everything was going to be okay so she wouldn't be scared. In truth, I was afraid enough for the both of us.

I don't remember much past her shirt being torn open and sticky electrode pads being pressed down onto her chest as the machine beeped, signaling it was ready to dispense a shock. The lady pulled our joined hands apart and pushed me back.

Not knowing how to help her was the single most devastating moment of my life—at least up until that point, anyway.

You can learn a lot in a ten-minute ambulance ride. For instance, you discover what it feels like to watch your girlfriend's heart failing in front of your eyes. The EMTs had let me ride with her, firing questions at me at an alarming rate—her name, age, preexisting conditions, medication, and allergies—all while hooking her up to various machines.

Her heart had been restarted as a result of the lady from the Bait House's quick thinking. The EMT had told me that those patients who received CPR and or a shock from an AED before being hospitalized had better survival rates. I think the guy was trying to reassure me, he'd even leaned over and squeezed my shoulder, but all his words served to do was alert me to the fact that my girlfriend could be about to die.

Eighteen-year-olds weren't supposed to have heart attacks, especially not when they were as fit and healthy as Harlow was. I'd left instructions for Sal to call our parents and have them meet us at the hospital. I might have physically been a man, I had the strength and build, but inside I'd never felt smaller. I was a scared, helpless child that needed his mom and dad.

If I'd thought that sitting in the ambulance with Harlow was bad, it was nothing compared to arriving at the emergency room and not being able to stay with her. I argued powerlessly with one nurse while a porter held me back. I struggled against him, still holding onto her fingers, as another nurse helped him to restrain me, and she was pulled from my grasp.

A team of medical staff wheeled her through a set of double doors and out of sight. I hated them for it. All I could think was that if anything happened to her, I wouldn't be there. I was directed to a waiting room where a nurse promised to update me as soon as she could. That's where her parents found me sitting, crying into my hands and not having a clue as to whether or not Harlow was even alive.

Dianne seemed to morph into calm and collected mode. She headed straight for the nurse sitting at the station set up in the corner of the cold, antiseptic room. Mike seemed to be handling things about as well as me: not good. He looked like he'd aged ten years since I saw him yesterday. I guess that's what fear and worry will do to you. I handed him the paperwork one of the nurses had asked me to fill out, I hadn't even attempted it, but Mike looked like he could do with the distraction.

"She's being sent for an ECG and tests," Dianne proclaimed as she hurried back to us. Mike immediately stood and hugged his wife, the pair of them close to tears.

"She'll be okay, Dianne; she's a tough one," he told her.

"The nurse couldn't say anything more than we already know," she lamented. "Someone should be out to see us soon."

So, we waited.

Hospitals are cold, uninviting places. Have you ever noticed that? There's never a moment when you're in one that you sit back and think, *well this is a nice comfy seat,* or, *what a cozy room.* All the rooms are painted the same washed-out nondescript blue, or pale green. The nurses always look exhausted, because they're juggling too many patients with countless mounds of paperwork. The doctors don't walk; they jog everywhere, too busy to stop and talk to anyone, and if they're talking, they're still walking.

Then there's always that one nurse who's probably never genuinely smiled a day in her life, and who makes you feel like a criminal for wanting to know if there's any news. She'll attempt a smile for you, but it's practiced and fake. She'll tell you that as soon as she has any news, she'll be right out to let you know. Only you can see it's a lie because you've heard her say it to every other person in the waiting room. Yet there we all were—stuck and clueless.

The plant sitting in the corner of the room was a fake. I stared at it for the longest time wondering why it was bothering me so much that the only decoration was a plastic ficus. I wondered if it was because the room had no natural light, being illuminated by fluorescents, which probably meant that it was hard to keep a real ficus alive. The thought that they couldn't maintain a plant's health in a place where keeping people alive was their job didn't just worry me, it fucking terrified me.

"Love is space and time measured by the heart."

— MARCEL PROUST

CHAPTER

TWELVE

Shock Waves

Harlow

The hardest thing in the world is to truly love somebody even when they're no longer around. Harder still if you don't want to like them at all. A decade of telling myself I was over him, of training myself to not compare every other man in my life to Ellis, is undone the moment our laughter arouses feelings I'd told myself I must have imagined because I hadn't experienced anything akin to them since him.

His fingers push through my hair and leave a trail of fire across the back of my neck. My body is alight with sensation, and I'm putty in his hands, desperately drinking up every ounce of passion he's pouring on me. Kissing this Ellis, the older, hardened, rougher version of the man I once knew is even more fantastic than I feared it would be. What a punishing and unfair life I've lived being denied this feeling for so long.

I was eighteen years old when I first learned that life wasn't always fair. I like to think I've always been a glass-half-full person, but sometimes no amount of optimism or positive thinking can prepare you for a blow you have absolutely no control over. I've often wondered if maybe I was a bad person in a former life, because once the punches began rolling in, I don't think they ever stopped.

I was the child that never really got sick. I'd had one bad bout of mono, but in general I seemed to be the only member of my family who managed to dodge colds and sickness bugs. Jared and Jake were like beacons for every illness: if something was making the rounds at school you could bet your last dollar at least one of them would catch it. I was pretty athletic; I was on the school varsity swim team and loved to skateboard. I spent most of my time outdoors and was healthy. Except, I wasn't. I just didn't know it.

The day of my collapse, I'd been feeling a little off, but nothing that worried me. I'd been tired and felt a little dizzy. I was on my period, though, so nothing out of the ordinary, given my monthly cycle. On the way to the skate park that Saturday the dizziness had subsided, and I'd been feeling fine right up until challenging Ellis to race.

I never won him, but I'd always try. My legs started feeling tingly and began to shake, but I ignored it. I was skating as fast as I could; I didn't for a second think anything sinister was happening. Once I pulled in front of Ellis, I knew something was off. I started feeling odd. My chest became too tight, and suddenly I couldn't breathe right. I remember coming to a stop and bending to catch my breath; I could hear Ellis in the background taunting me.

Before I knew what was happening, my vision faltered. It was as if I'd stared directly at the sun. I remember telling Ellis I couldn't catch my breath and vomiting all over my shoes, but most everything after that is still just a blur. The next thing I knew I was laid out in a hospital bed and my chest felt as though someone had rested a ton of bricks precariously atop of me.

"Miss Stevens, you suffered a massive heart attack," the doctor had told me, with little in the way of a gentle build up. The heart attack may not have killed me, but I'm pretty sure the shock of realizing that's what had happened could quite easily have triggered another. I was scared and confused. Nothing made any sense; surely I was too young to have had a heart attack? I was still a teenager. Heart attacks were reserved for middle-aged, overworked, overweight, and severely stressed adults who probably drank too much. I was none of those things.

I wasn't prepared for the battery of tests: ECG's, MRI's, X-rays and blood work. I had wires and electrodes sprouting from every available patch of skin, while machines beeped in the background and nurses came and went, recording results on clipboards and making notes. I felt like a lab rat in some strange science experiment. My parents didn't leave my side, and if they did, it was only to trade places with Ellis or my brothers. Our conversations dwindled into stilted rundowns of my stats, and a barrage of false compliments. *You're looking much better today, Harlow. You seem to have some color back in your cheeks. You're so brave. You're doing really well.*

I hated all of it.

The answers soon came, though, and when they did, I'd rather have gone back to my blissful ignorance. The news irrevocably altered my life in an instant.

I had something called myocarditis, possibly stemming from what the doctors called mononucleosis, which is basically mono. Apparently an EBV (mono) infection can occur if symptoms last for more than six months. I'd been hit with it pretty bad, going to and from Dr. Peterson's office, but it finally sub-sided, and I thought all was well. Everyone did. Apparently, we were all wrong. EBV lies dormant in the blood cells for the rest of your life, and can occasionally reactivate, even without symp-toms, the doctors explained. It was ridiculously rare, but wouldn't you know, I'd be the person to prove the statistic.

I sat dumbfounded. Myocarditis was inflammation of the heart muscle—my heart muscle. It's responsible for contracting and releasing, pumping blood in and out of my heart and the rest of my body. Because it was inflamed from the virus, its ability to pump blood lessened, causing my heart attack. As if that wasn't the kicker, the damage my heart had sustained had altered its rhythm.

"We feel that in your case, Miss Stevens, given the extent of the damage to your heart, you would benefit from being fitted with an ICD—a defibrillation device."

I stared at them, not understanding a word of what they were telling me.

"What do you mean being fitted with a device? Like a pacemaker, you mean?" My head was swimming with the thought of needing to have surgery. I was all right. I felt a little dizzy and collapsed. How could that equate to heart surgery?

"Arrhythmias cause your heart to beat either too quickly, too slowly, or in an irregular pattern. That's what you're experi-encing at the moment, Harlow. They can happen suddenly and unexpectedly, and sometimes people die as a result. You were very lucky that you were with someone when you collapsed. Your boyfriend getting you help so soon most likely saved your life. We're recommending an ICD because it can give your heart electric pulses, or shocks, to get your heart rhythm back to nor-mal."

Hearing a doctor tell me that I almost died wasn't some-thing I was prepared for. Emotion overcame me, and to my dismay, I began to cry in front of a room full of near-perfect strangers.

"The ICD would be inserted just under your collar bone." The male doctor that looked like a slightly older, rounded version of Jake carried on. "It looks similar to a pacemaker and is a little bigger than a matchbox. It's made up of a battery powered electronic circuit and electrode leads which are placed into your heart through a vein."

I couldn't hear anymore. I held my hand up for him to stop talking, and asked if I could see my parents. I needed someone here with me. "Actually, if it's okay, could you find my boyfriend too?" I added. I needed to see him. Not only to make myself feel better, his presence always had a way of calming me, but to thank him too. Ellis had saved my life.

The three-week hospital stay I'd been made to endure altered my state of mind, and not in a positive way. Between bouts of crying and lashing out at anyone within a ten-foot radius and reverting to a scared ten-year-old that wanted her mom, I'd had just about all I could take. I was horrible to everyone for the smallest of things. I'd bitten Ellis's head off the third time he brought me a fruit basket and magazines. He didn't even look upset that I'd turned into a mega-bitch, just picked them up off the bedside table, casually walked out of the room and knocked on the door next to mine.

"What did you do with them?" I asked when he returned a minute later.

"Gave them to the old lady next door, Jean. I haven't seen many people visit her, so I took her some flowers last week. She's sweet. She reminds me of Logan's grandma."

I'd wanted to slap myself at his admission. Instead, I bit my bottom lip and tried to stop myself from breaking down. Again. I was doing an alright job until he leaned over, kissed my forehead and told me he loved me and I could cry or shout or do anything else I wanted if it made me feel any better.

My brothers visited a couple of times, and I made an effort to not yell at them too, but it was hard. I felt sorry for myself. Dad kept telling me how amazingly lucky I was to be here, but all I could focus on was just how unlucky I was. All the things that I couldn't do anymore occupied my mind, leaving no room for appreciation.

Nobody seemed to understand that I was grieving. I'd lost the Harlow Stevens that I was just three weeks previous. I'd have to quit the swim team, skating was out of the window and the likelihood of me being able to go for a run on any given morning, or play fight with Ellis, or have a tickling match until we both collapsed in a heap was suddenly a thing of the past. It felt like everything about who I was had been snatched from me, and I was mad. Instead of Harlow Stevens, happy-go-lucky, always ready to try something new, I was Harlow Stevens, cautious and careful. I had become the girl who couldn't do anything too strenuous or tiring. I had to remember to take various medications at different points throughout the day. I had to change everything about who I was. It wasn't fair.

"I've never seen her like this," Ellis had said to my Mom, not knowing that I could hear them talking outside my room. "She's just so depressed, and I don't know what to do or say to make her feel better. She looks at me like she wishes I'd just go away and leave her alone."

What was left of my weak and damaged heart was broken by his words.

"She's been through a lot in a very short time, Ellis. She's just scared and coming to terms with what this all means for her. Give her time. She'll come back to us," Mom had replied.

I hadn't heard Ellis cry since that day I shot him in the knee when we were ten. But I could hear muffled sobs out in the hall and my mom making soothing, shushing noises. My heart giving out hadn't killed me, but the sound of Ellis Hughes crying felt like maybe it could.

I was self-conscious about my scar. It wasn't like me to be bothered by something so superficial, but the puckered, raw skin served as a reminder of everything I needed to give up. I had a three-inch scar running down the inside of my left arm from falling off my board when I was twelve. I'd been trying to land a kickflip and misjudged the whole thing. I'd tripped and thrown my arms out to catch my fall, but I landed awkwardly. My left arm had taken the majority of the impact, breaking in two places.

I'd laid, sprawled face down for a few seconds after the impact, knowing that I'd broken it. It was a strange sensation; the shock and adrenaline kicked in almost instantaneously, and it hadn't hurt at all until Ellis had lifted me up and I could see the new and unnatural angle the bones had created. The instant my eyes dropped to my forearm, the pain registered.

Ellis carried me home. He wasn't much bigger than me at the time, but he'd hauled me up and made his way shakily over to my house to get help. My Mom looked like she was about to pass out when she'd taken in the jutted-out position of my arm. Dad had to drive me to the emergency room because Mom had gone dizzy. I needed surgery, and a plate and pins put in to fuse the bones back together.

Never once had it bothered me, not like this one. This scar served as a reminder of everything I'd just lost. I didn't want Ellis to see it. It was a little higher than my breasts, but the bubbled up, purple incision line stood out dramatically against the paleness of my skin. Ellis liked to pay my chest attention, maybe liked is too weak a word—loved would be more accurate. The unsightly blemish made me feel almost disfigured, and I wondered if it would repulse him as much as it did me. The thought alone made me want to hide it from him. I didn't want him to look at me differently, and I certainly didn't want him to treat me any differently.

Doctor Foster, the one that reminded me a little of my brother, had come to check on the incision and make sure that the ICD was working correctly. I'd asked my mom and Ellis to leave the room when he'd announced his intention to check on the scar. They left my room to go and drink bad coffee in the cafeteria, and I breathed a sigh of relief.

Between Ellis's family and my own, they'd devised a tag team system so that I was never left on my own for too long. At first, I'd been thankful for it, the nights were long, drawn-out affairs. It took forever to try and ignore the noises of the machines and relax with a million and one things happening around you. I'd finally begin to drift to sleep, and then someone would be in to take my observations, or there'd be a commotion out in the ward. Sleep and hospitals do not go together. Did I mention I'm kind of a bitch if I'm overly tired?

"How are you feeling today, Harlow?" Dr. Foster had asked. "We can administer more pain medication if you're feeling uncomfortable or a little sore."

I wasn't feeling too bad until he began removing the white gauze taped over my chest. The tape pulled and stretched at the skin around my stitches, revealing the tenderness I hadn't registered previously,

"The incision is looking nice. It's a neat, small scar," he mused, and I closed my eyes, willing myself not to get upset. He began waving a paddle across my chest, which bleeped and registered my vitals across its face.

"This is all looking good," he proclaimed. Your stats are satisfactory, the anti-arrhythmic drugs seem to be working well, and you're stable enough to be discharged." I sighed dramatically in relief, and he chuckled. I'd wanted out of the hospital from the very first moment I'd woken up in it.

"Some things you need to know, Harlow, before you're released. I'd recommend you waiting to have a bath or shower for three or four days. It's important that you keep the arm on the same side as the defibrillator below your shoulder level until after your first ICD check-up, just because there's always a small chance the leads can move. It's perfectly okay for you to then do gentle arm and shoulder exercises to keep the arm mobile. We don't want you getting sore and stiff, now. That all sound okay with you?"

It sounded anything but okay, but I nodded anyway.

"Excellent. Well, I'll let the nurses know to begin organizing your discharge papers. I'll have someone come by with all the relevant information you'll need for your outpatient care." He smiled and walked out of the room to go visit with the next poor schmuck that had landed himself in the cardiac wing.

I'd thought that being home would improve my mood, but my mother's fussing put a dampener on what glimmer of relief I'd had to be discharged. Apparently having a heart attack had pushed her over the edge, and she'd quickly become over protective, over attentive, and completely overbearing. She meant well, everything she was doing for me was out of love, but despite knowing that I couldn't stop myself from snapping at her the fifteenth time she'd popped into my room to fluff my pillows and ask if I needed anything.

"I'm not a baby, you don't need to keep checking on me!" I yelled. She immediately took a step back from her task of trying to force another pillow behind my head and smoothed down the front of her blue cotton dress. A piece of her shiny blond hair had fallen across her face from the chignon it was neatly pressed into, and she blew it away dramatically before placing her hands on her hips and sighing.

"You'll always be my baby, Harlow. I'm sorry if I'm annoying you, I just want you to be comfortable." Her eyes looked slightly glazed over, but she stood straight and spoke clearly. I think my Mom was the one who coined the phrase, "stiff upper lip." She liked to be in control of a situation and wasn't someone who showed weakness quickly. "I'll leave you to rest, just holler if you need anything."

She slipped quietly out of the room, and I lay back looking around at all of my belongings, things that had always brought me comfort: photos, a ratty old stuffed bear from when I was a baby, and the quilt my mom and I had made in 7th grade. It had been a project that she'd persuaded me to help her with. The parts I'd sown were glaringly obvious and stood out against the perfect squares that Mom had made, but I'd actually enjoyed seeing it all come together, even if my thumbs did resemble pin cushions for weeks.

I pulled the blanket over me, sinking down into the mattress, and stared out at my skateboard propped up against my closet door like nothing had changed. I closed my eyes trying to ignore the slither of panic that crawled over my skin, willing myself not to think about my heart attack, the ICD in my chest, or what might happen if I collapse again.

My breath hitches as Ellis's hands move slowly from the small of my back to my hips. I stumble forward as he breaks our connection, pulling his mouth from mine. I feel drunk and heady with arousal as he bunches my nightshirt in both fists and drags it up and over my head without any protest from me.

His eyes are fixed on the faint white scar on my breast. It's not like he hasn't seen it before, but suddenly I'm that shy teenager all over again.

"Don't do that."

"Do what?" I ask, letting my hand fall from where I'd absently been rubbing over the scar.

"Try and hide yourself from me," he says, taking a half step closer and running his finger across the raised skin above my breast. The lightness of his touch makes my skin tingle. "This bit," he presses his lips to the scar, and speaks his next words onto my skin, "it's one of the best bits of you."

"Really?" I ask skeptically, "and, why's my ICD one of the best parts of me?" His face is still buried in my chest, but my tone is reflective enough of the confusion on my face.

"Because…" Kiss. "It keeps…" Kiss. "Your beautiful heart beating." Kiss.

I swallow around the lump that's formed in my throat because I remember him saying something similar once and I'm not so confident that my *beautiful heart* can survive Ellis Hughes twice.

"Through love all that is bitter will be sweet, through love all that is copper will be gold, through love all dregs will become wine, through love all pain will turn to medicine."

— RUMI

CHAPTER

THIRTEEN

Dessert First

Ellis

Getting to experience this moment with Harlow brings back the memory of the time I took her to The River Boat Landing. Somehow I've managed to jump in at the best part—the way we skipped straight to dessert all those years ago. I've missed out on everything we needed to work through, all the conversations we needed to have—and still do. I'm not even sure if this is all just a dream. If it is, I pray that I never wake up.

I don't deserve to be here touching her, tasting her, but I'm not going to deny myself the pleasure of it; the way she's looking at me tells me this is all that matters. The feel of her skin as I trace her scar sends me into an altered state of consciousness. I know what I want, and I'm certain at this moment that Harlow wants it too, but I can't gloss over that she's still hurting. How can she not be? But what do you do when you know the person you love is hurting? You go all in and try to make them feel better. The blood coursing through me is setting my skin ablaze. I know without hesitation that if we had sex right now it would feel amazing, and God do I want to, but would it really make things better? Would it be right?

"What's wrong?" Her voice is small and unsure.

I lift my eyes to hers. "What?"

"You've turned pensive all of a sudden."

I hadn't realized it, but she's right. Her arms slowly wrap around her waist, in a movement that signals she's protecting herself. Is she waiting for me to reject her? Surely not.

I lean forward so I can rest my forehead against hers. "I guess I can't quite believe this is actually happening."

My eyes drift closed when I register the warmth of her breath fanning over my neck, and then I let myself remember another time when I felt like this. When all I wanted was to make her feel good.

1998

Harlow was in a bad place the weeks following her heart surgery, and everyone was starting to worry that it was more than just a phase she needed to pass through.

"She's not returned any of my calls," Molly exhaled, examining her nail polish as she dangled her legs from the top of the half pipe. She'd found Elliott and me sitting at the skate park. It was dark out, ice practice had finished a couple of hours earlier, but I wasn't ready to go home. I needed a distraction, something to keep me busy and stop me from obsessing over how to revive Harlow's spirit. However, the day before had been a good day. The first one in what felt like a while.

"She's still recovering," I defended. "I'm sure she'll call you back when she's feeling up to it, Molly. She was in good form yesterday; maybe she just forgot that you'd called. Try her again tonight."

I'd been making excuses for her for the last week or so. It was as if the life was slowly bleeding out of her. If it weren't for her good mood when we'd gone to one of her follow-up appointments, I'd be more worried. She'd needed to go so that her ICD could be checked, and I'd offered to drive her to give Dianne a break. Harlow's mom was like superwoman, but I'd overheard her telling my parents that she and Mike had missed a ton of work while they were with Peewee in the hospital. And when Dianne wasn't trying to catch up on work, she was fussing and running around after her daughter like a headless chicken. The whole Stevens family looked like a fainter, tired version of themselves.

I'd pulled up to Harlow's doctor's office, trying to park as close to the entrance as possible. The slightest exertion tired her out and stole her breath something fierce. Every time she walked somewhere or climbed a few stairs it happened, and she looked more and more depressed when it did.

"I know that you like to live an active lifestyle, Harlow, and I'm not saying that you can't carry on being active, but the levels will need to change. You simply can't partake in anything physically challenging at the moment. You need to let your body recover. I'm sorry," Dr. Foster had explained when she'd inquired about upping her exercise.

My chest ached for her. I hated seeing her so downbeat, but, I'd take that any day over the alternative. I'd been having a recurring nightmare since the day Harlow was admitted to the hospital. It started out with her collapsing, just how it happened in reality. Except in my dream when the paramedics showed up, they loaded her into the ambulance and let me ride with her but refused to treat her. I'd be sitting by her side and she'd be unconscious, but gripping my hand tightly, and the paramedics would pronounce her gone, even though I'd be screaming at them that she was squeezing my hand.

The first night I had the dream I woke up covered in a cold sweat, not being able to distinguish whether or not it had actually happened. It unnerved me so much that I left the house and sneaked over to the Stevens'. I'd crept in through the back door and padded as lightly as I could straight to Harlow's room. I needed to make sure she was still there, that she was okay, and it was all just some horrible dream.

I didn't wake her once I slipped around her bedroom door. I sat at the end of her bed and watched her sleep for at least an hour. My eyes were fixed on the rise and fall of her chest, making sure that she was breathing right. My mom had once told me that she used to do the same thing with me when I was first born. She'd place me in my crib and then sit and watch me sleep, just to feel secure in the knowledge that I was all right. I'd laughed at my mom when she'd told me that story. I even think I may have told her she was a little nuts.

I didn't get it then, but I did now. I'd never contemplated how terrifying it could be to love someone. The thought of anything happening to them was too much to bear. So I sat, and I watched Harlow breath in and out, in and out, just like she was supposed to until all thoughts of losing her slipped away.

"So, I should leave my skateboard where it is and probably cancel my swim meets then?" Harlow said with a forced lightness to her voice.

"For now, that would be advisable." Dr. Foster smiled. "We'll get you back to being able to do your sports, it's just going to take a little time. We can discuss it further at your next appointment, okay?"

I looked over to Harlow, and there seemed to be a ghost of a smile pulling up her lips. It was enough for me. I hadn't seen a genuine smile from her in far too long.

"Okay, thank you," she answered, pushing her chair back to stand.

"Wait, that's it? You just wave the paddle over her, and we can go?" I asked confused. I thought her checkup would be decidedly more thorough, given it was her heart that they were making sure was in working order.

"Yes, like I told Harlow, the results are all within an acceptable range, and her incision isn't giving her any trouble." The doctor spoke nonchalantly like he was talking about what to have for lunch, and not about my girlfriend's health. "As long as you're not experiencing any nausea or shortness of breath when you're not doing anything, I'm happy. Of course, if you do start to present any of the symptoms that we discussed, Harlow, I'd like you to call right away so we can have you checked over."

She grabbed my hand and gave it a gentle squeeze in reassurance.

"Yep, I know. Thank you, Dr. Foster."

I followed her out of the room and back into the waiting area while she booked her next appointment. We were the youngest people in the room, by far. The folks that sit in cardio clinics generally look like they need to be sitting there. Harlow didn't, and I think that's what scared me the most because looks can be deceiving. I didn't know what was going on inside her body.

"You alright? You're acting strange," she asked as we climbed into the beat up old Honda I'd bought the day after I passed my driving test. The faded red body had more rust than metal, but she had a good reliable engine that ran smooth. It occurred to me that I'd picked a car that was exactly the opposite of my girlfriend.

"I'm good, I was just expecting that to take a while longer. I think I'd have preferred it if he'd taken his time and had a better look at you," I admitted.

"What, so you're openly telling me you wish he'd have checked me out nice and slow while you watched?" she asked and shook her head. "Dirty boy."

I laughed at her attempt at a wink. Harlow could pull most things off quite well, but winking wasn't one of them. She hadn't mastered how to not make it look as though she had a nervous twitch or dust in her eyes. I loved it.

I pretended to mull the thought over and nodded my head with a smirk.

"You little perv!"

"You brought it up," I quipped as she buckled herself into the seat. "But seriously, though, that didn't seem very thorough. I guess they know what they're doing better than I do, right?"

"Of course, now stop worrying. I'm alright," she smiled. It was a bright, toothy, sincere one. The kind that used to be permanently etched onto her face, and it made me want to take advantage of her lighter mood.

"You wanna go on a date with me, H?"

Her eyes and nose crinkled adorably in confusion. "What, tonight?

"Nope, like right now."

"Um, sure. What do you have in mind?"

I moved over my seat and cupped her face, pressing her head back onto the rest and kissing her like I'd been wanting to since she'd come home. My mouth moved over hers, reveling in her taste. I nipped at her bottom lip until she gasped and then moved back to my own seat, hoping I'd left her wanting more.

"You'll see."

I headed to The River Boat Landing. It looked like a small, rustic Italian restaurant, with its pale blue walls, red awnings and mini private balconies that looked out over the water. It served all of Harlow's favorite foods. Lunchtimes were always quieter than evenings, so I was hoping we'd get lucky and be able to grab a balcony seat.

"You're scoring points already, Mr. Hughes. I love this place," she said with a grin. The waiter had gone to see if there was a balcony free, and he waved us over a few seconds later.

"I don't think I could ever get tired of this view," I mused, once our drink order had been taken.

"I know, right? I love the water. There's something so soothing about listening to the waves crash against the deck, don't you think?"

Her head was turned toward the river, and the breeze was blowing her crazy hair away from her face. She was watching people walk by, some were families out with their children, some, tourists admiring the boats moored up and posing for photos.

I hadn't been talking about the view from the balcony; I'd been talking about the one sitting in front of me.

"Yeah, I do." My eyes dropped to her hand mindlessly rubbing at the spot where I knew her scar was. Apart from a few chaste glimpses here and there, I hadn't really gotten a close look at it. I could tell she didn't want me to see it, which bothered me a little. I didn't know if it was because she wasn't comfortable with it herself yet or something else, so I'd let it slide and didn't press her. She would in time, I hoped.

Harlow turned back to me and noticed where my gaze was focused. She immediately stopped rubbing the spot and adjusted the collar of her blue striped shirt, making sure that everything was covered, just so.

"I think I'm going to order dessert first," I announced, trying to keep the atmosphere from turning somber.

"You can't, that's the wrong way around. You'll spoil your lunch."

"Nope, I disagree. I'm looking forward to dessert way more than I am a club sandwich. Why delay the gratification? You only live once, and I want apple pie and pecan ice cream." I sat back in my chair and pushed my menu away—watching a bemused look take over her beautiful face.

"Okay, in that case, I guess I'll have the same."

"You can't, it's the wrong way around," I mocked in a high-pitched girly voice.

She stuck her tongue out and blew an enormous raspberry, right as the waiter appeared with our drinks. Her face immediately turned the same color as the bright red napkin she'd placed over her knees.

"Nice!"

"Shut up, Ellis," she whisper-shouted, although her embarrassed grin gave away that she'd found it almost as funny as I had.

By the time our sandwiches arrived, we'd gorged ourselves on our super-sized apple pie, and I couldn't finish my first bite. Harlow hadn't even attempted to pick her sandwich up.

"I think I ate too much ice cream," she exhaled and slumped back into her chair. "I kind of want to undo the button on my shorts now, and take a nap."

"I could go for a nap," I agreed.

"See, this is why you shouldn't eat dessert first. I'm stuffed, and I haven't eaten one thing that can be construed as remotely healthy. My doctors are going to be so proud," she groaned.

"Apples are fruit," I supplied and laughed at the overly dramatic eye roll I received in answer. "Let's get these bagged up to go, and we can head down to the beach and lay on the sand. I won't even complain if you want to unbutton your shorts, or you know what? I promise not to grumble if you feel like you just want to go right ahead and take them off completely. I'm a gentleman like that."

"I can think of a few things, Ellis, but a gentleman wouldn't be one of them. Try horn dog, or pervert."

"I prefer sexual deviant, it makes me sound badass."

"No baby, not badass…just a regular ass."

I loved the easy banter we'd fallen into—it made things feel like normal.

We had the food bagged and made our way down to the beach, walking at a leisurely, slow pace while people-watching and commenting on what we thought their lives were like behind closed doors. It was one of Harlow's favorite games when we were out and about. She'd make up ridiculously intricate, and speculative assumptions about what people got up to in their spare time. With each person she commented on, the story grew wilder.

An enormously built guy that looked like a linebacker who'd snap you in two with no effort, but secretly cried at Disney films. Or, a mousey, bookish-looking woman would lead a double life as a dominatrix for wealthy high-flying corporate suits who liked to dress in diapers and be led around their homes on a leash at the weekends. My girl had a vivid, and sometimes scarily warped imagination.

"You want to sit here?" I directed her over to where the rocks made a little cove, partially shielding us from sight.

"Sure, looks good."

I dropped down onto the sand, grabbing hold of her waist and pulling her with me so that she landed in my lap. I loved it when she straddled me. I could quite happily spend the rest of my life with her legs wrapped around me, and her face pressed close to mine.

"I think we should stay here and make out until the tide comes in. You game?"

"People are walking about, they'll see."

In all honesty, I didn't give a damn if people could see us or not. I pressed my lips to her throat and began planting lazy kisses in a path toward her jaw.

"You're not playing fair," she murmured, tilting her head back, exposing more of her skin. "I've missed this."

I carried on with my task, up and over her jaw until I made my way to her lips. "Me too," I whispered before pulling her closer and separating the seam of her mouth with my tongue. "So damn much."

I could feel her heart drumming against my chest and pulled back, worried. Her eyes opened slowly, her lips looked swollen as she caught her breath.

"What's wrong, Ellis? Why did you stop?" She pulled back to see me better.

"Your heart's racing so hard I could feel it against my chest, and you seem out of breath."

She grabbed my hand and placed it over her heart, and then took hold of my other, and placed it against my own.

"It's not just me, Ellis."

I waited for a few seconds, trying to register if my own erratic heartbeat felt any different from hers, and she was right. It was drumming just as fast, and I was out of breath from kissing her, too.

"You always make my heart beat faster, especially when you're kissing me like I'm the last meal you'll ever have. I'm fine. You don't need to worry that you're about to trip my ICD by putting the moves on me."

I felt like kind of an idiot.

"I'm sorry, H, I just panicked that I might be hurting you."

"You know, when I had the ICD fitted, and the doctors explained about resting and not over doing things—they gave me a list of stuff to avoid. It was the usual, no running, no high-impact sports, no extreme sports, you know the kind of thing. When they finished, I sat for ages wondering about sex and kicking myself for not asking. I didn't want them to think I was some sort of slut."

She grinned.

"I finally got the balls to ask and called in one of the nurses. She didn't even flinch, just told me that most everyone asked that question too, which made me feel like much less of a brazen hussy. Anyway, it's fine as long as I don't overexert myself. So, unless, Mr. Hughes, you intend on working through the karma sutra with me, you don't need to worry."

I wanted to cry out in relief. I'd been wondering about it for weeks, but what kind of insensitive asshole asks the "what about sex" question when their girlfriend's recovering from heart surgery? Plus, up until today, Harlow wasn't acting like she even wanted to be looked at, never mind touched.

I pressed my forehead to hers. "That's pretty awesome news, but I'm okay with whatever you want to do, whenever you want to do it. I wanna take things at your pace."

"I'll tell you if I need a break, but right now what I need is for you to kiss me again. Make me feel like myself."

She asked, so I obliged. We spent the rest of the day like I'd joked—making out at the beach until the sun started to dip in the sky and the waves began rolling in.

"To conceal anything from those to whom I am attached, is not in my nature. I can never close my lips where I have opened my heart."

—CHARLES DICKENS

CHAPTER

FOURTEEN

Back to the Beginning

Harlow

He's changed his mind; I can see it in his expression. A few minutes ago he was ready to take me right here, but then he undressed me and somewhere between the two seconds it took for him to slide my nightshirt off, he's had a damn epiphany. I need to make a decision: should I cut and run or call him out?

What I'd like to do right now is punch him in the face for no other reason but to make myself feel better about his imminent rejection. I'm frustrated, turned on, and seething mad that I only have myself to blame. I was sure we were on the same page; the intense look on his face spurred me on. I don't know how I could have misread the signals. I mean, he's standing in his boxers, and there's not much room for misinterpretation with a pair of tight-fitting Kleins. His feelings about our current situation stood out. Literally.

Almost naked and standing in my mother's kitchen, my skin is still damp from the milk Ellis is covered in. An involuntary shiver makes my body convulse, and I notice as I look down that my nipples have hardened. In any other circumstance I'd be embarrassed, but my body's reaction isn't due to lust, it's the chill of spilled milk on my skin. Suddenly I'm all too aware of what a ridiculous situation I've put myself in. The last time I can remember feeling this stupid and unsure I was a silly eighteen-year-old that still believed Ellis and I would live happily ever after. I was convinced he didn't want to make love to me then, too.

1998

"I don't think Ellis dares to have sex with me," I proclaimed walking out of my bathroom.

Molly had been sitting on the end of my bed waiting for me to finish trying to tame my hair. She'd persuaded me to go watch the hockey game Ellis was playing tonight. It was at home, so the lure of not having to travel had closed the deal. I hadn't really been out much since my surgery, and when I'd finally gotten around to answering one of Molly's calls, she'd unleashed holy hell on me. It was refreshing, to say the least. Everyone had been pussyfooting around me like I was a damaged china doll ready to fall to pieces at any moment—except Molly.

"That's way more information than you needed to share, Harlow," she laughed, looking a little mortified. Our relationship had never entered the realm of talking about sex or guys. I'm pretty sure she thought I was still a virgin by the shocked expression on her face.

"I know, but I need your advice," I simpered. "You've had way more experience with guys than anyone I know."

"Wow, way to make me feel like a whore!" She picked up the stuffed, ratty, old bear from the side of my bed and hurled it at my head.

"Ouch! That came out wrong—you know what I meant. I think he's reluctant to sleep with me because he thinks he's going to trigger another heart attack or something."

"So, he's not modest about his performance then? He must think pretty highly of his bedroom skills if he thinks they're worthy of a cardiac arrest."

I laughed in spite of myself. "He's got skills," I mused. "I've already told him that I spoke with my nurse, and she said it would be okay."

"Maybe put the moves on him, then, you know? Set the tone and reverse the roles. Pick him up, take him out and then book a room somewhere." Her nose wrinkled in disgust. "You know, I've known you two for a long time. You're practically family, and family talking about sex is just weird."

"You used to live for girl talk like this," I mused. I never took Molly for such a prude. She'd had her fair share of boyfriends throughout school. I assumed this was the kind of thing that she spoke about with her other girlfriends. I guess I'd been wrong.

"A girl can change her mind." She was right I supposed. I smiled at her attempt at a wink. "Okay, I won't bring up my sex life again."

"That'd be great, thanks," she said standing. "You ready to go?"

I fixed my shirt in the mirror, making sure that my scar wasn't on show.

"Am now."

The hockey match blew, and not just because our team had gotten their asses handed to them on home turf. It blew for a whole new reason, and one I'd never dealt with before. When you have two older brothers, and most people deemed you as "one of the guys" it cut out a lot of talk about you. But when you almost drop dead of a heart attack your senior year the gloves are off and everyone assumes they have free reign. I had to endure a whole match with people pointing and whispering. I didn't hear anything particularly bad, but having what felt like an arena's worth of people talking *about* you and not *to* you doesn't feel nice.

The final buzzer sounded and I made my way out into the parking lot like the building was on fire. I told Molly that I'd catch a ride back home with Ellis and that I'd pass on going for pizza. She didn't look too happy about me wanting to leave alone, but I assured her I'd be fine. I found Ellis's Honda and climbed in. He never locked it. Both our dads had chastised him about the fact, but I had Ellis's back on this one. Nobody would steal his car, not when there were a million other better-looking ones to go at. The Honda looked like it was ready for the junkyard, but I loved it. It wasn't pretentious or gaudy like Ellis's buddy Elliot's car. His parents had bought him a brand new shiny black BMW when he'd passed his test. It took him almost a month before he'd wrapped it around a signpost in town. His parents wouldn't pay for the repairs, and so he drove it around with a huge ass dent in the trunk. The Honda had so many lumps and bumps you'd never know if a new one appeared. That was the beauty of it, or at least that's what Ellis claimed.

"What are you doing in here all by yourself?" he asked opening the passenger door and almost dropping his kit bag on me until he noticed I was sitting there.

"Waiting for you. I wanted to take you someplace, so you can either let me drive, or I'll direct you."

He climbed into the driver's seat and moved across to kiss me hello before settling back in his seat and buckling in.

"What do you have planned? I was kind of hoping I could coax you back home to my place; Mom and Dad are at one of Dad's work friend's retirement dinner. I have the place to myself."

"You win. Let's go!" I said with a laugh and pulled my belt on. "I was going to get you to drive out to Bleacher's Point, but this works much better."

His eyebrows shot to his hairline, and he stalled turning on the engine, a small smirk playing on his lips.

"You wanted to go to Bleacher's Point? There's nothing to do there but make out or have sex in your car."

"I know," I shrugged. "But that was before I realized that we could go back to your place and have sex without the worry of some dog walker slash jogger catching us."

He laughed at my crudeness, but pulled out of the parking lot like a horse out of the stalls.

The moment we pulled up to his house his hands were all over me, but there was still an air of hesitancy in his touch. I wasn't sure whether he second-guessed himself, worried that I wasn't yet physically up to the task at hand, so to speak, or if the problem was with me. Maybe I was so focused on everything that he was doing that I read something in his touch that simply wasn't there. I was beginning to obsess over trivial things like how long or short his kisses lasted, or whether he was purposefully avoiding touching my chest because of the scar. He hadn't ever asked to see it once. At first, I'd been happy about it—I hated how it looked and felt, and the thought of Ellis looking at it and being turned off scared the crap out of me. Something strange had transpired, though, because the more time that passed without him showing any curiosity toward it, the more I worried that it actually *did* repulse him, and suddenly I was eager for him to see and touch it.

We stumbled through the dark hallway kissing and fumbling, without paying attention to anything but each other. His hands were in my hair one second, and then on my ass the next as we blindly maneuvered the stairs to his room and fell through the door of his bedroom. Literally, fell through. Our lust-filled panting and moaning were replaced with a burst of laughter. Ellis had cushioned my fall and was sprawled between his bedroom and the landing with me perched on top of him.

"That was smooth," he said with a groan. I didn't realize the door was already open when I leaned back to open it.

"You just couldn't wait to get me to the bed," I chortled. "Admit it."

"That's kinda true."

I crawled over him and stood, still laughing, disheveled and slightly out of breath. "You know that's not what people mean when they say, 'sweep her off her feet,' right?"

He picked himself up from the floor and stood filling the doorframe. His blond hair was still damp from showering after the game and looked a dark golden brown. His jeans were riding low on his hips, and my eyes flashed to the tan-defined lines of the V that disappeared under the waistband of his boxers.

"Having a good look?" His eyes were sparkling as I drew my gaze lazily up to meet his.

"You're so pretty," I mused, batting my eyelashes at him. His lopsided grin flattened instantly.

"Pretty? That's not a way to describe a man. Girls are pretty. Flowers are pretty. Not me."

I bit down on my lip, trying to contain the smile fighting to burst free.

"You are, too! Men can absolutely be classified as pretty."

He huffed in exasperation. "You're not getting it. I'm rugged, or handsome, or hot has fuck!" he exclaimed. "Calling me pretty is as bad as naming my junk after a Care Bear. It deflates a guy's ego."

I couldn't contain the laughter after that, and he rushed forward, picking me up in one clean swoop and depositing me into the middle of his bed. He began tickling me and demanded that I called him hot. I writhed from side to side trying to avoid him reaching my ribs, squealing like a little girl for him to stop.

"Babe, you're hot, you are hot, okay! Now stop before I pass out," I squirmed.

His hands fell away promptly, almost as quickly as the smile on his face. "Do you feel like you're going to pass out? Shit, Harlow, I'm sorry. I didn't think." He grabbed my arms and began looking me over, no doubt for signs of distress.

"I'm fine! I just don't like being tickled," I told him in a huff. The mood had turned south rapidly.

"Okay, I just forgot that I need to be more careful with you now." He pressed a kiss to my forehead and moved to sit next to me rather than directly in front of me.

"You do realize that I hate that people are treating me differently," I whispered. "I don't want you to second-guess tickling me, or kissing me until we're both breathless. I want you to want me the same way you did before this." I pulled at the neckline of my shirt, indicating the ICD.

"Harlow, trust me when I tell you that I want you just the same, if not more than I did before your surgery. I just don't want to do anything that will compromise your health. I couldn't live with myself if that happened."

"And I can't live with feeling like a shadow of myself. Just treat me like you always have and trust me to tell you if I need to slow down, Ellis. Don't take that away from me. Please." I moved from the bed and pushed his legs apart so that I could stand between them. I liked the tables turning and being the one that got to bend down to kiss him. He was so much taller than me that it only ever happened if we were in this position.

I ran my fingers through his damp hair and moved his head back so I could kiss him how I wanted to be kissed. I guessed that I'd need to be an example, do what Molly had suggested and take the lead.

So that's exactly what I did.

"Lift your arms in the air," I whispered as I bent down, gathered the hem of his white t-shirt, and began slowly pulling it up and over his head. I wasn't particularly versed at seduction; I'd never had to be. We were always in tune when it came to initiating sex; it was a steady and almost seamless evolution from making out, to tumbling between the sheets. I don't recall either of us ever having asked the other one to make love to them. That's not how we worked, so me instigating what I hoped was about to happen felt strangely new and exhilarating.

He didn't say a word as he obeyed my command, but his crooked smile urged me on. The blue in his eyes darkened as I dropped his shirt at my side and then took a step back and slowly began unbuttoning my own. I'd seen women do this in movies hundreds of times; they'd maintain eye contact while making a show of undressing. I had managed three buttons before the fourth got stuck. I had to avert my stare so I could concentrate on unbuttoning the rest. By the time I brought my gaze back up to Ellis's I could see the humor dancing over his features. My stomach clenched as I slowly let my shirt slide down my arms and gather in a pool at my feet, hoping to steer the atmosphere back towards sensual instead of amusing. His humor quickly subsided as his jaw tensed and his throat bobbed as he swallowed.

"I've missed this," he said grabbing hold of the back of my thighs and pulling me to him until his forehead rested between my breasts. I shivered as he placed a light kiss on the highly sensitive spot of skin just below my breasts. I loved when he kissed me there—it always gave me chills. His hands moved north to palm my butt, squeezing slightly and causing me to gasp.

"Me too," I agreed, reaching behind me and tugging on the white lace to unclasped my bra.

The second it was gone Ellis stood, scooping me up with his movement and depositing me on the bed, then maneuvering over me to drop his head to my chest. I was waiting for the moment his soft, warm mouth would close around me, but it didn't come. Instead, he laid lazy feather-light kisses in a path up between my breasts until he reached the small purple scar that bore testament to my heart condition. My fists curled into the cool cotton sheets, and my breathing stilled, waiting for him to bypass the area. He didn't. He caught me completely off guard as he lowered his mouth down and his lips gently skimmed over the incision. My body was on fire—from sensation or relief I couldn't be sure. He repeated the movement letting his lips linger for a few seconds more. The gesture shocked me a little. I was so sure he'd avoid it, as though somehow it tainted what was otherwise so good. I blinked and felt the warm trickle of a tear slide down across the side of my face and betray my anxiety. My chest expelled a heavy breath as the realization that he wasn't sickened by it began to seep in.

"I think that's my new favorite spot," Ellis said, letting his gaze wander from my chest back up to my face. His eyes narrowed at the tear making its way across my jaw.

I shook off his admission, wanting him to know that he didn't need to try and make me feel better. "You don't have to say that, Ellis." My voice sounded rough with emotion, even to my own ears.

"I'm serious," he said resting on his elbow and bringing his other hand to my face, swiping another traitorous tear from my cheek. "I wouldn't ever tell you something like that if it weren't the truth, H. I know you're self-conscious about it at the moment, but do you wanna know what I see when I look at it?"

I didn't. Not really, because all I saw when I looked at it was loss. It represented living a censored version of my life, or at least it did up until he spoke his next words.

"I see second chances. I see a future that for a terrifying few days I was sure had been stolen when you collapsed. I don't think I've ever been as scared as I was that day; my life only makes sense if you're in it." He traced my incision with his index finger before moving to lace his hand with my own. "This scar means that I don't have to. It means you're here. How can I not love something that gives me you?"

My throat bobbed, and my chest tightened. I didn't have an appropriate response to show him how relieved or how loved he made me feel. His words were like a balm, cooling and soothing the ache that my condition had left within me. It never occurred to me when I looked in the mirror to see anything beyond the negativity and depression the scar made me feel inside. Ellis had just inadvertently given me a small ray of sunshine. Something positive to hold onto when it felt like all the light in my life was being blocked out by the gravity of my heart problems.

"You're pretty amazing, Mr. Hughes," I told him, letting go of my anxiety about him touching me there, and relaxing deeper into the soft mattress.

"You're not too bad yourself, Ms. Stevens."

I looked down to where our jean-clad legs were tangled and pouted.

"What's wrong?" Ellis asked, pursing his lips.

"We're wearing entirely too many clothes, and I can't decide if I want to strip you or watch while you do it yourself," I said, flashing him my biggest grin. It no doubt looked more menacing than sexy, but he'd just made me feel like me—the normal carefree version—and I hadn't felt like that since my heart attack.

"You do me, and I'll do you," he quipped smugly as he lifted his weight from me.

I lunged forward grabbing the waistband of his jeans and wrestled them half way down his thighs before he could even blink. His words had lit a fire in my belly, every nerve ending felt electrified and my skin prickled with the desire building inside. I brought my hands up to his jaw, pulling his lips to mine and falling backward, dragging him down with me. My feet scrambled to kick down his jeans further as he made quick work of unbuttoning mine and sliding them off along with my underwear, demonstrating far more finesse than I'd shown.

His hands found my center, causing my back to arch dramatically and my thighs to quiver. Each measured movement of his adept fingers made my pulse race faster and my body more alive than I could ever remember. This is what I needed, I thought as Ellis bent down and claimed my mouth roughly. He was doing exactly what I wanted by trusting me to tell him if this was too much. I pushed my fingers into his hair, holding on as he breathed light back into me.

"Thinking of you keeps me awake. Dreaming of you keeps me asleep. Being with you keeps me alive."

—Unknown

CHAPTER

FIFTEEN

Bitter Sweet Symphony

Ellis

I've dreamed of being in this very situation—not the specifics but the circumstances. I've closed my eyes each and every night praying that my sleep would be filled with this fantasy, the one where Harlow forgives me for the past and still holds promises of a future. I'd close my eyes as the cell door locked behind me and try my hardest to recall every detail of her face. Each single freckle and the unruly way the waves of her blonde hair tumbled in uncontrollable masses over her slim shoulders. I'd lie still, doing my best to ignore the sound of keys rattling, deadbolts grinding metal against metal, and guards reprimanding rowdy inmates. I'd picture her smile and hope that my subconscious wouldn't take over, peppering my sleep with the horrible fragments of my new reality.

I want to savor this moment of Harlow standing in front of me, wanting me, and the fact that it's real and not a fantasy. But that's exactly what's made me stall: I'm not so sure that it is. I remember my mother always telling me to never make a decision when feeling especially emotional, and I know that's what Harlow's doing now. I've lived with the burden of regret, and I'll be damned if I inadvertently force her to do the same. I want to make love to her more than I want my next breath, but I'd rather die a thousand deaths than cause her any more pain.

"We shouldn't do this." The words slice at my throat as I force them out, but I make sure I say them loud enough to be clear. They hurt almost as much as the look of embarrassment that has her scrambling to pull her shirt back on.

"It's not that I don't want to, Harlow. God, if you only knew what I wanted to do to you right now."

"But you won't." She smoothes the fabric over the top of her thighs, brings her eyes back up to meet mine and verbally slaps me. "You don't want to hurt me, right? Well, news flash, Ellis, that ship sailed a long time ago."

"You'll regret it—this. If it goes any further you'll end up hating me even more."

She must know that I'm right because I catch the way her shoulders drop the smallest fraction, and this win suddenly feels like a massive loss. I reach for her, not knowing if I'll be met with hostility or apathy, and not really caring. I just want to touch her. The tip of my index finger brushes down her forearm and over her wrist. I'm so preoccupied with the prickling of energy that sparks over the pad of my fingertip that my eyes trace the line I'm drawing to her palm. When her hand catches mine and she steps into me, pulling my arm around her back as she presses her face into my chest, I have to resist the temptation to change my mind and drop any sense of morality to the floor along with her panties.

"I'm kind of struggling here," I whisper into her hair. "You don't make it easy to do the honorable thing when you let me hold you like this." I rest my cheek against the top of her head and squeeze her tighter to me, shamelessly hungry for any form of contact I can get.

"I should clean this spilled milk. The whole house will start to smell, and it's late. I need to go back to bed." In spite of her words she makes no effort to acknowledge my admission or pull away from our embrace.

"I'll help."

Neither one of us moves for a solid five minutes, despite the fact that we're both covered in goose bumps and beginning to shiver. I'll let Harlow decide to break away first. I think if it were up to me, I'd never let her go again.

I figure coffee is always a good ice breaker, and Harlow could never function very well in the morning without it. I busy myself brewing a pot when I hear the floorboards above me squeak, letting me know she's about to come down. I didn't want to up and leave without seeing her this morning, especially since I'm not sure when I'll get another chance. I don't even know where she lives anymore, but her overnight bag clued me in on the fact that it isn't here.

"Morning, sunshine!" I say with more familiarity than she looks comfortable with as she enters the kitchen.

For a second she looks somewhat shocked before she notices my actions and makes her way toward where I'm pouring two cups of coffee. She snatches the closest cup and hugs it close to her chest, inhaling its aroma like an angry little caffeine junkie. I physically try to suppress my amusement by dragging my hand over my face, tempering my urge to smile. I'd forgotten just how moody she is when she first wakes up. If you ever need the definition of an anti-morning person, it's Harlow Stevens.

While she tentatively sips at her coffee I steal glances over my own cup, letting my eyes wander over the woman that stands in place of the girl I left behind. My reasoning had seemed so clear and sound in my own mind when I decided that pushing her away would be the best thing for her. It's what got me through the time I spent locked up. I wanted the best for her, and I'd proven unequivocally that wasn't me. I believed that fact, clung to it when I wanted to cave and write to her, begging her to come visit me. Looking at her now, my reasoning doesn't seem quite so astute. I may not be viewing her in the best of circumstances, and I know that ambushing her hasn't helped any, but she doesn't look happy or full of vigor, she doesn't even look overly well. What she looks is bone tired, and weary.

"How are you feeling this morning?" I ask conversationally, hoping that the unease settling in my gut is unfounded. The pallor of her skin causes me concern, and I quickly realize that I don't know this Harlow or at least this version of her. I noticed her taking her medication last night, but never pressed for information and I'm now observing that I probably should have.

"Been better," she says taking a seat at the kitchen table.

At least her level of sass is healthy.

"You're not looking too good." I move over to where she's sitting. "Do you need to take anything?"

"I'm fine, Ellis."

"If there's one thing on this earth I know to be true, it's that when a woman tells you she's fine, you're screwed because she's anything but." I grin—a small attempt at baiting her into opening up—but she looks away instead, and it does nothing to make me feel any better.

"The new drugs I'm on don't make me feel too great if I haven't eaten. I'll be okay once I've got some food in me." There's a sad tone to her answer that stops me from pressing any further about her health. I know she's not telling me something, but I don't have the right to demand she explain what it is, no matter how much I want to know.

"How about I take you to breakfast? We can kick back and watch the scandal it causes over pancakes and bacon?" It's a long shot to get her to spend more time with me, and in truth I'm amazed I've managed to stretch things out this long. So when she agrees, I almost choke on my coffee.

"Fine, but you're buying. I can't be too long either, I have stuff I need to do today."

"No, great. That's great," I stammer, draining my cup and placing it in the sink as I pass. "I'll go grab my jacket."

I race up the stairs, taking them two at a time, and round into the room I spent last night in before she can change her mind. It's only when I spin around that I realize I wasn't even wearing a jacket last night. I push my hands through my hair and take a deep breath, forcing myself to slow down. Her agreeing to breakfast is because she's hungry, and I can't let what almost happened in a confused moment of haste fog the reality of our situation. I notice my cell on the bedside, snatch it up and make my way back downstairs with a fraction more composure and renewed sense of reality.

"Let's walk," she says zipping up the red parker she's slipped on over her cream sweater. Her jeans are rolled at the ankle and true to form she's wearing a weathered pair of blue Chuck Taylors. I'm still wearing the slacks and white shirt I'd arrived in yesterday, the only difference is a day's worth of scruff over my face and a watery mascara tearstain by my shoulder. I'd rubbed it with a wet towel, but it seems it's there to stay—a reminder of what I do to Harlow.

"Sure, you want to head over to the Bait House?"

"Best pancakes in town—where else would we be going?"

"That's good with me." I gesture toward the door. "After you."

I follow a step behind, allowing myself the luxury of watching her without making her feel uncomfortable, or at least I hope I'm not. I hadn't lied when I said that pancakes sounded good, but every step closer to the Bait House reminds me that it's a step closer to having her tell me goodbye. She's already said she has plans today, and I don't want to leave her yet but I don't have a good enough reason to stick around if she's not going to be here. This place holds the best and worst memories of my life, and there's not a single one that doesn't involve Harlow.

We've almost made it to the pier before she finally breaks the near silence neither one of us seemed in a rush to fill. "This feels strange, like déjà vu, don't you think?" The wind rolls across the frothy whitecaps of the Atlantic, whipping her hair over her cheeks as she turns toward me.

My hands stuff themselves deep into the pockets of my slacks, my arms rigid at my side warding off the early morning chill from the ocean. "It's déjà vecu," I say pensively to myself rather than answering Harlow.

She stops, turning entirely to look at me now, making a futile effort to push her hair behind her ears and stop it from distorting her vision. "What was that?" she asks, looking confused, while fighting an impossible war with the wind.

"I said it's déjà vécu, not vu. It's what most people are experiencing when they think they are feeling déjà vu."

I'm greeted with a telling blank stare. She has no clue what I'm talking about, so I carry on. "Déjà vu is the sense of having seen something before, right? Only, that's not what this is. This is déjà vécu, the experience of having seen an event before, but in great detail, so much so that you can even recognize the smells and sounds. We must have walked to this pier, what, maybe a thousand times? We've smelled the salt in the air, and listened to the ocean lap and break against the legs of the pier without even consciously realizing it. That's what's brought on the sudden sense of familiarity…déjà vécu."

She blinks a few times, the ghost of a smile appearing. "That's probably one of the most nerdish things I've ever heard you say. Why would you even know that?"

I laugh a little at the way her expression has knitted her brows together. "I've always been a wealth of useless information; you know that."

The moment I say the words aloud, I catch something pass over her that steals the tiny smile from her lips and triggers the realization that she used to know that. These days we don't really know anything about each other at all.

The gulls circling above cry out, harmonizing gently with the whistling breeze and crashing waves, a bittersweet symphony that makes me ache with regret. "Let's go," I say, pointing in the direction of the Bait House and gently guiding her elbow. She turns to face forward while I do my best to stop from looking back.

Sitting in our old booth overlooking the water, while trying to have light conversation to avoid the heavy one we should be having, is harder than I expect. The waitress, thankfully nobody I knew, took our order swiftly but has yet to return with our drinks. Harlow's fiddling with the corner of her blue paper napkin and I want her attention on me.

"I feel like I have a million and one questions for you, but I can't think of where to start," I admit.

Her eyes flick up from the table, and she crosses her arms in front of her. It's a defensive move, but her face doesn't display the same guardedness her body does. "Go for it, what do you want to know?"

I'm not expecting her forthright response and now I'm on the spot, wondering how deep I can delve. Should I jump in with both feet, ask about her relationship status? Enquire about her heart condition? Casually ask if she thinks she could ever love me again? I settle for a paltry. "Okay, where are you living these days? I noticed you had an overnight bag with you yesterday."

"I'm not far," she answers, adjusting herself in her seat. "I moved to Raleigh after graduation. I'm still close to the hospital for work, but I'm a little closer to Mom, so it works well."

"You work at the hospital, where? Duke?"

"Yeah," she says with a smile that I can't help but mirror. "I'm a counselor."

An acute sense of relief washes over me, and something in my chest feels instantly lighter. I've carried a certain amount of dread with me for so long that what I did—how I left—altered her life for the worse. Not that the event itself didn't completely blow her world wide open, but the fact that she went on to achieve her goals, even after the damage I caused, makes me so incredibly proud of her. I want to tell her that, but I don't know how to voice it without it sounding contrived or condescending.

"That's great," I murmur. "I bet you're fantastic at it."

She snorts and unfolds her arms. "I wouldn't go that far, but I definitely enjoy it. It has its rewards."

I'm about to ask her more about that when her cell rings, and I catch sight of the display as she retrieves it from her jacket resting over the seat next to her.

"Sorry, I need to get this." She looks a little uncomfortable and angles herself away from me.

Martin. Whoever's calling is named Martin, and she looks uncomfortable. Is he her boyfriend? Oh, God. Suddenly I feel overwhelmingly sick. Where the hell was the waitress with our drinks? I need something to push down the bile I can feel rising up at the prospect of her being with someone else. Why had I just assumed she wouldn't be in a relationship? Oh Christ, what if she's married? Why hadn't that been my first question? I can feel my throat closing up as I lean to the side so I can get a look at her ring finger.

Gloriously bare.

I can breathe now.

That doesn't mean that this Martin person isn't her boyfriend, though, and the reprieve at the absence of a wedding ring is short lived when I tune in to her hushed conversation.

"How's my baby boy been? I hope you managed to get some sleep last night and he didn't keep you up too much."

It's as though the world tilts with that one sentence and throws me completely off my axis.

"Yeah," she continues. "He's going through that clingy phase."

The waitress appears and places a pitcher of water between us. The glasses clatter as she deposits them from her tray onto the table, obscuring what Harlow is saying to Martin. *Fucking Martin.*

"Whose is the decaf coffee?" she asks, and I stare vacantly at the name badge on her navy Bait House shirt, not knowing how to make my voice work.

Harlow lifts her hand signaling it's hers as she continues to talk on her cell and I continue to suffocate slowly in my seat, letting her words murder me internally while she laughs at something *Martin* just said.

"Sorry about that," she says once the call has been disconnected and her cell placed back into her jacket pocket. She must register my internal anguish when she brings her attention fully back to me because she asks, "Are you alright?"

No. Not even close. I almost bark. "Everything okay at home?" I challenge instead, not bothering to hide the hurt obvious in my voice. I'm waiting for her to confess that she has a baby. A baby, and no doubt a boyfriend too. A family she didn't think to mention when we almost fucked in her mother's kitchen last night.

Harlow's eyes narrow, her posture stiffening with the action. "Yes, everything's fine."

I can't believe she's not going to elaborate. My blood runs white hot under my skin; I have absolutely no right to be mad, but I am. I'm furious, and devastated and a thousand other emotions that I don't have time to label. I spit my next works like they're poison on my tongue.

"Who's Martin?"

She shifts but doesn't look remorseful, not even a little. *Goddamn it.*

"Sharpe, you've met him, remember?" her words are delivered low and cool, an exact opposite to mine.

Martin Sharpe? I roll the name around in my mind, waiting for some form of recollection. "Martin...from Duke? Your old counselor?" I feel like I'm about to pass out. "You had a baby with Martin." It's a statement, not a question and it takes her by surprise. She drops the water pitcher she's holding.

"What? No!" Incredulity is laced through those two small words, and it colors her cheeks. The water sloshes over the side of the jug, but miraculously it rights itself and doesn't topple over.

"But, you just said—" I let my words trail, completely perplexed.

"What are you talking about, Ellis? He called to ask what time I'd be home because he's dog sitting my new puppy."

I've never wanted to kiss her as badly as I do right now. My pulse is almost painful as it throbs rapidly under my flesh. I drop back, sagging in my seat as the tension ebbs across my shoulders and scrub my hand over my face.

"So you're not with him?" I clarify as an afterthought.

"I think his wife and kids would have a problem with me if I were."

I reach over and take a long drink of water from her glass, almost draining it in one gulp.

"What's gotten into you?" she asks as I place the glass back down between us.

"I'm sorry, Harlow, I don't know." I laugh humorlessly. "I heard you say something about a baby and, and, I don't know, I guess my mind sort of ran away with itself."

"You look like you're about to have a heart attack, Ellis. Which is kind of ironic if you think about it, since I'm the one sitting here with heart failure."

She winks and re-pours herself another glass of water.

"Heart failure," I echo. "What do you mean you're sitting here with heart failure? You're joking, right?" I ask the question already knowing she's not. I can feel it, and don't ask me to explain; I just know it's the truth.

Harlow's mouth tips down at the sides and the back of my throat and nose begins to burn as I watch her countenance soften. I try my best to swallow down the panic as she meets my worried eyes with ones that hold an acceptance I'm in no way prepared for.

"I need a heart transplant, Ellis, and I need one soon."

I hold my breath; it's not a conscious action, I just somehow stop breathing as I process her words. A thousand questions fight their way to the forefront of my mind, causing a surge of confusion and fear to careen into me, threating to knock me down. I don't trust my voice to not break if I try speaking any of them. I don't want to believe that this is real.

My stunned silence must unnerve her.

"Are you going to say something?" she urges after a long moment.

"I, I…" my mouth opens and closes like a goldfish. I shake my head, trying to settle on just one thought and failing. When I meet her eyes again, I know what I want to ask. "Are you scheduled for a transplant? Are you at the top of the list?"

Her eyes drop to the floor taking my heart along with them. You don't look away to answer a question like that if it's good news. She lets out a soft, almost inaudible sigh and doesn't look at me when she answers with only one word.

"No."

"The heart will break, but broken live on."

— LORD BYRON

CHAPTER

SIXTEEN

Conversation Killer

Harlow

I shouldn't feel guilty about speaking my truth, but I do. I've become so accustomed to my inner circle of friends and family knowing the intricacies of my medical condition that I don't need to worry about shocking them with my blunt honesties about my ailing heath.

Ellis is different. He used to be a part of my inner circle. Hell, he was the center of it for long enough. Not anymore, though. Yes, he knows about my history but only to a point. There's so much he hasn't been around for, but that was then and this is now, and I have a whole new catalog of problems he's not been privy to.

My delivery was callous, and regardless of our past or even my inability to decide on an appropriate emotion toward him now—hatred, contempt, God, even love?—I shouldn't have said anything. Not here. Not like this.

Of course, the moment I realize all of this is a second too late. I've told him I'm dying without any forewarning; no gentle ease in or steady build up, and it's undoubtedly the reason for my guilt. To my horror, it manifests in an entirely unexpected way—my eyes begin to well. I've cried more these past twenty-four hours than I have in the last decade and it's not me. I'm not the person who wears her emotions on her sleeve. I abhor it; I'm stronger than this.

Maybe it's the distraught contortion of his face that summons my tears, or the unmistakable aura of helplessness that rolls from him in heavy, suffocating waves. He rests his elbows on the table and his head in his hands. I watch the way he drives his fingers roughly through his hair and into his scalp, his knuckles whitening with the force.

I blink, hoping the traitorous tears won't spill from my bleary eyes. I know it's all in my mind, but I swear that everyone in the diner is listening in and watching for my next move.

"You're dying."

The words are whispered so softly I'm not sure he meant to speak them at all. Certainly not to me, he hasn't even lifted his head. They feel like a lead weight sitting on my chest, and I'm shocked at how much they scare me, how much they still hurt. I've voiced them to myself an inordinate amount of times, but other people don't say them. I'm paralyzed for a moment, shaken to my core. Whoever said that a healthy dose of reality every now and again is a good thing is an asshole. It's not like I'd forgotten my heart was irrevocably broken in every sense of the word, but I must have anesthetized my own mind to it. Watching Ellis's response makes me feel like I did when my doctor first told me things had gotten worse: powerless.

"We all are really, if you think about it." His head snaps up, his eyes red and his mouth set in a grim line. "I just have a heads up, is all."

I slip into my counselor role, one I'm comfortable in. The one I can control. The need to soothe him takes precedence over the bad blood between us. It's not a feeling I have a conscious govern over, it's intrinsic, no matter my plight with him. My life could be written as a Shakespearian tragedy; my only love actually is sprung from my only hate, and as much as I wish it weren't true, I may never have enough time to make my peace with that.

"You say that like you don't think you'll get a heart," Ellis says, reaching across the space between us to rest his hand over mine.

I should move it, but I don't. Instead, I ignore the fizz of electricity flowing up my arm.

"It's not that," I respond. "I'm just a realist. I'm not at the top of the transplant list yet, and even if I were you know as well as I do that my blood type dramatically lowers my chances of finding a good donor match. I'm hoping for the best but prepared for the worst."

"But there's still hope that you'll find a match, right?"

I don't have the strength to give him the stats and reel off the probabilities, so I do what I know I shouldn't. I placate. I tell him what he wants to hear versus what he needs to hear. It's an omission rather than a lie, and I do it as much for him as I do for myself.

"Yeah, Ellis. There's always that chance."

Breakfast was a fucking disaster of epic proportions. Once we'd both finished pushing food around on our plates that neither of us could stomach, we'd talked a little more. I know now that he's been living in an apartment in Greensboro since his release from Morrison Correction in Hoffman County. The realization that it's only an hour's drive from home sits uncomfortably in the back of my mind. We walked back to my mom's, and I dropped him off at his car before I could screw my mind up any further. I was so desperate to lighten the mood that I'd plummeted us both into the dangerous waters of reminiscing, and now I feel worse than ever, wondering if we'll come back up for air. Kissing him last night has awakened a sleeping giant, and recollecting happier times with him now feels akin to placing a band-aid over a gaping shotgun wound. Futile.

2000

It had taken my entire first year at Duke to figure out who and where I wanted to be in my life. Spending so much time at the medical center talking with counselors, doctors, and other people with similar heart conditions to mine had opened my eyes. I started attending group sessions for people with heart complications a few months into my first semester. Ellis had pushed a pamphlet under my nose that he'd picked up at Dr. Butcher's office. I'd been sitting in the center of our bed, tangled up in the yellow comforter feeling sorry for myself. My parents had left a little while before, and I was completely drained, both mentally and physically.

They visited more often than was probably accepted as normal, but it had its perks—Mom always brought food. I missed her homemade pies; the couple of times Ellis and I had ventured away from anything that needed more than microwaving, it never ended well. I could burn water, and if Ellis deviated from the three or four things that he knew how to cook, he'd wreck the kitchen so badly that it looked like we'd been burgled. The cupboards would be bare, and there wouldn't be a single piece of kitchenware left unused. The cleanup operation was a bitch, and if the food was worth the labor I could overlook it, but it never was. Ellis was pretty awesome at most things—annoyingly so—but cooking wasn't one of them.

My parents grilled me each and every time they visited. Had I been to my appointments? What were my results? Was I taking care to not overdo things? It was like the Spanish Inquisition: Mom fired questions, I answered then Dad over-analyzed what I'd just said, and questioned me further. If the FBI were ever recruiting middle-aged interrogators in our area, Mom and Dad would have been snapped up in a heartbeat. I knew they worried about me and were only trying to ease their own minds, making sure their little girl was okay, but their visits were exhausting.

"You look tired," Ellis had said as he passed me the pamphlet and crawled onto the bed, pulling me down onto his chest. "I picked this up for you, I thought you might be interested. There's a group that meets every couple of weeks on Thursday nights. From what Dr. Butcher said, it's a great place to go and talk with other people that understand what you're going through."

"I'm kind of over talking about myself and reassuring everyone that I'm okay," I bit out more harshly than I intended. He was comfy and warm, and there were better things we could be doing in bed than talking. I stretched over his wide chest, tossing the paper onto the bedside table.

"That's the thing, though, Harlow. You're constantly trying to reassure me, your parents, even your friends. This group wouldn't be like that. They're not expecting you to turn up and try to convince them all that you're fine and that you don't really want to throat punch the next person that asks if you're feeling all right. They already know what it's like. They live it too. I think it would be good for you. You should at least give it a try, even if it's only one time."

He'd been tracing figure eights on my shoulder as he spoke; he knew it was basically like hypnotism to me.

"I'll think about," I conceded, and he paused and kissed the top of my head. I wriggled to get him to carry on with the stroking, and he let out a soft chuckle.

"You're like a lazy house cat that just wants to be petted."

I lifted up onto my forearm and looked at him. His gray t-shirt made his eyes look stormier than their usual clear blue depths. He had a severe case of five o'clock shadow, and his golden hair had grown so long that it had a distinct wave to it, and when I pushed my hands through it I could grab a thick handful. It was unfair how soft his hair was, or how impossibly long his eyelashes were. Guys shouldn't be allowed to be as effortlessly hot as he was. He woke up looking like an advertisement for Abercrombie. I woke up looking like I'd been dragged through a hedge backward, and that was on a good day.

"I feel like a burden. You're always taking care of me," I admitted, shocking myself. I hadn't meant to say it out loud, but the second it passed my lips I realized that it was the truth. I'd spent months waiting for him to get pissed with being my babysitter. I was scared that he'd start to resent me. That he felt like he was trapped in a situation he didn't want to be in but was staying out of obligation. What guy our age wanted to stay home on weekends and spend his free time going for gentle walks, instead of partying 'til all hours and doing dumb shit like the rest of his friends? I was holding him back.

He pushed backward up the bed to sit against the dark wooden headboard, looking at me like I was a puzzle he couldn't quite fathom.

"Why would you think like that?" he asked, the hurt evident in his voice. "You could never be a burden to me."

I wanted to believe him, but there was a small part of me that couldn't wrap my head around him not tiring of worrying about me.

"You say that but I'm not stupid, Ellis. You run around after me like I'm your responsibility and I'm not. We've thrust ourselves into a situation that most people don't end up in until way after college. Think about it. We live like an old married couple, and I keep waiting for the moment that you figure out that it doesn't have to be like this. You're not the one who has to live this lifestyle."

His expression darkened, the softness morphing into annoyance as he pinched the bridge of his nose. He was quiet for a few beats, taking in what I'd said, and I shifted uncomfortably, waiting for him to agree.

"You really think I'm that shallow?" he asked but didn't give me time to respond. "That I'd walk away from us because you have health issues? I'm not in any situation that I don't want to be in. I live with you because I want to wake up next to you every day—not because you have a heart condition and I'm too chicken to walk away. Jesus! Is that what you think? I'm here because I daren't not be?"

He'd run his hand through his hair and expelled a frustrated breath through his nose. I hadn't expected his reaction; the whole time Ellis and I had been together I could probably count on one hand the number of times that I'd seen him look pissed. He was always laid back; I couldn't even remember the last time we argued, or what it had been over.

"I try my best to take care of you because I love you," he sighed. "That's the only reason I do anything. You're not, and never could be a burden, Harlow. Granted, you can be a pain in the ass and stubborn as hell sometimes, but never a burden."

I swallowed the lump that had formed in my throat. My heart pounded painfully in my chest as I digested his words. My relief was mixed with a pang of guilt for doubting him, but when you have someone in your life that's seemingly perfect, you can't help but look for faults. He shook his head and rose from the bed to walk out the room. I watched him as he looked back to where I was sitting, the disappointment clouding him like smoke. He didn't say anything else, just walked out of our bedroom leaving me feeling like the most ungrateful girlfriend a guy could have, drowning in her own self-pity. That was the night I decided to give the Hearts & Minds group a go. I owed it to Ellis just as much as I owed it to myself to give it a chance. I had no idea when I walked through the door a week later that it would end up changing the course of my future forever.

"Fresh meat! Welcome, come and grab a drink," a girl with green dreadlocks shouted as I stepped through the door in the medical center. It had a whiteboard with "Hearts & Minds, tonight 7-9pm" written on it.

I looked around hoping her comment wasn't directed at me, even though I knew it was. My pulse thrummed as I twisted my hands together nervously and gave her a weak smile. I made my way slowly around the circle of blue plastic chairs until I reached the foldaway table that had been set up in the corner of the room. Tall glass jugs of juice and plastic cups had been haphazardly stacked high on it. I noted the plate of cookies, most of which had already been demolished despite it only being 6:55.

"Hi, I'm Tori," the girl with the dreadlocks offered, thrusting her hand out for me to shake.

"Oh, um, hi. I'm Harlow." I shook her hand before moving past her to busy myself pouring a drink. I scanned the table looking at the different containers, trying to deduce where the coffee was.

"It's juice or water, I'm afraid," Tori said, answering my unspoken question. "There's no tea or coffee. I guess they don't want any of us to drop dead from the caffeine," she said rolling her eyes. I nodded and poured myself an orange juice.

"This is your first time then," she stated rather than asked. "The guy with the black Henley on over there is Richard." She pointed to a guy sitting in one of the plastic seats. He looked a little older than me, but not by a whole lot. I'd have guessed mid-twenties. "The guy he's talking with, that's Teddy. The older lady sitting over there is June, she's like the momma bear of the group, and the quiet girl with the black hair sitting beside her is Larissa. She's not very vocal in the group, but if you happen to bump into her at Shooters, well, it's like meeting a whole different girl."

"Okay," I nodded, taking in the different names and knowing that I'd probably forget them within five minutes. "So who leads the actual group?" I asked assessing the people she'd pointed out.

"Oh, that's Martin," she said with a smirk I didn't quite understand. "He's not here yet, he's never been on time once."

I took a sip of my OJ and placed the cup back down on the table.

"So how long have you been coming to the group, Tori?" I suddenly felt like I needed to at least attempt to make polite conversation. What I wanted to do was take a step back from her so I could take her in all at once. It was like looking at a rainbow. Her bright green dreadlocks hit just above her waist, and she was wearing what looked to be a homemade-knitted sweater that was every shade of orange and red you could possibly imagine. Her gray jeans had different pieces of fabric sewn all over so they resembled a patchwork quilt and she was wearing a pair of bright yellow Doc boots. She should by all rights have looked ridiculous, but she didn't—everything seemed to fit together perfectly.

ELLE BROOKS

"I've been coming for just under a year," she said almost as brightly as her clothing, ignoring my blatant stare. "My mom convinced me to come after my bypass—I think she was worried that I wasn't ever going to leave the house again."

"Bypass?"

"Yeah, ASD." She pointed to herself. "It's basically a hole in the part of the septum that separates the upper chambers of my heart. I never knew I had a problem until I collapsed at a music festival. I think everyone just thought I was drunk or high because the group of friends I was with at the time was both. Thankfully, someone realized I needed help and before I knew what was happening, I'd had surgery to correct the problem and now here I am."

I wanted to respond but wasn't sure what to say. I mean, what can you say to that? I took another sip of my juice as the door flung open and a guy I could only assume was Martin rushed in.

"Sorry I'm late, guys," he said dumping a brown satchel and a hefty load of papers down on one of the empty chairs, then pulling out the one next to it to sit down.

"That's our cue to park our butts," Tori whispered, steering me into the circle. I pulled out the chair nearest to us, and the legs scraped along the gray tile floor, sounding like nails on a chalkboard. Suddenly every pair of eyes in the room was trained on me.

"Sorry," I offered lamely, feeling my cheeks flush as I bit the corner of my lip and sat down on my hands. I wasn't normally a shy person, but I didn't feel particularly comfortable in my surroundings yet and was hoping that I could slip in and out of the group unnoticed. No such luck. Martin smiled widely as he looked me over.

"Ah, we have a new face tonight, people," he declared. If anyone hadn't noticed me yet they sure as shit did now. *Great.* "My name's Martin Sharpe, I am a cardiac nurse here at Duke

Cardiology EP Clinic. And, yes, you heard me right. I'm a nurse," he smiled. "Contrary to popular belief, men can be nurses too. I've been here almost six years and took over the group around eighteen months ago. The group is for anyone who's experienced or is currently living with chronic cardiac illnesses. We meet once every two weeks here at the center to provide people with a venue to discuss any fears and anxieties they might have."

Martin didn't look like a nurse, not that there were any predefined specifications, but he just didn't. He was clean-shaven, had large owlish brown eyes, and a buzz cut. He had what I guess you could call a baby face, so his age was hard to determine. The only telling sign that he was a little older than most of the group were the crinkles that formed around his eyes when he smiled. It had taken a minute before I realized that the group had gone silent while I'd zoned out, analyzing Martin's features. I turned to Tori, who was stifling a smile.

"He's waiting for you to introduce yourself," she somehow managed to whisper without moving her mouth. She'd make a great ventriloquist.

I looked back to the group. "Oh, hi. I'm Harlow Stevens," I announced and gave a lame little wave.

Martin waited a few seconds, allowing me time to elaborate and no doubt spill my story. I didn't oblige, and when it was clear that I had no intention of baring my soul five minutes into my first visit, he glossed over my aversion to sharing and carried on with the session.

Two things happened that I wasn't expecting. The first was that hearing everyone speak was inspiring. I'd been so sure listening to them talk about their experiences would be depressingly monotonous, but it wasn't the case. Most people focused on the progression they were making and shared their triumphs no matter how small or inconsequential they seemed. The second was that I found myself wanting to talk. I held back, listening to the others but the urge to join in had taken me by surprise, and the fact that I left that night knowing I'd be back was oddly exciting.

It took three sessions for me to feel comfortable enough to share my own story with the group, and five before I spoke with Martin and decided I wanted to major in psychology. I liked the feeling of freedom that came with discussing my condition with the group, and I quickly decided I wanted to be the person that helped others to find that same openness.

"Doubt thou the stars are fire, Doubt that the sun doth move. Doubt truth to be a liar, But never doubt I love."

—WILLIAM SHAKESPEARE

CHAPTER

SEVENTEEN

Head Spinner

Ellis

I t's not like I didn't know that this day might come. I've always had it in the back of my mind; Harlow's health has haunted me just as her dad's face has. I guess you can't ever really prepare for the news that someone's dying. It seems so much crueler if you love that person, and the purest form of evil when they have so much living left to do. Harlow's in her thirties; she shouldn't need to worry about her own mortality.

I've been sitting in my rental car for an hour and I can't make myself turn the key in the ignition to actually start it up. My whole body feels numb. My fingers curl into my palms and my fists clench tightly of their own accord. Why am I being punished? When will it stop? I was in shock back at the Bait House, now that I'm alone I'm angry. Rage courses through my blood and swells the veins in my forearms to the extent that they pop out from my wrist to elbow. My pulse hammers so hard in my ears it's a wonder I don't explode.

I give in to my frustration before I know what's happening and start beating down hard on the steering wheel, punches falling in an insistent surge of anger, causing the car horn to sound and my knuckles to ache. Flailing and writhing in the front seat, all I can do is scream out my helplessness in a string of curses and profanities. I lose myself in anger and hurt. I know I need to stop and calm down but I can't because my mind's racing, taunting me with possibilities that are too painful to consider and too real to ignore. The only thought I can make sense of is that I know I don't want to exist in a world where Harlow doesn't.

It's exhaustion that finally claims me. When I'm breathless and can't hit the steering wheel anymore, the tears start. It took all my effort not to break down in front of Harlow at the Bait House. I'd held my head in my hands so I didn't have to look at her face. One glance before I had pulled myself together would've been all it took.

A woman walking her German shepherd falters when she notices me in the car, and quickly picks up her pace. The discomfort of seeing a grown man cry is clear in her gait. She crosses to the opposite side of the street and throws inquisitive glances back at me until she finally reaches the street corner and disappears out of sight. A group of what looks to be college-aged kids notice me next. A small brunette girl accidently makes eye contact as she walks by the car and a second later the whole group is turning their heads in my direction. I rub my hands down my face, take a deep breath and turn the key in the ignition. I need to get out of here. I pull out, passing the group of kids who are laughing and smiling like they don't have a care in the world.

God, I wish I could go back to being their age.

High school had ended in a blur for Harlow and me. While Logan, Elliott and the rest of my friends were trying to recreate *American Pie* and see high school out with a bang—pun intended—I'd been preoccupied with hospital appointments and supporting H in a bid to convince her parents that deferring college for a year wasn't necessary.

From the moment we'd been pushed to start considering colleges, my goal had always been Duke. It was a great school that wasn't too far away and had one of the best pre-law programs in the country, according to my dad. It didn't hurt that Duke athletics were pretty stellar and Durham's cost of living to quality of living ratio made it seem like a total no-brainer. When Harlow was diagnosed with Myocarditis and we were forced to re-examine our college choices, making sure to pick somewhere close to a good hospital specializing in cardiology—our searches all pointed to Duke University Hospital—sealing our fate.

I'd always maintained a picture in my head of what I expected our college experience to be. Harlow and I would be together, that part was never up for debate, but we'd decided that we wanted to spend our freshman year like any other teenager away from home for the first time: drunk, hungry and eager for new experiences.

Neither of us was interested in going the Greek route, and Harlow was as far removed from a sorority chick as you could probably get. She was a tomboy who'd rather spend the night watching sports and scarfing down pizza than waste three hours getting her hair and makeup ready to be seen at the "cool kids" parties. Which, by default made her cool in her own right. Guys loved her, and not just because she was beautiful, but because she could hold her own in a room full of hockey players. She wasn't afraid to damage her rep by telling it like it was. She called a spade a spade, and if you were talking crap, you'd better believe she'd let you know.

The plan we'd made in high school had never factored in medical issues, though, so instead of living in separate dorms with strangers we were expected to forge lifelong friendships with, we opted for an off-campus apartment. Our parents didn't go for it immediately, but I'd sold them on the fact that by living together off campus I could make sure that Harlow's medical needs were taken care of. There'd be no random strangers or peer pressure to drink when it was the last thing she should be doing with her daily medication regimen. I'd be with her pretty much 24/7, which meant that she'd always have someone nearby that knew exactly what to do if her health began to deteriorate, and would constantly be looking for the signs. It made perfect sense and was a win, win scenario in my eyes. I'd get to spend every night with the girl I'd been in love with since she'd shot me in her back garden the first week I'd moved to North Carolina.

So, that's what happened. We left for college, just like most other kids from our senior class. Molly scored a scholarship at Brown, Elliot moved to Chapel Hill and attended UNC, quickly pledging for Phi Delta Theta and by some magic, or more likely bribery, he actually got in. As for Harlow and me, 509 Willard Street became our home, and for the first three months of our freshman year we locked ourselves away in the small two-bedroom apartment and survived solely on sex and ramen.

"It's basically high school round two," Harlow told her mom over the phone. Dianne had made me promise to make sure that Harlow called her every two nights to check in—and by "made me promise" I mean she threatened me. For such a slight and pretty woman, Dianne had a glare that could reduce a grown man to tears. That's no joke; I'd seen her rip into the twins on more than one occasion and leave them tearing up. There were two things I knew with absolute certainty. One, never, never answer yes if your girlfriend asks if she looks fat in a particular item of clothing. Two, always stay on the good side of Dianne Stevens.

College wasn't shaping up to be what I thought it would. Sure, all your average clichés about frat parties were sadly and irrevocably true. But, I felt kind of cheated by Hollywood. In every college-based film I'd ever seen, and granted while it wasn't as many as most it was still enough to con myself into thinking I had an educated opinion, students hung out in coffee shops discussing the next big event on their social calendar. Well, newsflash! Students do not have copious amounts of free time. Go figure. My schedule was insane and it was only going to get busier. I'd been truly duped by movies that portrayed college as a non-stop rager; in my experience, it was an academic institution that wouldn't think twice about ejecting your ass from their program if you didn't toe the line and actually do the work.

Where were the movies that showed kids like me spending all their time in class studying, or interning for some local law firm for free—all so I could claim a small semblance of experience? Can anyone say office bitch? It was less *Law and Order* and more free labor exploitation. I spent all my time filing or fetching coffee and sandwiches. It sucked on an immeasurable scale. The summer I'd spent mowing the neighbors' lawns in ninety-five-degree heat with a killer case of hay fever when I was thirteen, just so I could save up to buy my own computer capable of connecting to the world-wide web, was more enjoyable.

Harlow was living a different college experience than mine. Whereas I was focused, had my major in sight and was heading for it with guns blazing, she wandered aimlessly through her entire year. What's more, she wasn't the slightest bit panicked by it. Over the course of a few months at Duke, she'd gone from obsessing about her health limitations, not being able to join the swim team, or party like most other freshman, to a full-blown embrace of her situation. I'd be lying if I said I wasn't a little envious of how happy-go-lucky she seemed about college. I get that she was probably just happy to be there at all, but somehow the tables had turned and I'd inadvertently taken on all of her anxiety.

When we first moved in we lived like students. We ate like students. Embraced the whole lifestyle, ridiculously late nights and caffeine-fueled morning seminars included. It wasn't until one of her check-ups when the doctor told us they needed to make adjustments to her medication because her stats had slipped that I paused long enough to realize we weren't normal students. She hadn't asked me to take care of her; I'd put that on myself as her boyfriend. I needed to do it, if only to settle my own nerves. I set my alarm thirty minutes early every day, even when I didn't have class. I would get up bleary-eyed and put out her pills on the kitchen counter so she wouldn't forget to take them. I'd memorized all the leaflets the doctors had given her about leading a healthy lifestyle and made sure that the apartment wasn't stocked with only junk food. I was happy to assume the role of caretaker. I needed to feel like I was helping. The image of her unconscious in the back of an ambulance was so deeply ingrained in my memory I was hell bent on making sure I never had to relive it.

Harlow wasn't one for taking things easy or living within a pre-determined set of guidelines, even though they'd been set out by a team of exceptionally qualified medical staff. She was a free spirit, a firecracker and determined to push the boundaries and not be held back—a quality I both loved and loathed in equal measure.

"When Dr. Foster diagnosed Myocarditis, I'm sure it was firmly recommended that you completely avoid all competitive and highly physical sports for at least six months, Harlow. Only resuming them if or when your cardiac tests showed complete recovery," Dr. Butcher reiterated.

Harlow nodded her head, her unkempt blonde waves spilling from the loose clip she'd fastened it with. A strand dropped out over her cheek, catching at the corner of her mouth and I moved unconsciously, sweeping it away with my thumb and tucking it behind her ear. She gave my knee a tiny squeeze, and I gazed down at the spot she was holding and took her hand. I couldn't help noticing her own knees bobbed up and down impatiently waiting for the doctor to make his point.

"We've looked at your results and at present I'm not in a position to advise that you increase your physical activity any further," he told her, settling his sympathetic eyes on the paperwork in front of him.

A slither of dread unfurled itself deep in the pit of my stomach, making me shift forward in my seat and grip H's hand a little tighter. I was aiming for reassurance, even though I knew I was missing the mark.

"But... But it's been more than six months. I'm feeling really great," she countered. "I'm almost never out of breath when I go through the exercise plan you gave me. I could probably do it twice without even breaking a sweat. I'm not asking for you to clear me to go climb mountains or anything," she said with a laugh, looking from him to me, and then back at him. "I just want to be able to do more. I miss being allowed to run, I'll even settle for jogging. Heck, power walking would do," she confessed hopefully.

I could tell Dr. Butcher didn't want to dash her hopes, but I could also see that it was exactly what he was about to do. I kept my eyes trained on the doctor, trying not to witness the sadness I knew would be settling into place over her pretty face. I didn't need to look at her to know she'd be biting down on the corner of her bottom lip. I knew her hazel eyes would turn glassy, but she'd rather die than let a tear fall in public. I knew the light that rested somewhere behind her smile wouldn't be making an appearance today, and that thought alone crushed me.

"Harlow, abstaining from physical activities shortly after any type of inflammatory heart disease is recommended because viral persistence could last for several months. Six months was given as a guide and we've reached it, but I'm afraid we need to move it back a little further. All the beneficial principles of ACE inhibition, beta-blockade, and the diuretics we've been administering aim to unload the burden on your heart, but we have to afford them the time to do so. Different people react in different ways, some more slowly or quickly than others with the same prognosis. It's a very delicate balancing act, trial and error for want of a better phrase, to find each person's equilibrium."

"So really this is just a little bump in the road, right? You're not saying that she can't ever resume more physical activity, just not right now?" I asked, trying to inject a positive note into the conversation.

"That's right. Not right now," Dr. Butcher said pointedly, looking directly at Harlow. He seemed to know as well as I did that just because he'd given her the facts didn't mean she would listen to them. He gave me a curt nod when she didn't acknowledge his answer, knowing that I was taking note at least.

I liked Dr. Butcher; when Harlow and I had first met him, we'd laughed at how unfortunate his name was, given his profession. Nobody wanted to associate their heart doctor with a butcher.

"I keep imagining him behind his desk with a stethoscope in one hand and a meat cleaver in the other," I'd said sniggering as we waited in the reception room at the Duke Cardiology EP Clinic.

"Ouch, what was that for?" I whined as Harlow's elbow dug into my ribs.

"I'm about to meet my new cardiologist, and you're freaking me out with the butchering jokes," she whispered. "I'm already nervous. Now I have an image of some Leatherface looka-like in a white coat and apron covered in blood!"

"Leatherface?"

"*Texas Chainsaw Massacre*," she replied. I gave her a blank stare and shrugged.

"The dude with the chainsaw, he was Leatherface—you know, because he'd wear a skin mask, and he used to work as a butcher at the meat factory with his brother, the cook."

"How do you even know all that?" I asked. Half of me was intrigued, and the other half was a little terrified of how her brain worked.

"Seriously, Ellis, you've watched it with me. How can you not know that stuff?"

Neither of us saw or heard the moment Dr. Butcher entered the waiting room as we slouched together on the hard plastic seating, talking about dudes wearing masks made of human remains.

"Ms. Stevens," he said in a commanding voice loud enough to make us jump right out of our skin. As a heart doctor you'd think he'd be a little better at not inducing heart attacks in his patients or their chaperones. We turned to take a look at the man with the booming bass tone and couldn't hold back our muffled sniggers. We had to feign a few coughs to calm our surprised laughter. Dr. Butcher was about five-and-a-half feet tall and looked like he weighed eighty pounds soaking wet. The guy was tiny, and yet his voice carried like a supersonic jet engine. It was utterly disarming.

It took three weeks of taking it easy before Harlow began to push her boundaries again. She'd jump on her board and skate to class, and when I pointed out that wasn't a good idea, she'd shrug and tell me she coasted ninety percent of the way, and to trust her. It wasn't about trust, though; I knew if she started to feel tired that she'd stop and rest. It was the fact that she was so willing to take the risk at all that irked me. My girl was sneaky. She would push a little more each and every day; before I knew it, she'd be seconds away from joining the damn track team, and I'd have to reign her inhibitions back in.

Freshman year turned out to be mostly a year of testing our limits.

"Let's go out," Harlow had said one Saturday night, half-way through Fall semester. "Katie from my English Lit class has a boyfriend that works at Shooters. He'll serve us for sure. I need to get out of this apartment, and you do too. I can't remember the last time we had a night out," she said, hands on hips.

"We're like a forty-year-old married couple trapped inside the bodies of twenty-year-olds."

I laughed at her assessment and stretched out my arms lazily unleashing a yawn.

"You should invite some of the guys, it'll be fun." She was wearing a dazzling smile full of hope that made my tired-ass self want to groan. I couldn't say no to her once she switched up her tactics and pulled out the big guns—huge wounded puppy eyes. I was beyond tired, but the prospect of letting off some steam and having a few beers appealed to me more than I thought it would.

When I'd taken on the internship at Goldman and Burke's I hadn't planned on staying past the initial three-month placement. But once that was up, and they'd exacted as much free labor as they could from me, they offered me a paid position. Mrs. Feldstein, their legal secretary who'd worked for the firm since what I assumed would have been the dawn of the dinosaurs, was falling behind in her productivity. Since she didn't want to retire, and the partners didn't have the heart to replace her with a younger, newer and more efficient model, they enlisted my help. I picked up the slack, assisting with the preparing and filing of legal appeals and motions that Mrs. Feldstein couldn't get to. My previous role of tea bitch became a thing of the past. Mrs. Feldstein wore a hearing aid, had a penchant for mint crisp cookies and had a bit of a drinking problem—if adding whiskey to her mid-morning coffee was anything to go by.

But, despite having to shout over the radio she constantly had blasting at noise levels I'm sure broke some form of pollution code, Mrs. Feldstein was a lot of fun to talk to. I never had a grandma, but I imagine she would've been the coolest granny on the block. She swore like a sailor and none too quietly either. She was pretty much buzzed every day by 2 pm, and I think half the time she closed her office door she was actually passed out asleep at her desk.

Harlow loved her. Every time I'd come home from work the first thing she would ask for was a run down of what crazy and politically incorrect words Mrs. Feldstein had managed to drop into conversations throughout my day. It was a rarity if she didn't at least let one cuss word slip while there were clients in the office. She was hilarious.

"I'm up for it, but I need to shower and change first," I said hopping up from the sofa and bending to kiss Harlow's head on the way to the bathroom. She'd apparently not expected to win me over, and her mouth popped open like I'd suddenly grown a second head.

"What?" I asked laughing as I unbuttoned my gray shirt, peeking out around the bathroom door.

"Nothing, I just expected you to be too tired. I'll call Katie and let her know we're going."

I dropped my shirt to the floor and was unbuckling my belt when she stopped in her tracks and placed the phone back down on the counter. I raised a brow as she shamelessly assessed my body, raking her gaze from my head to my toes.

"There's room in the shower for two," I called, walking back into the bathroom to turn the hot water on, knowing she'd be right behind me.

There's nothing quite like hot shower sex to get you in the mood for a great night, even if it is rushed. We'd strolled into Shooters twenty minutes later than planned, but by the look of things we hadn't been missed. Katie was leaning across the bar, her long white-blonde hair spilled over the counter as she talked animatedly with the guy serving drinks, whom I assumed was her boyfriend. Jace and Matt were huddled up by Katie's roommate, Rebecca, whom I'd met only a handful of times before. She was a dork magnet if there even was such a thing. Standing at least six feet in her Docs, and possibly the only female in the bar wearing a Star Wars t-shirt, she stood out. Her bright red hair was clipped back with hundreds of tiny little black clamps, and her spiky chokers screamed, "back off!" while her smile said, "come closer." She was a giant contradiction. The guys were drawn in by her ability to talk comic books and gaming, neither of which were my thing, but my friends ate it up all the same.

We made it to the bar, pushing through the throngs of students in various states of inebriation. The music was loud enough that I could feel it echo through my chest and I gripped Harlow's hand, guiding her toward Katie.

"Hey, you made it!" she shouted, turning to introduce us to her boyfriend, Kyle. I ordered a beer hoping Kyle wouldn't ask for my ID. I was in luck, he passed over a Miller Light without so much as batting an eyelash, and I turned to ask Harlow what she wanted to drink.

"Rum and Coke."

She tossed it out nonchalantly like it was something she drank every day of the week. I held my hand up to stop Kyle from reaching to fill a glass from the rum optics and looked at Harlow with an expression that asked whether she really thought it was such a good idea. When all she did was widen her eyes at me, I shook my head. "You know you're not supposed to have alcohol. Or too much caffeine, for that matter."

"Ugh! Ellis, I'll only have one. Relax, I know what I'm doing."

I didn't like that she seemed intent on drinking, it had never bothered her to abstain before. I didn't want to make a big thing out of it in front of her friends, so I nodded despite my unease.

"Make it a vodka orange," she shouted to Kyle while still focusing on me.

"I'll drop the Coke, that way the caffeine's not an issue, and I promise I'll only drink this one." She pressed up onto her tiptoes and kissed the side of my jaw. "Don't worry."

I sighed, and resigned myself to the fact that it was just one drink, what harm could it really do?

"Let's ride the mechanical bull," Jace said, handing over another round of shots. I'd lost count after the first five, and my buzz was quickly turning into full-blown tanked. I wasn't a big drinker; I wasn't even a small drinker. I'd always needed to be sober for hockey, and with Harlow not being able to drink I limited myself to one or two tops. The alcohol had been in full flow that evening, though, and it felt good to cut loose and not worry for a little while. I didn't have practice, work, or classes the next morning, and the more I drank, the more relaxed I began to feel. You never truly appreciate just how drunk you are until you need to take a trip to the toilet, I discovered. I had to brace myself against a wall to keep from swaying and I was acutely aware that maybe it was time to switch to water.

"Twenty dollars says my guy can hold on longer than you, Jace," Harlow chirped from under my arm a short while later.

"Oh, you're on, little lady!"

"Wait, I don't think I'm built to be a bull rider," I admitted, swaying slightly.

"I've got to agree with Ellis on this one, guys," Katie offered. She was looking from me to the bull at the far end of the bar. "My money's on Jace." She lifted off her stool, pulling a twenty from her back pocket and slapping it down in the center of the table.

"What you betting on?" Kyle asked as he leaned to collect the tray of empties from our table.

"Who do you think will ride the bull the longest, baby?" Katie answered, pointing between Jace and myself.

"Your man here has the advantage," Kyle said, clapping Jace on the shoulder. "He's shorter, his center of gravity should be better."

Jace grinned at me smugly, and ran his hand through his messy dark hair, sending it shooting out in all directions. We'd met in our first ethics class, and bonded over our mutual appreciation of our lecturer. She was smoking hot and looked way too young to be the teacher, but once she'd opened her mouth and unleashed holy hell on a group of guys that had walked in late, we'd quickly named her The Dragon and feared her more than fancied her now. He was only a few inches shorter than me, and was lean, but built smaller through the shoulders.

"Ellis is a skater, his balance is awesome, and his limbs are longer, so he should be able to wrap around it better," Harlow countered.

"Okay, you're on. Put me down for twenty on Jace. I'll take your money, Harlow, if you're so intent on losing it."

Within minutes we had a book going on who'd get his ass served to him by the bull, and I was pretty confident that it would be me landing quicker on the inflatable red crash mat surrounding the machine. I rolled my shoulders, psyching myself up. I almost collapsed in a fit of laughter when Jace began trash talking with Harlow like we were weighing in for a boxing title.

Rebecca and a few of the people she'd been talking with had joined in too, and to Harlow's delight were joining "Team Ellis." Before I knew what was happening, the whole bar was enthralled as Matt took to the DJ booth and announced our battle.

Katie insisted on a coin toss for who'd go first and set the bar. Jace called it, and made his way over to the inflatable mat and mounted the bull like he was a pro rider. I watched through hazy eyes as he wound the rope tight around his right hand, taking a firm grip and then leaning down low. The concentration on his face was epic; he was taking it as seriously as if he'd just mounted a real bull. Cheers erupted as the machine swayed into motion to the sound of "Dead or Alive".

"Huh, he moves pretty well with it," Harlow mused as her eyes traced Jace's actions, his hips rolling back and forth as the bull bucked beneath him at an increasing tempo.

"Oh, the boy's got skills!" Katie howled, stepping up on the crossbar of her stool so she could get a better view over the crowd. "Who knew? Whoop, go, Jace!" she called out before turning back to us all.

"I feel like I'm watching him get lucky—I mean, just look at his face. I bet it's his sex face," Rebecca added. Everyone within a five-foot radius began laughing as we watched the bull pick up speed and its movements become more erratic.

"Oh, he's going!" Matt boomed over the PA as Jace began to slip from the bull's back, and clung to its side like his life depended on it.

"How long's he been on?" Harlow asked Katie.

"Forty-seven seconds, forty-eight, forty-nine...and he's down!"

The crowd cheered as Jace's grip slipped and he was flung to the mat like a sack of potatoes. His shirt was riding up and his wrist flamed bright red with rope burn, but he stood up wobbly on the inflatable mat and threw his hands in the air like he'd just managed a solid eight seconds at a Professional Bull Riders event.

"Shit, that's way harder than it looks," he gasped reaching the table and taking a pull of the beer he'd left. "Good luck, man."

Harlow pushed up from her stool and kissed my cheek. "Okay, Ellis, go show him how it's done." She patted my ass and bounced on the spot as I took a final drink from my bottle, placing it down on the table with my wallet and keys.

"I can't believe you're making me do this," I groaned over my shoulder as I moved through the throng of students littering the ringside.

"Where's Ellis Hughes at?" Matt's voice carried over the bar. I threw my arm up stepping into the ring and toeing my sneakers off.

"Get on up, bro, you got forty-nine seconds to beat."

"Make me proud, Hughes!" Harlow called from back at our table.

Have you ever experienced that feeling of know something's a stupid idea but throwing yourself into it headfirst anyway? Knowing it will end badly but relying on hope to carry you through? That was the nervous sensation that settled in my stomach as I threw my leg over the side of the bull, twisted the rope over my hand and looked out to the crowd. I've never had motion sickness, and I like adrenaline sports. I'm no pussy when it comes to trying new things and I told myself I'd be fine, but the second the bull jerked to life and completed its first revolution I knew I was screwed.

"I Will Survive" was blasting over the speakers, and I couldn't help thinking it was an omen. I tried to lean backward and let my hips flex with the seesaw motion, but the spinning combined with the shots and the too-warm air in the overcrowded bar suddenly felt overwhelming. I scrunched my eyes up, hoping to steady my equilibrium but it didn't help. I needed to focus on watching the bull to adjust my position and hold on. The music was blaring and I could barely make out the muffled sounds of cheers as blood rushed in my ears.

The bull bucked.

My stomach rolled.

Saliva flooded my mouth.

My throat tightened as I realized what was about to happen, but I was powerless to stop it. The machine pitched forward, jerking me into an upright position at the same time as it spun violently to the right, putting me in full-face view of the crowd. I clamped my lips shut as tightly as I could, but the force of the jerking caused me to expel the contents of the night's binge drinking at full force into my audience. The bull made two full revolutions before someone had the foresight to kill its power, stopping me from spraying the entire bar with regurgitated Sambuca and Miller Light.

The giant red countdown clock had been paused on fifty-four seconds. I was still sitting tall in the center of the machine, but the spectacle of people retching and gagging around the room overshadowed the win. The lucky ones who'd avoided the splash zone were dry heaving and covering their horrified faces, but a hoard of people—mainly guys—were bent double, laughing and clutching at their sides.

My eyes scanned the bar in search of Harlow's face. I crashed with her dumbstruck expression and watched as she shook her head in bewilderment. I unraveled the coarse rope from my fist, the burn not registering nearly as much as my embarrassment. I slid from the bull on shaky legs that didn't feel like my own. They were weak from gripping the side of the bull so tightly. Harlow had made her way through the sea of angry and disgusted vomit-soaked students, stopping short of the ring. Matt barreled down from the DJ booth with tears in his eyes— either from laughter or the smell that was permeating the stifling room, I couldn't tell.

"Are you okay?" Harlow mouthed with something akin to a wince and a smile.

"Hughes, what the fuck?" Matt shouted.

"I won, though, right?" I answered shrugging.

"You want to claim this as a win?"

He shook his head assessing the carnage still unfolding in front of us.

"A win's a win," I said, stepping forward. The inflatable mat hadn't escaped the disaster, and my foot slid from under me. I hit the padded barrier full force—with my face.

"Let's go out," she'd said. "It'll be fun," she'd promised.

I'd initially panicked when she wanted to drink, worrying that we'd end up in the emergency room. My fears were justified, although somewhat misplaced. It was a blessing, and a curse that I'd consumed so much alcohol—drinking so much had caused me to fall but had also helped numbed the pain of my broken nose. Turns out, I should have been paying more attention to my own limitations, and not badger Harlow to recognize her own. Duke could keep its so-called college experience. If the night had taught me anything, it was that sometimes a win was actually a loss, and I was a sore loser.

Literally.

The only silver lining was Harlow got to play nurse instead of patient, and she made for one hell of a nurse.

"There is no remedy for love
but to love more."

— DAVID HENRY THOREAU

CHAPTER

EIGHTEEN

Coffee and Other Drugs

Harlow

I learned more than a few survival skills throughout college:

1) Befriending the dining hall staff is the best thing you can ever do for your college career. If you can't cook to save your life and your boyfriend thinks ramen can be eaten morning, noon, and night, it pays to have friends in high places...like the kitchen.

2) You can only learn your true alcohol tolerance level through trial and error.

3) Beer pong never ends well, even if you have stellar hand-eye coordination.

4) Taking an afternoon class that has no appeal other than a distinct lack of early morning lectures can turn out to be the best damn thing you ever do.

I never had an overt interest in psychology; I'd pretty much always deduced that people acted a certain way because it's how they're wired. In my head, it really was as simple as that. It never occurred to me to analyze their behavior and look for reasons why they acted the way they did. I initially enrolled in the Psychology elective because it fit well with sports science, and, probably the main reason, the lectures happened to fall in the late afternoon. I'd do anything to keep my mornings as free as I could. If it hadn't been for that one lazy decision, coupled with Ellis pushing me to join Hearts & Minds, I wouldn't be doing what I do today.

Being a counselor means I'm involved in helping people come to better terms with their lives and experiences through exploration of their feelings and emotions. It's kind of ironic that I find it almost effortless to help others, and yet I can't practice what I preach. In my work I'm expected to provide a confidential setting in which to listen attentively to my clients. I'm good at my job, not because of my ability to empathize, show patience and respect, or analyze a person's issues. I'm good because I care. I genuinely want to help. As cliché as it sounds, I've sat on the other end of that big scary counseling sofa. I know what it's like to feel helpless in your own body and judged for how you handle yourself. I'm not at liberty to give advice, but I can offer help and support.

It's a mentally exhausting career, but not an entirely selfless one. There's a certain buzz you get from feeling like you've truly made a difference in someone's life, and it would be a falsehood to claim that I didn't love that feeling. Because of the intimacy of my work, it's crucially important I'm fully self-aware. My ability to self-reflect and remain emotionally detached from relationships that develop with my clients is perhaps the single most important trait I possess as a counselor. I've never once felt like I was faking it.

Until now.

It's been almost two months since I spent the evening with Ellis and to say that I've overanalyzed every aspect of every damn minute we were together is the understatement of the century. He's consumed my mind, entirely. I think about him when I'm at home. I think about him when I'm at work, and if I do finally manage to fall asleep at night, guess who pops up in my dreams?

Ellis-goddamn-Hughes.

I made the fundamental mistake of exchanging cell numbers with him before he left. I told myself I'd delete it after a whole night staring at my phone and willing myself not to call or text him. I didn't delete his number. Instead, I've let it sit on my contact list for the past eight weeks taunting me. I wonder if he's been doing the same thing? I'm not an idiot and I knew I wasn't over him, not really. We never got to have the closure I needed to walk away and leave that part of my life behind. I just hadn't realized how completely not over him I was.

"Harlow?"

I scribble in a figure eight at the top of my yellow legal pad, watching the blue ink darken as I retrace the shape over and over again. The symbol of infinity: a never-ending loop, just like my torment.

A cough snaps me out of the trance I'm in.

"Hmm?"

"I said is our time up?"

It takes me an embarrassingly long second to assess my surroundings and regain my equilibrium. I realize that my patient

Jennifer, who's sitting back in her chair, is waiting for me to dismiss our session. A session in which I have no clue what she's just professed. I don't think I've asked her one solitary question since she's been in here, and our sessions run for an hour.

I try my best to calm my demeanor and look a little less flustered than I'm feeling. *Oh, God. I hope I at least made some form of acknowledgment, even if it was a misplaced nod or hmm to her single-sided conversation... Crap.*

I'm further mortified to realize that I haven't made any notes. Not one meaningful word. The only thing covering the notebook in my hands are random doodles. I tilt the pad toward my chest, hoping she doesn't see that I've done fuck all in sixty minutes except space out. At least I have the foresight to tape our sessions. I'll need to revisit this one for sure. I feel absolutely terrible.

"Yes, that's it for this week," I answer as brightly as I can, standing and walking toward her chair. The slim tightening in her face gives away her annoyance at my falsely chipper response. She knows I have no clue what's happened in here, and just as I'm about to apologize for my unprofessionalism and absence today, she leans gingerly forward and touches my hand.

"Are you okay, Harlow?"

Jennifer has been coming to see me for just over two years. She's a sweet woman, only a few years older than me, with a list of medical conditions as long as my arm. She has MS, and her deterioration since the first time we met has been a cruel, steady journey. She's now wheelchair bound and is slowly losing function of her fine motor skills. Her speech is a little slurred, not so much that you can't understand her, but enough to make her harder to comprehend than my other patients. She requires more concentration, and this alone makes me want to cry for how this session has gone. She is more than deserving of my full attention. Physical contact and interaction are against our code of ethics. I'm here to listen, not to dole out hugs and false assurances, but Jennifer's attempt at what I feel like is intended as a hug causes me to pause and smile. I give her hand a quick squeeze in appreciation.

"I'm fine, thank you," I say pointedly, as I move past her and open my office door. "I'll see you next week."

She doesn't say anything further, just fixes me with a stare that speaks volumes about her ability to know when I'm talking crap. I wait until her chair disappears down the corridor before closing my door and letting myself flop down onto the plush patient sofa. I huff out an exasperated exhale, annoyed at how distracted I've been these last weeks. I pull my phone from my pant pocket and am about to call and schedule an appointment with my own therapist when my alarm sounds, signaling I need to take my meds. I pinch the bridge of my nose, listening to the incessant beeping and decide I really need a break. Not just from work, but from my own mind—hell, from my life in general. Of course, what I really need is to stop thinking about Ellis, but that's like telling yourself to stop breathing. You can only hold your breath for so long before your survival instincts kick in and you gasp for air.

Texts I almost send to Ellis before deleting:

Do you want to meet for coffee?

Hey, How are you?

Hi, Ellis. Just wondered if you'd maybe want to meet up to talk?

Why did you give me your number? You knew I'd obsess over using it. You're an asshole.

Hi, Ellis. Are you free, today?

I press send on the last message before I drive myself completely crazy. Collin tilts his head inquisitively; he probably thinks I'm a nut, shouting to myself. His stubby white tail swishes back and forth as he tries to decide if this is a cue that I'm about to start playing with him. I look up over the rim of my phone, and he must decide it's not, because his fat little head falls back down on top of his paws, his floppy white jowls spreading out over my floor and no doubt concealing a puddle of drool. I lean forward, ready to pet him when he breaks wind and I quickly need to go and open a window. The lady at the pet store had said that switching him to a dry food only diet would help with his terrible flatulence. I'm still waiting to feel the benefits of that particular piece of advice. I'm not convinced that it wasn't just a ploy to upsell me on dog food twice the price of the product I was initially buying. Collin doesn't move, just traces my movements with lazy, contented eyes.

I'm sure I've landed myself with the K-9 equivalent of a languid, overweight beer-swilling husband. The type that sits around on the couch all day, one hand down his pants while the other cradles a beer. I never had any intention of getting a puppy. In fact, everyone thought I was insane when I told them I'd taken him on. I'd argued in Collin's favor, of course. English Bulldogs are perhaps the laziest and most exercise shy breed of dog that there is. On paper we were a match made in heaven. I also kind of liked being defiant. Heart patients and dogs aren't usually a sensible mix. I'd been assured he was about as much work as a goldfish from the sweet little old man who'd persuaded me to take him. I realized after twenty minutes of getting Collin home that despite the man's cutesy, little-old-pensioner appearance, he was a liar. He'd won me over by saying he'd have to take Collin to the pound, and me being the complete sap I am, looked into the tiny white bulldog's wide puppy eyes and was sold.

He ate two pairs of sneakers, one whole rain boot (the left foot) and the bottom step of my staircase in the first week I'd owned him. He wasn't overly active; at least that part had been true. He hated his leash, and our walks usually ended in me carrying the pudgy little pain in the ass home. Once he's made up his mind, he's stubborn as hell. If he doesn't want to walk, he simply stops and lies down. Even if you attempt to drag him he stays flat, like a dead weight, until you pick him up. I first discovered this while walking across the road a little way from my house. He'd obviously had enough, and collapsed right there in the middle of the street. A cherry red Nissan, almost hit us but the blaring horn didn't even startle Collin into standing, and I'd almost had another heart attack dragging him to the curb.

Hi. I'm free as a bird, what do you have in mind?

The reply from Ellis feels strange. It's almost too familiar, and yet impersonal and distant at the same time. I stare at the cracked screen of my cell (another product of Collin's affinity for chewing) and berate myself after a moment for obsessing over text messages. I'm not a teenager, for heaven's sake.

Want to meet me for coffee? 11:30 am at Joe Van Gough's in Durham. It's the one on Broad Street, not the Duke shop.

JVG is my favorite coffee house. There are two huge coffee chain stores within a half-mile of my home, but I still jump in my car and drive almost all the way to work on my days off for the scent of their fresh ground coffee alone. The place always smells amazing, and just because I can't drink too much caffeine doesn't mean I can't bask in the aroma of it once in a while. It's where I tend to go when I need to get away and think. It's gotten me through many long days after little sleep and it's within walking distance of work, which is both a blessing and a curse. Half my salary must be spent in there. They have local art on display, too, which I love. It's almost like a home away from home. My mom always comments that if Pottery Barn did coffee shop chic, my living room would be the product.

I'll see you there.

His text is simple and to the point—unlike our relationship. I don't even know what I want to say to him once I see him. What I do know, however, is that since he showed up again I seem to have forgotten how to function. My therapist thinks that talking with Ellis will be a positive step for me. Talking I can do—that part's manageable. It's the same thing I would encourage my own clients to do. It's what the talking might lead to that has me torn up inside. No matter how inconvenient it is to still have feelings for the person responsible for your father's untimely death, that is exactly what's happened.

The attraction has always been there. It had morphed into love long before dad dying, and somehow it hasn't disappeared over time. I thought that my feelings for Ellis had evolved over the years, not necessarily into hate, but something close—animosity maybe? But, seeing him didn't validate those feelings, and instead reminded me of what it was like to have your whole body set ablaze by just a look. He'd brought me back to life when I hadn't even realized how dead I was inside. The feeling was intoxicatingly addictive. The trouble with addiction I've found is that if not fed, you slip quickly into withdrawal. I've tried going cold turkey for the last two months, and it isn't working. My work and my mental heath are both suffering. So, now I'm attempting to reintroduce Ellis into my life before weaning myself off of him slowly. At least that's what I'm telling myself I'm about to do.

But then again, we all know junkies lie.

The coffee shop is uncharacteristically quiet for a Saturday morning, and I'm not sure if that unnerves me or makes me feel better. I guess this way there's less chance of bumping into anyone from work.

"The usual?" Marcus, the barista, asks me when I make my way to the counter.

"Not today, thanks. I'll take a spiced chai latte, and a cinnamon bun."

The adrenaline coursing through my body is enough to have my heart working overtime. I don't need coffee adding to that. I came here for the familiarity of the place, not the drinks. Anticipation over seeing Ellis has me trembling, and I'm doing my best to appear unaffected by my anxiety. I'm like a swan swimming across a quiet pond. On the surface I appear almost graceful, gliding effortlessly, but if you peeked under the water my legs kicking frantically to keep myself afloat would tell a different story.

I hand over my card to pay and Marcus motions for me to go take a seat.

"I'll bring your order over," he tells me, turning to grab a cup.

"Thanks."

I walk over to a small round table nestled in the corner by the window. From this angle I'll be able to see Ellis arrive. Knowing that he won't be able to catch me off guard this time oddly calms me a little and makes me feel more in control. I pull my red parker off, draping it over the back of the worn brown leather chair and take a seat. There's a tall girl with a slight hint of Asian parentage in her beautiful complexion who catches my eye. She's sitting at the table across from mine, bent forward in cahoots with a much smaller but equally pretty girl with flame red hair and more freckles than I've ever seen on a person before. Their conversation is carrying across the room as they talk animatedly about someone I'm assuming isn't with them. From the gist of what they're saying, I'm guessing that they don't approve of their friend's lack of interest in choosing a college major. I smile to myself, because once upon a time they could have been talking about me.

Unlike Ellis, I began my first year of college with zero clues about what I wanted to major in. I'd decided to take as many varied and random classes as my schedule would allow until I found something that ignited a spark and made me tick. It was a risky strategy. I'd always planned on swimming through college and had all but decided to major in sports science. I didn't have a comprehensive plan of what I wanted to do, but the opportunities that a degree like that would have opened up appealed to me. The only problem was that I wasn't physically able to put that plan into place, and spending my time around people that were doing activities I couldn't partake in seemed a little sadistic.

Instead, I decided to immerse myself in and amongst activities I could do. Slowly but surely I began to see things in a brighter, more positive light. I didn't need to be so doom and gloom about my prognosis and finally accepted that my life was what I made of it. That realization set free some of the resentment I'd let fester within me deep below the surface. It was the part of me that I tried on a daily basis to keep locked away, hidden from myself just as much as the people around me. I'd never been the girl who felt sorry for herself before, and I wasn't comfortable in my own skin when I sensed myself slipping into that persona. I goofed around, made people laugh, even if it was at me rather than with me. It took a while for me to grasp that I didn't have to stop being that person, and the recognition and acceptance were invigorating.

Over the years I've had plenty of reason to slip back into that sad and broken girl. For a while, after my father died and Ellis was gone I slipped so far into the rabbit hole of my despair that I worried I'd never find my way back out. But I did it. I pulled myself out, and every time an issue with my health threatened to push me back down, I managed to summon the strength to stand fast. Maybe that's what has knocked me sideways about Ellis turning back up in my life. He blindsided me, and my own emotions pulled the rug from beneath me. The contempt I thought I'd feel for him was replaced with relief, which only made me stumble further. I'm hoping that meeting him today will help me find my footing. I can't deny that his ability to knock me clean off my feet terrifies me, but the tiny adrenaline junkie within me has been awakened and is shouting, *bring it on!*

"Love recognizes no barriers. It jumps hurdles, leaps fences, penetrates walls to arrive at its destination full of hope."

— MAYA ANGELOU

CHAPTER

NINETEEN

Coffee House Confessional

Ellis

s there a way to combat nervous anticipation? If there is, I wish
to God somebody would clue me in on it. Meeting Harlow
without knowing why she wants to meet is brutal. Knowing she
must have some agenda and not being in control of the outcome
has reduced me to a nervous wreck. I read somewhere that a
calm mind promotes inner strength, but hell if I can stay calm.
There are too many variables that can affect this get-together.
Her health is the biggest one, and it scares me to death if I'm
going to be truthful. Maybe she has good news, and she's about
to tell me that she's found a donor? Hope blossoms in my chest
before rationality takes a hold and squashes it back down. It

would be more likely that the opposite ws about to happen, and do I really want to hear it? Can I hear it?

I've tortured myself with researching her condition every day since seeing her last. There isn't a website or medical forum I've left unexplored. There's no escaping that Harlow needs a donor's heart, and I've poured over all the information accessible to me, hoping I could find something to ease the anxiety—a statistic, anything I can grasp onto that offers hope. I found the statistics I was looking for. I challenged them, looked for evidence that they were wrong, but was only left feeling more inept for it. The odds of Harlow first finding a donor with a compatible blood type, and then her body accepting that heart, are less than five percent. It's a horrifying figure, given that it assumes Harlow is at the top of the donor register and she's not.

Get a grip, Ellis.

I pull a black t-shirt over my head, followed by my dark gray sweater and push my cell and wallet into the back pocket of my jeans. I quickly take a glance at my appearance in the mirror. Insomnia has been kicking my ass, and I look like hell, but at least I've shaved. I dip my fingers into the pot of styling wax resting on the vanity and rub the stuff haphazardly through my hair before quickly making my way out of my bathroom. I walk through the bedroom (which also happens to be my living room and kitchen) and grab my keys from the hook as I exit through the front door of my studio apartment. The whole journey takes less than twenty strides. Still, this place feels positively huge given the square footage of my last permanent residence.

I take the steps in the hall two at a time, dropping heavily onto each one until I'm on the ground floor and opening the hefty scratched-up metal door that leads from the back of the garage workshop I live above. The smell of motor oil hits me square in the chest, its consistent existence oddly soothing. I walk around the building to the back where the customers drive in and leave their cars. My bike rests in the far corner of the lot. I haven't gotten around to buying a car yet, and Manny, the guy who owns the garage, sold me an old Triumph Bonneville America in exchange for labor. It had been his, but his wife refuses to let him drive it now that they have children, much to his chagrin.

I've been helping out when I have free time away from my mind-numbingly boring job, but beggars can't be choosers—or maybe that should be felons can't be choosers? Manny's a nice guy, he's not prejudiced about a person's past. There are not too many people willing to give a guy a break when they find out he's just done a stretch inside for killing a man. He's the older brother of a friend from Morrison. Santi had given me Manny's number and told me he'd help me out with work if I needed it on the outside. It was startling how quickly I'd realized I needed to take him up on that offer.

The drive over to Joe Van Gough's takes me forty minutes, which is roughly enough time for me to run through every plausible reason Harlow could have for wanting to meet up. I kick my bike stand out, shake out my shoulders and make my way to the door, trying to portray a coolness I in no way feel.

I've wanted to call Harlow every day since we exchanged numbers, and frankly, I'm amazed that she was the one to contact me. I would have done it a million times by now if I'd known what to say to her. Instead, I've been casually driving past her work every day, hoping to catch sight of her. It's my way of making sure she's still okay, without bothering her. At least this way I can still love her from afar. I hadn't actually thought about how creepy that might seem until now. It's not like I'm stalking her or anything. I just wanted to put my mind at rest that she's okay. The days that I catch her walking from the building or pulling out in her car are the ones when I sleep better at night.

I pull the door open and step inside the coffee shop. I haven't been in this place before, and I'm hit with a waft of hot air as I pass over the threshold. My nose is invaded with the pungent and almost overwhelming perfume of fresh coffee. I look around scanning the tables, and my eyes immediately catch on the small blonde in the corner staring straight at me. Her presence is like a homing beacon, always has been. I smile, my nerves easing that she is actually here, and raise my hand in a self-conscious sort of wave. I make my way around the tables to where she's sitting, trying to gauge her mood and plan my greeting. Her face is completely impassive until I reach her and the tiniest of frowns creases her forehead. It almost causes me to pause, but then she smiles and mouths hello, urging me on.

All my game is gone—not that I had much to begin with—and standing in front of her has shrunk me from the man I am to the boys I was. To prove that point, the most obstinate greeting ever played out ensues. I automatically lean in to kiss her cheek in greeting. She reads me wrong and gives me a very awkward shoulder clinch like she was maybe going to hug me then changed her mind at the last moment. We're doing a strange kind of robotic dance, trying to anticipate the other's movements and it's uncomfortable as hell.

"Oh, my god I'm just going to sit down," she says in a high-pitched squeaky voice.

I straighten my posture, looking down at her peering back up at me and I can't help myself—I grin.

"Well, that was all kinds of awkward."

"It really was, wasn't it? I don't even know what I was attempting," she confesses before taking a sip of her drink to regain her composure.

I pull the seat opposite out and drop myself down into it, not breaking eye contact. Her lips are still twitching, and her eyes are sparkling, I notice. That has to be a good sign, I hope.

"How are you?" we both ask at the same time.

"Okay, you first," I tell her, sweeping my hand out in front of us, gesturing for her to go ahead.

"I'm good, thanks, Ellis." There's a false cheeriness to her voice that contradicts her answer, and even if there wasn't I'd have known she was talking bull. She was always a lousy liar. I suppose if this is the tact she wants to take I should indulge her.

"That's good to hear."

"You know what," she says before taking another sip from her cup. "That's not entirely accurate."

The hair on the back of my neck stands on end; I wasn't expecting her to call herself out. I hold my breath in preparation for whatever she's about to hit me with.

"I've been kind of distracted lately, and well, honestly, I'm blaming you."

Now that's definitely not what I was anticipating, but she doesn't sound annoyed, and her body language is still open and positive.

"You're blaming *me* for you being distracted?"

"Yep. You see I'm not big on surprises anymore. Go figure, right?" She cocks an eyebrow, staring pointedly at me.

I lean back, crossing my ankle over my knee, and she takes the opportunity to slowly scan me from top to toe. I clear my throat to mask my amusement at her lack of subtly, and an eruption of deep pink pigment blooms instantly over her cheeks. I love that I can still do that to her. My pulse kicks up a notch, my body reacting to hers like they're somehow still in sync.

"Seeing you has kind of messed me up."

The warmth spreading through me is extinguished in that one sentence. I drop my foot back down to the floor, lean forward and place my hands over hers nursing the coffee cup she's holding between us. The small contact sends a huge blast of adrenaline through my system.

"Harlow, I'm so sorry, I never meant for—"

"Stop." Her hands slide from under my own as she swipes an invisible hair behind her ear, then settles them under her thighs. She's literally sitting on her hands to keep them out of my reach. *Wow, that stings.*

"I'm not looking for an apology, I'm just being honest with you. We used to be good at it—it was easy—do you remember? I've been kind of a mess, and I think it's because I wanted to pretend that you weren't around, you know? Just carry on like the other month never happened. But it did happen, and I can't stop overanalyzing it. The more I tell myself that I don't miss you, that more I kind of do? I don't know, I guess I'm not making much sense. What I'm trying to say—and failing miserably—is that I miss you, Ellis. I've missed having you in my life, as problematic and screwed up as that is. I thought I was done with feeling like this years ago, but apparently not."

The world falls away at her admission. The soft coffee house jazz is suddenly muted, the art covering the walls blurs together, and the only thing in focus now is Harlow.

"There hasn't been a day that we've been apart that I haven't missed you too. It might not be how or what you want to feel, but I don't want you to beat yourself up over it."

"Yeah, well that's easier said than done."

Don't I know it! I pray every night that I might somehow wake up with no memory of her, my slate completely wiped. How sweet it would be to not be tortured by an overbearing, continuous sense of longing. It's the little things that get me—like knowing the way it feels to wake up beside her. Not feeling her soft sleepy breath against my skin, or having her crazy hair all up in my face—that's the stuff that hurts the most. I can't escape my memories no matter how hard I try, and the good ones are more painful than the bad.

"You wanna get out of here?" I ask on a whim. Everything feels so weighted between us. "How about we go get some air? We could try spending some time together without focusing on the baggage."

Her nose crinkles from the way her brows knit tightly to-gether.

"You think we could do that? Spend time without letting our past get in the way?"

Probably not, but I don't say that, of course. I nod instead. "I'm willing to try if you are."

The chair scrapes across the tile as I push it back and stand, holding out my hand to her. I want to tell her to take a chance and grab hold. I can't promise that I can make her feel better, but God if she'll just let me, I'll try.

She's frozen in place, looking at my hand and making no ef-fort to take it. The pause feels embarrassingly long. *Should I withdraw? Sit back down? Why isn't she doing anything?*

"Don't die wondering, right?"

Her words are spoken in a soft whisper that sounds almost contrite. I'm not sure if they're meant for her or for me, but she takes my hand anyway. Her fingers push through mine, her soft, warm palm flattening against my much larger rougher one. Our hands fit together effortlessly like they, at least, remember how to exist together.

"Where would you like to go?" I ask, pulling her in step with me as I head for the door.

"I thought you had somewhere in mind—you're the one who suggested getting out of here!"

"And that's what we're doing, getting out." I grin as I reach over and hold the door for her. "But the next part is up to you."

The door is still slightly ajar, and I hear Harlow say in a low motherly tone, "Okay, mister, come and meet my friend, Ellis."

I'm surprised as hell that we've ended up at her house. We walked around Durham until Harlow was too tired to go any further, which was way sooner than I'd imagined. Then she suggested I come and meet her and Martin's illegitimate child. It took me a while to realize she was referring to her dog.

The sound of paws clattering over hardwood in a scurried frenzy is preceded by a stubby mass of wrinkled white and tan skin, and a downright squashed snout. It looks like someone's opened a door into the poor dog's face.

"He's a bulldog?"

"Yeah," Harlow answers, following him into the lounge. His little legs are sliding out in all directions as he tries to move across the floor with all the grace of a one-legged man in an ass-kicking contest. The poor little fella can't walk for shit on this floor.

He finally reaches me, and I'm waiting for him to fuss around my feet, but he lazily takes a quick sniff around my ankles before collapsing down next to me like he's just run a marathon.

"What's his name?" I ask rubbing his head. His skin moves and droops over his eyes, but he doesn't seem to mind it.

"Collin," she says affectionately, looking at him collapsed beside me. The droopy part of his mouth is splayed over my left foot.

"You named your dog Collin? What kind of name is that for a dog?" I tease.

"The best kind, thank you very much!"

He's one of those pets you'd describe as ugly cute. Like, he's so ugly that it's endearing. He definitely looks like more of a guy's dog. If you tried stuffing him into a purse to carry around town like celebs do, you'd throw your back and shoulder out for sure. What he lacks in height he sure makes up for in girth.

"Hey, come here, mister," Harlow calls. He lifts his head and looks at her for a moment before deciding it'd be way too much work to get back up. He does the doggy version of a "you gotta be kidding me" look and rests his head back down.

"I think he likes me more than you," I muse.

"What, no way! He's only known you for twenty seconds. Come here, Collin, come on."

Collin doesn't move.

"Aww, you want to stay with me, don't ya, boy?" I give his head another little rub, and he lets out a grunt of pleasure, followed by enough wind to gas out an entire football stadium.

"Jesus Christ, what do you feed him?" My eyes literally begin to water as I cup my hands over my nose to guard against the stench.

Harlow's face splits into a big grin. It's only seconds before she's in stitches. Her arms are wrapped around her waist; her chest bent forward, and head tilted back. She always used to say she hated her laugh, but every time I hear her bark out in abandonment and snort adorably I feel myself fall a little more in love with her.

Moments like this make me wonder if all that's ever happened is nothing but a lie, and this is how were meant to be.

"I'm sorry," she gasps. "Quickly, open that window before we both pass out."

The infectious guffaw she can't seem to control conveys more energy and pure unadulterated joy than I've witnessed from her since reconnecting a couple of months ago. I'm futile in my attempts to keep my nose shielded, and despite my best efforts to hold it in my own laughter explodes from my pursed lips.

"It smells so bad! Seriously, this can't be normal." I'm genuinely baffled as to how such a small creature can produce anything like this.

"Ellis, the window!" Harlow giggles hoarsely, shooing me into action.

I don't make it to the window, though. The sound of a door slamming closed jolts me. I turn to see who it is and all signs of laughter die in my throat as my heart literally stutters and sinks deep within the cavern of my chest. I stand tall, snapped into place by my own cowardice.

"Ellis?" Dianne proclaims, stunned.

"Mom!" Harlow gawps.

Not now, I think to myself. Not like this. I don't want the memory of today—the first good day we've had—tainted by what's about to happen. I knew I'd have to confront Harlow's mom eventually, but selfishly I wanted more time.

"Hello, Dianne."

"Darkness cannot drive out darkness; only light can do that. Hate cannot drive out hate; only love can do that."

— Martin Luther King, Jr.

CHAPTER

TWENTY

Brace for Impact

Harlow

regularly tell my patients that humor eases your worries. I have a whole spiel about how it enthuses your hopes and connects you to others. There's a reason we refer to laughter as the best kind of medicine—it's not a bunch of hocus pocus—it's because nothing balances your nervous system faster. Mother Nature's most powerful antidote to stress, anxiety, and conflict. I even have a framed poster in my office that reads: "Always find a reason to laugh. It may not add years to your life, but will surely add life to your years."

It feels like I haven't truly laughed for a long time; not like this anyway, with pure abandonment. With so much power inside to heal and renew, I'm an idiot for not letting go more. I have plenty of friends and colleagues who are always trying to coax me out with promises of a good time. "Come out, tonight, Harlow," they say. "We'll have a laugh." And I do, I put on a smile and make an effort to join in and have fun, but there's always been something missing. I'm starting to realize that something is Ellis. I'm somehow more alive when I'm with him.

My giggling is hideous, and right at the point I'm sure I sound like a demented hyena, Ellis's whole body language does a swift one-eighty. I turn my head, confused at what's rendered him catatonic, and my mother's voice registers in my ears.

My living room shrinks in her presence, apprehension filling the space where the air should be.

"Mom, what are you doing here?"

I stand up from where I'm kneeling, one arm snapping across my waist in a bid to settle the jittery butterflies and my other hand shoots straight into my mouth. I bite down on the skin at the side of my thumb—a nervous habit from my childhood. There's a heavily pregnant pause as my mother's gaze flits between Ellis and me.

"I, err..." She's stumbling. My mom never stumbles over her words; Dianne Stevens is the epitome of perfect poise under duress. "I was passing by," she finally manages to push out. "I haven't seen you in a few weeks."

That's because I've been avoiding her. My mother knew Ellis was back in town before she'd even returned from her trip visiting with my brother and his family. We'd had a stilted conversation about him attending Mrs. Adkins' wake, and I made my excuses to end our call at the first possible instance. Ashamedly, I've deflected her at every opportunity since, and have only exchanged texts with her these past weeks. I needed time to process my own feelings about Ellis being back before attempting to digest or even recognize what his return might do to her. I try to live my life without regret, but I'm choking on a hearty dose of it now.

What was I thinking letting her find him here?

Mom's demeanor shifts and the moment she regains control over her shock is visible in the quick shake of her arms and intake of breath. My pulse hammers in the base of my throat as she squares her shoulders and takes a tentative step further inside the room. The cause of Ellis and my laughter must register with her because she gives Collin a quick look of revolt before settling her glare back on Ellis. I almost feel as sorry for him as I do for my mom. I watch the scene in front of me unfold with a strange sense of suspended animation.

"Ellis," my mother says again. Her voice is quiet but clear and concise. She's always had a no-nonsense air about her.

"Dianne, I'll leave, I'm—"

"Leave, no, no don't do that," she rushes out in a quick breath.

Ellis's face is pure misery. He runs his fingers through his hair, and drags them down his face, squeezing his chin for a moment. He's no doubt trying to come up with something to explain why he's here with me in my house. Collin's grunt as he rolls onto his side, trying to find a comfier spot to rest his head, registers at the volume of a supersonic jet engine. It's loud and obtrusive in the otherwise somber atmosphere of my living room.

There are a thousand images passing through my mind in the millisecond it takes for my mother to lurch forward, throwing herself in Ellis's path. My breath hitches as I wait for her arm to sail through the air and slap him. *Why else would she rush him?* I let out an unexpected noise, a startled inhalation at her advance; I smack my hand over my mouth trapping the sound, but my panic's unwarranted. She's not lunging toward him in an attack. Instead, she embraces him. Her arms fling around his stunned body, trapping his own by his side, and she presses herself to him. I watch with incredulity as she hugs him tightly for a long, strange moment.

There are very few times I can recall throughout my life when my mother has shocked me quite this much. I'm completely dumbfounded by her display of affection toward him. My brain is having very real difficulty comprehending it. As punitive as it sounds even in my own mind, he killed my father, her husband. And, yes it may not have been in a cold-blooded attack, but I'd always assumed that she hated him for it. She's continually avoided speaking about him in font of me, and here she is in my living room, hugging him like she's yearned to do it dearly. I'm so confused. Has she missed him? Why would she let me believe she might actually loathe him when she so clearly doesn't?

I moved home for a while after my dad died. I couldn't stand being in the apartment I'd shared with Ellis at Duke. His absence was oppressing, and I needed to be somewhere that I could ignore the hollowness he'd left. Home didn't feel like home with Ellis gone either, and my heartache doubled. I'm not sure my mom knew how to take care of me; Ellis had done it for so long. My parents once told me how worried they'd been at how seemingly dependent on each other Ellis and I were. I'd laughed in their faces. I get it now.

Our love started out exceptionally simple, and as time passed it only grew. People's emotional states at some point in their relationship reach outside the boundaries of politeness, or unwillingness to offend or upset each other. They begin to fight, or start to believe that they've lost the spark they once had. That wasn't true of Ellis and me. Sure, we didn't agree with each other all of the time, hell, not even half the time, but we never really argued. It didn't feel like we needed to work to retain our spark—it was always there. Of course, after Ellis went to prison my emotional state was unstable, to say the least. I was trapped on a roller coaster I couldn't get off. My feelings for him were suddenly an intense paradox of love and hate. For such a long time I've believed I was alone in simultaneously missing the only person I've ever had a true reason to abhor. Witnessing the grief projecting from my mom, I'm hit with an awareness that threatens to knock me sideways. *I wasn't alone.*

"You're not angry?" I don't mean to speak my thoughts aloud, but that's what happens; they slip out like an accusation. I guess they are.

"Angry?" my mother intones, bemused. "Of course I'm not angry. Shocked, yes. I have to admit that I wasn't expecting to ever walk in on the two of you again, but I'm not mad if that's what you're implying, Harlow?"

"Dianne," Ellis carefully slips from where my mother still has a hold of his wrists. He guides her to the sofa and sits down beside her. "I should have sought you out by now, and I'm truly sorry that I haven't. I just, well, I guess I didn't know what to say to you. I still don't," he admits. "I wish I had the words to express the regret I feel, and how sorry I am. It was one impulsive moment, I ruined your lives and if I'd just walked away..."

He can't finish his sentence. Whatever he was trying to say is lodged in his throat, and he coughs to clear it. I swear I can almost feel the sense of shame he's experiencing. I want to comfort him, but I don't. I stay motionless, paralyzed in trepidation that if I attempt to console him I might start crying and never stop.

"Why wouldn't you let us visit with you, Ellis?"

I can only see the back of my mom's graying blonde chignon from where I'm positioned, but I have a perfectly clear view of Ellis's face. I'm sure mine is the mirror image of his; startled and sad.

"I was scared."

His response is raw and honest. Ellis is a foreboding figure of a man, intimidatingly tall and muscular, but his voice is still the same voice that used to hum horrendously out-of-tune ballads to me when I was restless and couldn't fall asleep. His arms are the same arms that would wrap around me reassuringly whenever I needed a to be admitted for a procedure, or more tests. He's still the boy I fell in love with in my backyard, and my mother must see it too because her next words floor me.

"You didn't need to be scared, Ellis. You were a part of our family. I loved you like I love my own boys. I didn't just lose Mike the day he died," she quickly turns to look at me fleetingly, and my legs crumple beneath me like a thin piece of paper as I sit back down, startling poor Collin. Her eyes are glossy with unshed tears, and I feel my throat begin to burn. "I lost my daughter that day, and I lost you too."

Ellis pulls my mother to him, burying his head into the crook of her neck while his vice-like arms envelope her slight frame. She whispers her forgiveness to him in a soothing voice as they gently sway. "It was an awful accident, that's all." There's not a single audible sound from him. It's only when I notice the small tremors sporadically running across his shoulders, and my mother begins to rub his back like only a parent can do, that I realize he's crying.

I am too.

It's dusk before I remember that I've not taken my afternoon medication, nor have I eaten since breakfast. My mother left thirty minutes ago, and Ellis and I have sat in a comfortable silence since she went. I finally move, my stomach grumbling to protest that I've neglected myself, and Ellis stands too, rubbing his stomach and stretching out his arms, causing the fabric of his sweater to rise and reveal a thin sliver of skin above the waistband of his jeans. I look away as quickly as I can, heading to my kitchen and calling to him that I'm about to make something to eat.

"Are you hungry?" I shout, not realizing that he's followed me into the kitchen.

"Starving," he answers in a much quieter voice.

"Jesus! Sorry, I thought you were in the other room." One more shock today and I'm not entirely sure my heart won't give out. I shake the morbid thought from my head, open my fridge and realize that I'm falling as an adult in every area at the moment. The sole contents of my refrigerator consist of a lone moldy lemon, a half empty carton of milk, a block of Swiss cheese, and an empty egg box.

"Grilled cheese?" I ask, holding up the Swiss.

"Always, where's your bread?" he asks scanning the counter tops. I pull the cupboard door open above his head to show him, and it smacks him in the face.

"Oh, Ellis!"

"You're a damn liability, Stevens. You should come with a public health notice," he retorts good-naturedly, before reaching in and pulling out the loaf.

"You should probably sit over there, while I make these, I don't want to kill you."

I could swear I hear him whisper that I already do—kill him, that is—but he obeys my instructions and takes a seat at the breakfast bar.

I busy myself making our sandwiches as Ellis tells me about the garage owner, Manny, who he does odd jobs for when he's not doing his regular job.

"What is your regular job? I just realized that you haven't told me."

"I flip burgers at McDonald's," he says nonchalantly.

My mouth literally falls open. I can't imagine Ellis working at a fast food joint; he was studying law at Duke before he, well, just before. I attempt to school my face impassively so as not to give away my astonishment.

"Oh, that's good, err…"

"I'm messing with you, Harlow, I just started working for a small accounting firm in Greensboro."

My shoulders sag in relief. Not that there's anything wrong with working at a fast food chain, but Ellis was always so driven, the thought of him flipping burgers saddens me.

"I can just see you in a McDonald's uniform, I bet you'd look fab in a hair net," I tease, poking my tongue out at him. I slide his sandwich from the pan to the plate and push it forward to him.

"I can tell you for a fact that I look amazing in a hair net," he jibes. "We had to wear them when we worked in the cafeteria at Morrison. They were horrible blue nylon things, but they really brought out the color in my eyes."

As if for effect, he bats his eyelashes dramatically at me.

"I bet they did." I grin imagining it. I was always envious of his eyelashes, thick, dark and impossibly long. Mine reflect the natural color of my hair, a slight strawberry blonde. I don't even look like I have any lashes at all unless I paint them on in black mascara.

I position my plate next to his at the counter and then walk over to my medicine cupboard and begin pulling out the medication I should have taken earlier. I place six different pill bottles out on the counter and start shaking out the pills into a little pile, ready to take.

"You want me to fix you a drink?" Ellis asks preparing to move out from his seat.

"No, it's fine I've got it. Eat your grilled cheese before it goes cold," I order.

"Yes, ma'am."

I roll my eyes at his mock salute and pour myself a glass of water from the faucet.

"Today has not been what I expected when I first looked at your text," he says around a mouth full of food.

"Really, how so? What were you expecting?"

"Truthfully?" He swallows his next bite. "I thought I'd covered every possible scenario on the ride over to the coffee place, but I never factored seeing your Mom into any of those scenarios."

I finish popping my pills at the counter and drain the last drops of water from my glass before moving to sit down.

"I'm sorry about that. I feel terrible, for you and my mom actually. I didn't know she'd be dropping by and she's not usually big on impromptu visits. I should have told her that I was seeing you, that way neither of you would have been ambushed."

He nods in contemplation, and I take a bite of my sandwich.

"I'm kind of glad it happened; it needed to, you know? I've got to admit I thought it would go down a whole lot worse than it did."

"I'm pretty sure I was as shocked as you were," I say to myself, more than him.

"This is strange, isn't it?"

"What is?" I ask, peering up from my plate. He's wearing a sort of bemused smile that makes me swipe at my mouth just to make sure I don't have food stuck to me.

"Sitting here eating with you. It feels strange."

"Not to me," I answer. "It feels natural."

His eyes widen at my candid response. I could lie and agree with him that eating together feels strange, but it doesn't. Not at all. A small part of me likes it too much, certainly more than my conscience thinks I should. Every time I catch myself beginning to feel comfortable around him, I'm hit with a tiny pang of guilt about my dad.

Collin slips and slides into the kitchen like a toddler on ice and Ellis laughs at my poor little dog making his way to his water bowl.

"I need to take him out for a walk. If I don't, he'll likely pee all over the place."

"Can you not just let him out back into the garden?" Ellis asks, craning his head back to look out of the kitchen window, no doubt assessing if that's a viable question.

"I could, but watch this." I hop down from my stool, and walk over to the back door, opening it wide. "Collin, come boy. Outside."

Collin looks up from the rim of his water bowl and stares at me like I'm an idiot, waving my hands, trying to entice him to come forward. I try and call him again, this time coaxing him in a baby voice, but he stands frozen just staring at me. I look over to Ellis and shrug.

Ellis laughs and says, "He's the laziest dog in the world."

"He won't move from that spot unless I drag him and literally push him out the door. Then he'll sit there and cry until I let him back in."

Ellis looks over to Collin; sure enough, he's still glaring at me and hasn't moved a muscle.

"Want me to walk him for you?" he asks.

"I'm not sure how he'll react to that. Plus, I could kind of do with the fresh air, I think. Do you want to come along with us? I could actually use your strength for carrying him back." Ellis looks at me quizzically, his brow raising and a deep crease forming from the movement. I smile. "You'll see."

"Keep love in your heart.
A life without it is like a
sunless garden when the
flowers are dead."

—OSCAR WILDE

CHAPTER

TWENTY-ONE

Man Up

Ellis

It's the third time this week that my call to Logan goes straight through to his voice mail. I have to stop myself from slamming my phone against the nearest wall as I leave another tight-lipped message to my best friend.

"Logan, it's Ellis, again. Where are you, man? You were supposed to be calling me on Friday about the documents from the hospital. Call me back."

I press end on my cell, throw it behind me into the middle of my unmade bed, then move toward the edge and sit with my head in my hands. He's having second thoughts—I know he is—

I've been questioning the decision too, but there's no other way I can figure out.

God, I wish it weren't the case.

Logan promised me that he'd do this for me, under duress, sure, and fuck if he hasn't begged and pleaded for me to reconsider. He knows I have no choice, though, not really. He'll help me because he knows that I can't be dissuaded. Not when it comes to her. I'll do anything for her. I've been back and forth from his practice, signing papers and researching other cases similar to mine. My last assessment at the hospital was yesterday, and I've put everything in place that I can to ensure things go smoothly. I rub the bruise on my forearm and screw my eyes up tight, I swear the more pieces I manage to get lined in place, the more distant he's becoming. I need to get him back on board and focused. He has to be ready because we're running out of time.

"Unless you love someone, nothing else makes any sense."

— E. E. CUMMINGS

CHAPTER TWENTY-TWO

Hulkamania

Ellis

ogan Smith has been my best friend for as long as I can remember. We'd grown up together back in Montana, and when
my parents decided to move our family to North Carolina I
was left with a Logan-shaped void to fill. At ten years old, your
whole life is your friends. Moving away to a new strange place
where I didn't know anybody felt like the end of my world. Harlow in time filled the gap that Logan left, and for an eleven-year-
old girl, she made a pretty great friend and sidekick. She was
literally a much better looking version of Lo. It wasn't until we
progressed into early adolescence that I began to realize my feeling for her ran much deeper than those you harbored for friends.

I think perhaps they always had, but my juvenile brain couldn't decipher that there was more than one type of liking somebody. Logan and I kept in touch; we regularly spoke on the phone, and nine times out of ten Harlow crept her way into our conversations. By the first time they actually met face-to-face they pretty much knew everything about one another. Logan loved Harlow almost as much as I did after ten minutes of knowing her, she was just that type of person. She acted like one of the boys but was way better to look at.

Any respectable eleven-year-old needed to have guy friends too, though, and that's where Elliott stepped up. We were in the same homeroom and quickly bonded over the usual stuff boys did; hockey, skateboarding and later down the line, girls. I'd met him the same week I met Harlow, and we instantly fell into an easy friendship. Elliott was the reason I tried out for the school hockey team, although our reasons for joining had differed somewhat. I wanted to make the team because I loved hockey, Elliott wanted to make the team because of the attention the team garnered from the girls at school. Our football team sucked, meaning the ice hockey team were the stars of our school. Elliott was a great winger, but if a cute girl caught his eye, his attention went to shit. The term "ladies' man" had been invented solely for Elliott Roberts.

In the few years between middle school and the start of college Elliott had morphed from a pretty average-sized kid to a complete monster. He was by far the biggest winger we had on the team; he even made our defensemen look a little scrawny. Despite his size, he still skated like a guy carrying half his bulk, which made him quick as hell and one scary-ass mountain of muscle gliding toward you on the ice like a freight train. We made a point through college of trying to all get together when Logan would visit. Logan pretty much thought the sun shined out of Elliott's ass since he was always surrounded by a harem of hot girls. The pair made a formidable force when they descended on our apartment. Harlow had pretty much given up on warning them to not bring random wasted chicks back and invite the whole campus around for drinks on a whim. She resigned herself to the fact that if Elliott and Lo were visiting, she'd better write off the weekend and embrace the mayhem that they inevitably brought with them.

When I was in Morrison, I'd flick through the photo album I took with me. It was one of the only possessions that brought me any comfort. I'd trace my fingers over page after page of pictures capturing Harlow, Elliot, Lo and all our friends in happier times. It helped me remember back to when everything seemed so much simpler.

2001

I was headstrong and determined when I got to Duke to embark on a JD Masters in Law. I wanted to be done with school as quickly as possible, so that meant working my ass off, leaving little time for anything else. I was spreading myself way too thin, and the strain was telling. I couldn't stay awake long enough some nights to talk with Harlow about how her day had been, and most of the time she was in the same boat. As soon as she'd decided to become a counselor, we became ships that passed in the night. Our schedules were completely opposite, and it meant for the first time in our lives we had to work at our relationship, making sure that we put time aside, no matter how fleeting, to spend quality time with one and other. When the guys came to visit it gave us both a chance to put down the books and just have fun.

Sometimes I'd come home from work or classes and find Harlow asleep in our bed. She'd look so perfect and beautiful, and all I'd want to do is crawl over her and wake her with my mouth pressed to every part of her flawless skin. But, I knew that she constantly pushed herself mentally and sometimes physically further than she should, so instead, I'd lower myself down next to her and watch her sleep. I had to battle with the desire to wake her up and do all the depraved acts that flashed through my mind as I watched her chest rise and fall in a beautifully hypnotic rhythm. Her lips were always parted when she slept, and she'd sigh and roll over into me, knowing I was there. I'd always found Harlow beautiful, but there was something about watching her sleep that completely undid me. Two minutes watching her and I'd be gone, my whole body humming with need.

"Harlow," I whispered, trying to wake her gently after receiving a text from Logan. He'd messaged to say that he was flying up for the weekend. It was probably the worst and best time he could come. Worst because we were two weeks away from midterms, and best because I was pretty sure I was at breaking point. I needed some serious R&R with a side of alcohol and about a month's worth of sleep.

"Hmm, yeah, what?" she asked nestling further down under the comforter.

"Logan is flying up."

She bolted upright so fast that I'd almost fallen backward off the bed. "What? Like, now?"

I couldn't help but grin. Her hair was matted and stuck to her cheek, and she was sporting some impressive creases along one side of her face from her pillow.

"Not now, this weekend," I reassured her.

Her face crumpled into a sort of bemused sneer. "Why are you waking me up to tell me this now then?" The mattress bounced as she dropped back down dramatically.

"Um, because it's four in the afternoon?"

She uttered something from behind the pillow she'd squashed over her face, and I couldn't make out the muffled sentence. Whatever she was saying seemed to include the words tired, reading, and jackass. I guessed I was probably the jackass for waking her.

"Come on." I dragged the pillow from her face and grabbed her wrists, pulling her back to a sitting position before bending and scooping her up over my shoulder. Her yelp was loud enough to burst my eardrums, and I playfully smacked her ass and told her to stop acting like a brat. She shouted at me to put her down, drumming her fists against the base of my back. If she weighed more than a hundred pounds, it might have actually hurt. Instead, I carried her through our apartment, laughing. If I thought she was really mad, I would have put her down, but her giggling was enough indication that she wasn't about to Chinese burn me for dragging her out of her pit. I deposited her on the small marble counter in the kitchen.

"Jesus, Ellis the top's freezing!"

The way she squirmed, rocking from one butt cheek to another to try to avoid placing her bare thighs against the surface was kind of hot. Her oversized t-shirt was twisted and looked almost as creased as her face.

"Here, drink this and take them." I passed her a half-empty bottle of water I'd been drinking from and her pillbox. "Were going to a party on Saturday with Elliott and Logan, and we need to go and find costumes before all the good ones are taken."

"A costume party! Oh my God, what are we, five?"

"Do you want to be the only person there without one?" I countered and tapped her nose. "Besides, you get to help pick out mine too."

She knew it was just a sweetener, but I lifted my eyebrows and hit her with my widest grin to try getting her onboard.

She pretended to ponder for a moment before letting out a bored sigh and saying, "Fine, what's the theme?"

"According to Elliott, it's 'When I Grow Up' so, whatever your dream job was when you were a kid, I guess."

"That sounds kind of cool actually," she considered, using her foot to hook around the back of my legs and drag me between hers. I thought I was about to get lucky until she rested her head against my chest, closed her eyes, and let out a massive yawn, using me as nothing more than something to lean on.

"What the hell are you supposed to be?" I'd asked opening the door to Elliott. The pants he was wearing were a sickly-checkered beige and brown and at least an inch too short in the leg. He had dressed in a white button-down with a pen in the breast pocket, and a pair of spectacles that had the thickest lenses I'd ever seen.

"You look like an eccentric old professor," Harlow said ducking under my shoulder and kissing him on the cheek in greeting.

Elliott stepped into the hall with a broad grin on his face. "Close." He flicked his glasses, bringing a magnifying lens in front of one eye. "I'm a gynecologist."

I burst out laughing, and Harlow punched him in the arm. "That's gross." She shuddered scrunching her nose. "What kid ever dreams of being a gynecologist when they're older?"

Elliott shrugged, his shit-eating grin still plastered in place. "Hey, it's a very reputable profession, and trust me when I say I've had a ton of dreams about it." He tapped the back of his glasses, so they moved up and down on his nose.

"Spoken like a true pervert," Harlow answered in mild disgust.

"We're still waiting on Logan," I said to Elliott as we made our way into the living room. "Want something to drink?"

"Sure, I'll take a beer. So, when are you guys going to get ready?" he asked, eyeing Harlow and me.

I tossed him a beer and dropped down onto the sofa.

"I'll go in a sec, but you'd better get your butt into gear," I said, looking over to Harlow. "That's a lot of spandex you need to wiggle into."

Elliott untwisted the cap from his bottle and took a sip before saying, "I like the sound of that."

I tossed a throw cushion at him, knocking the bottle into his teeth and making him spill.

"Ha, serves you right!" Harlow called as she made her way out of the room to get ready.

"What's your costume?" Elliott asked, wiping the spilled beer splatters from his ugly pants. I rested back into the sofa and brought my beer to my mouth before answering.

"You'll see as soon as Harlow's finished up in the bathroom." I grabbed the TV remote and flicked the channel to ESPN while we waited. Elliott was screaming at the screen for the soccer referee to be shot when the bathroom door flung open and Harlow came bounding into the room. She was a blur of sunshine yellow lycra and baby-oiled skin, hitting us with her best muscle man pose.

"Eat your vitamins and say your prayers, boys! Watcha gonna do when the Hulkster runs wild on you?"

I choked on my Miller and leaned forward coughing. "Oh my God!"

"Hell yeah!" Elliott shouted through his laughter. "H, you're my hero right now. Fucking Hulk Hogan—classic." He stood and high-fived her while I was still trying to cough up my lung.

"Please tell me you want to spar?" Elliott chuckled, and I threw him a dirty look in jest.

"What happened to the nurse costume?" I managed to ask when I finally stopped spluttering.

"Oh. Come on, Ellis. You know I've never dreamed of being a nurse. Jake and I used to watch wrestling religiously when I was like, eight or something."

"Yeah," I agreed. "But why Hulk? Didn't you want to be a girl wrestler?"

"Hello no!" She grinned like I'd just said something stupid. "It's Hulkamania all the way, brother!" She kissed me, and a hair from her fake blonde handlebar mustache stuck to my lip.

"Damn, facial hair feels weird to kiss."

"It's kind of a turn on. I like it when you haven't shaved," Harlow countered.

"Yeah, for me, not so much."

Elliott was still laughing his ass off when there was a knock at the door.

"I'll get it," he called, walking around the chair. "It's probably Logan, right?"

The sound of hysterical laughter could be heard from the hall, and I was worried for a minute that Elliott was about to piss himself. He walked into the room first, and I gave him a quizzical look. Then Logan appeared behind him in a yellow bandana, blond mullet, mustache, yellow spandex and a red Hulkamania wife beater.

"No way!" I burst out laughing at his expression when he noticed Harlow.

"Oh crap," Logan exhaled. "She's wearing it better than me."

"Trust you to steal my thunder, Smith." Harlow slipped my grip and immediately threw her arms around my best friend. I loved that they got on so well. "Good to see you, Logan," she said tackle-hugging him.

"You too, Hulk." He kissed her cheek before blowing raspberries like a toddler. "Damn. I just got a mouth full of your mustache."

"Now that's a phrase I didn't expect to hear from you," Elliott chuckled.

"Good to see you, man." I nudged Logan's arm as I passed him and made my way over to the fridge to grab everyone another beer.

"Where's your costume?" he asked following me into the kitchen.

"Just about to go put it on," I answered, passing him a beer.

"Give me five and I'll be back," I announced to the guys as I passed over two more beers and then jogged through to the bedroom. I reemerged a couple minutes later dressed as Father Christmas.

"You wanted to be Santa?" Elliott asked as I walked into the room.

"Yep, what kid wouldn't want to live in a toy factory and get to fly around in a magical sled?"

"Awe, I think it's cute."

"Thank you." I smiled at Harlow, pulling her up from her seat and then dropping myself into it and dragging her onto my lap in the process. "What time is it? I guess we should probably make our way over to the party."

"It's after eight, we should probably make tracks," Logan answered, so that's what we did.

Patron has a lot to answer for. It wasn't even past ten and Elliott and Logan were on their way to being wasted, and I wasn't too far behind. Harlow was the only sane and sober one among us, which was good because I panicked like crazy about her mixing alcohol with her medication. It's not that she couldn't drink at all while on her medication, just small amounts. Tiny amounts. Yeah, no, she probably just shouldn't drink. Ever.

"Why's your face red?" I asked Elliott as he dropped down onto the steps of the patio where I was sitting. The music from inside was still deafening, and I'd thought that the fresh air would sober me up. All it had actually done was make me acknowledge how much more buzzed I was than I'd realized.

"See that girl over there?" I looked up, and he pointed to a brunette who was glaring back at us with daggers in her eyes.

"Yep, what about her?"

"I offered her an examination," he said grinning like an idiot. "She declined with a slap."

"Are you surprised?" I asked incredulously. "Dude, that's super creepy. You're lucky she didn't mace your dumb ass."

"It's a numbers game, Ellis. The more girls I ask, the better the chances that one of them wants to play doctor with me."

"You do realize that if you get your ass kicked tonight by someone's boyfriend it'll be totally deserved, right?"

He shook his head at me like he couldn't comprehend that I wasn't down with his plan to harass every girl at the party and I laughed and nudged his leg.

"You're so whipped. I mean it, you're like a forty-year-old married man. No, worse, you're like my dad. It's college, Ellis. When else is it gonna be acceptable to hit on every girl in the damn room?"

I rolled my eyes so hard that I actually began to feel dizzy. "It's never acceptable, Elliott. That's the problem."

He made a whipping noise, and I just shook my head laughing. Anyone would think he enjoyed being slapped. "Hey, I'm going back inside to find Harlow," I told him, standing from the patio step.

I turned to make my way inside when he called out, "She was dancing in the front room last I saw her."

I made my way through the crowded kitchen, pushing past a Ken doll, GI Joe and Superman battling it out at beer pong. There was an astronaut passed out at the table, and Cinderella was patting the back of his neck with a wet towel while talking animatedly to a girl in surgical scrubs. I made it into the living room and had to take off my furry red hat and unbutton my coat—it was too damn hot in a Santa outfit. The house was crammed, the lights were low, and the music was vibrating through my chest. I caught a glimpse of a yellow bandana and blonde mullet and shoved my way through a multitude of drunken dancing classmates.

When I finally sidestepped a girl dressed as a flight attendant sucking face with what I assumed was a chef, I was positioned behind Harlow. I bent my knee into the back of hers making her stumble, then caught and tipped her back dramatically, like a well-practiced dance move. I quickly covered her mouth with my own and the crowd parted, cheering loudly. She tasted like beer and tequila and goddamn was she heavier than she looked! Or maybe I was just drunker than I'd thought. I opened my eyes and was met with bright ginger eyebrows and a pair of stunned eyes that didn't belong to my girlfriend. My mouth was still pressed on his. HIS!

"What the fu..." Logan murmured trying to crane his head far enough back to separate us. I let go on instinct, and he dropped to the floor in a heap before bouncing back up at the speed of light.

"Jesus Christ, I thought...I mean, you're wearing...and the hair! What the fuck, Lo? Why'd you take the wife beater off?"

"Because it's like a hundred degrees in here, Ellis! What the hell, man?" he shouted.

"I saw the spandex and the wig, I thought you were Harlow!" I answered taking in the horror on his face. We paused. The whole room was still cheering, and some dipshit was cat calling.

"Hmm, I always figured if you were ever to cheat on me it would be with someone a little less hairy," Harlow said from behind me. I spun at the sound her voice, and she was doing a crappy job of hiding her amusement. Her face was about to explode from the laughter she was trying to suppress.

"It's not funny."

"Oh come on, Ellis, this is *the* definition of funny," she retorted with a broad smile and crinkled eyes.

Logan's arm draped around my shoulders, and he looked at me before saying, "You're a shit kisser, Ellis. I think I feel a little sorry for you, H."

Harlow lost it then and began cackling like a traitor as I stood dumbstruck in a room full of people laughing their asses off at me.

"It's a good thing I love you two," I said looking from Harlow to Logan. I really meant it, and it wasn't just the beer talking. They were my people, and I'd do anything for either of them. "I don't just go making out with anyone."

"I love those who can smile in trouble, who can gather strength from distress, and grow brave by reflection. 'Tis the business of little minds to shrink, but they whose heart is firm, and whose conscience approves their conduct, will pursue their principles unto death."

— LEONARDO DA VINCI

CHAPTER

TWENTY-THREE

Revived

Harlow

Seventeen days, that's all it's taken. Seventeen days to be brought back from the dead. Resurrected. I thought I could introduce Ellis back into my life slowly. I'd told myself that I could phase him out gradually once I got closure.

I didn't find that closure, not even close. I found myself, or at least I feel like I am finding myself, when I'm with him. We're trying the whole slow and steady thing, easing back into being a part of each other's lives and it's been working, but God would it be so much easier to not love him. My head is telling me that being friends and going slow is healthy. My twisted heart is pushing for more. I'm a damn sadist.

Jarod's now not talking to my mom because he found out Ellis and I have been spending time together. He doesn't understand why she would let it happen, or that I would put myself through something like this. He told Mom that he refuses to watch the fallout when the shit hits the fan. I spoke with Jake on the phone last week, and he said he was indifferent about whether I want Ellis back in my life, just not to expect too much from him. He said he needed time to get used to the idea, and doesn't want to see Ellis anytime soon. I get it. I can respect it because I've felt the same.

Feelings change, and people alter, but I'm only realizing now that love is a constant. After all, you can only truly hate someone that you love.

"Tears come from the heart
and not from the brain."

— LEONARDO DA VINCI

CHAPTER

TWENTY-FOUR

Home is Where the Heart is

Ellis

'd promised Harlow that I would come over and walk Collin with her after work. I knock on the door but there's no answer. Her car's sitting in the driveway, and I'm pretty sure she wouldn't leave knowing I was coming over.

"Harlow!" I call out, opening the front door. "Hey, it's me!" I make sure to shout as I let myself in so she knows I've arrived. There's no answer as I walk through the house and head for her living room. I crane my head around the door noticing that the TV is switched on, a local news channel playing low in the background. I see a half-full cup of what looks like hot chocolate on the coffee table. I decide to check the kitchen, wondering if she's maybe out back with Collin. The dog is sitting in the middle of the kitchen floor when I walk through.

"Hello, boy," I say, bending to ruffle his head. That's when I notice her feet poking out from behind the island.

No, no, no, this can't be happening.

Panic grips me as I rush around the island to see her collapsed on the floor, her cell phone laying just a few feet away from her outstretched hand.

"Harlow!" I yell, grabbing her shoulders and turning her onto her back. She doesn't look right; her skin's always pale but has a rose tint to it. Today it doesn't—the pinkness is replaced with a sickly gray sallowness that sends my heart rate into overdrive. Her face is the same shade of gray as clouds before a storm, and she has a very distinct bluish tint to her lips.

God, no!

"Harlow, baby, can you hear me?" I shake her shoulders slightly, but she's completely unresponsive and limp. A tornado of dread forms in my gut, and I'm hit with flashbacks of her collapsing at the Bait House. I place my ear to her mouth and watch her chest. She's breathing, I can see her chest rising, but her breaths are far too faint and shallow to relieve my fears. I immediately go into autopilot and pull her over into the recovery position as I lean and grab her phone to call 9-1-1.

"You're alright," I tell her, trying to stop the tremble in my fingers as I attempt to dial. "I'm here, Harlow, you'll be fine."

The call goes through, the operator's voice merging with the ringing in my ears as she asks what service I require.

"Ambulance, I need an ambulance, now!" I bark out at the woman, putting the call on speakerphone and cradling Harlow. "Come on baby, wake up."

Harlow's eyes flicker before opening lazily as her head lolls to the side. I want to cry in relief as I answer the operator's questions and relay our location.

"Harlow, stay awake for me, keep your eyes open," I ask gently tapping her cheek in a bid to focus her attention on me. Her breathing seems more labored now that I've roused her.

Where the hell is the ambulance?

The first time this happened was different. Maybe it's because Harlow's now conscious, and there'd been no need for CPR that I left myself so unguarded against bad news. Or maybe it's because I didn't have anyone shouting out instructions about how to use a defibrillator, or fear that her heart wouldn't start again. Maybe that's why I assumed this time wasn't as bad. At the risk of sounding like a complete jackass, this time it seemed so much easier. Surely it couldn't be as serious because her heart was clearly still beating? She'd fainted, that's all. It hadn't stopped. Perhaps it was my naivety that was making the blow so much more painful. She didn't look as sick as when she'd had her heart attack, and even though I know how ill she is, how badly her health has deteriorated over the years, her sitting up and being conscious has wrongly given me a false sense of security. I thought it was a good sign. How could I be so fucking wrong?

I gulp, squeezing her hand. "The doctor told me you'd fainted, and for a second I was relieved. Jesus, this all feels like some cruel joke now."

Harlow's eyes are red, and there are thin purple marks running across her cheeks from where the string of her oxygen mask has bitten into her skin. It's now hanging loosely around her neck, and the clip on her finger is rubbing at the side of my palm where my hand's still resting over hers. I don't know how she's remaining so calm; she hasn't let a single tear fall. I wonder if she was expecting this news. I daren't look at her any longer, I can't disguise my pain as elegantly as she does so I rest my head against hers and screw my eyes shut as tight as I can. I kiss her forehead lightly, not knowing what else to do. One of her hands moves to her oxygen mask, pulling it from her neck and pushing it over her mouth and nose as she takes a deep breath. I move back, watching her draw in labored breaths, powerless to do anything other than be here so she's not alone to process what the doctor just told us.

Her body is shutting down.

"It'll be fine, Ellis. Don't worry."

My head whips back to look at her. She smiles. She actually smiles, and I can't comprehend how she can be so brave when I feel so weak. I should be the one to tell her everything's going to be okay. That needing a heart transplant is no big issue, and we can find a donor match inside of six to eight weeks.

Oh God, I feel sick.

Six weeks, that's what the doctor just said. Maybe a few more, but only if she's lucky.

Lucky, ha! What a stupid and callous word to use when you're telling someone how long they have left to live. I'm restless so I stand, then sit again, perching myself back down on the side of her bed, trying desperately to hold on to my composure and not break in front of her. I've just listened to the same ten-minute diagnosis that she has, but I seem to be taking the news much worse. I had to hold my breath as the doctor harped on about statistics and percentages. I've done my homework; I know what they mean. I watched her face stay smooth and unaffected as the middle-aged doctor—one I've not met before—told her how big of a drop there is in those percentages when you factor in her blood type. They say these things like we don't already know, and it infuriates me.

"There's a critical organ shortage, which means that we must strictly evaluate who should receive a heart transplant," he'd said. I wanted to grab his collar and shake him; scream that SHE should receive a transplant. "The major reason for transplantation is to improve our patient's survival. Being able to predict how a person will do after transplantation is the most important part of our selection process," he continued. I wanted to smack myself awake, I was sure it all had to be a bad dream, but I could feel Harlow's fingers squeezing mine, and knew there'd be no waking from this.

"Patients are divided into statuses and further divided between low, medium, and high risk. We're upgrading you to status one, Harlow. The final decision about listing you for a transplant will be determined by Dr. Butcher, he'll be by to come and assess you shortly."

That was only a few minutes ago, but I've replayed the words over and over. Harlow has been silent save telling me it'll all be okay. I don't know what to do. Should I say something? Should I let her sit here all quiet and numb? Should I give her time to process?

I can't take it. This is too unfair.

I just got her back.

"Do you need me to get you anything? Are you thirsty?" I ask standing and looking around the room for a jug of water. I need to do something, anything; I'm desperate to calm my anxiousness. I don't want her to see me like this. I want to be strong for her, and right now I'm having trouble faking it. The tension in my body has to be obvious.

She doesn't answer me and I turn my head, letting my gaze fall back to her. The only noise registering in the room is the hum of the machines and the steady beep of the monitors she's hooked up to. Dark shadows ring her sad eyes, pulling on every fiber of my being. I want to rip this room apart from one end to the other. I scrub a hand over my face and take a few steps over to the window. It faces out against a brick wall, and for some reason that makes me furious. But I remind myself that showing her how pissed I feel over this shitty fucking life she's been dealt won't do her any good. I need to make her feel better, not worse.

I take a deep breath and fill my lungs with the dry, sterile air that offers none of the refreshing sense of renewal I was hoping for. *God, I hate hospitals.*

"I'll go to the cafeteria and get you something," I say in a thick voice that scratches the back of my throat as I turn in confused circles. Her hand reaches out, grabbing my arm and steadying me.

"Will you stay? Just until my mom gets here?"

Her voice trembles and breaks my heart into a thousand tiny irreparable pieces. I don't answer with words. Instead, I envelope her body with mine and hold her as tightly as I dare. I swallow down my grief and despair at this cruel situation we're in, and inhale the scent of her skin, trying my best to commit it to memory. Softly, her cold lips kiss a brief path over my jaw in a slow and devastating caress that's more sorrowful than passionate. My resolve slips and I pull her closer than I think I have ever held her before.

Do not cry, Ellis. Hold it together—for her.

Her arms squeeze my waist, and her fingers press into my shoulder blades while I silently vow to never let her slip away.

The nurse who administered the inotropes told Harlow they'd take twenty-four hours to take effect and then she could go home. I'm not sure if she'll want to go to her place or her mother's, but one thing I am sure of is that I don't want to leave her. I need to stay with her—whether she wants me to or not.

Dr. Butcher passes by the doorway, and I take the chance while Harlow is sleeping to ask him what options we have for getting a donor. I'm a mumbling mess, not making much sense and I badger for answers to questions I already know he can't answer. Why is he so impassive? It pisses me off. I grab his shoulders, visibly shaking his calm demeanor.

"You have to help her now! She needs a goddamn heart now! Please," I beg. "Please."

He looks at me, his face betraying that he's not about to say anything I want to hear.

"Ellis." He gently pulls my hands from his shoulders and guides me to the brown plastic chairs lining the corridor. He sits beside me, resting the files he's holding on his knees as he raises his face to the ceiling and takes a deep breath. "I need to point out that to ensure donors' hearts are distributed fairly, there has to be a system. It outlines rules and considers time on the waiting list, the severity of a patient's illness, and then also the geographical proximity to the donor."

He adjusts his position, leaning forward and wresting his arms on top of his folders as he turns his face to look directly into my own.

"At the moment the average wait time on the donor list for a heart is around four months. That's for patients that are status one and do not have a rare blood type. I think that you need to prepare yourself for the fact that Harlow's body probably won't be strong enough to hold out while we wait for a donor, and if by some small miracle we do find a match, she still might be to too weak to survive the surgery."

I drop my head to my knees, tears falling faster than I'm able to blink them away as I grip the back of my head and sob. Not the quiet, reserved kind of cry, but the soul crushing, body wrecking moans that stem from the very core of you, stripping your throat bare and setting it on fire. My chest aches so bad that for a second I wish myself dead. Anything would be better than this feeling. Dr. Butcher's hand rests on my back, giving it a few pats before letting it fall still against my shoulder blade. I can't breathe, let alone speak, so I sit in the corridor bleeding out my sorrow and knowing there's only one way to make it end. There's no question anymore.

Last night was probably the longest night of my life, and I've experienced some pretty bleak ones before. They pale in comparison, every last one. I called Logan first thing this morning. He's on his way to my apartment and I don't know how I'm going to get through this, I just know I have to. Harlow's dressed and sitting on the edge of the bed when I walk back into her room.

"You ready?" I ask

"Yeah, my mom's finally given in and gone home. She said she'd be at my place tomorrow afternoon. I didn't think I'd be able to convince her to let me go home, she was pretty adamant that she wanted me to come stay with her."

"Yeah, I had to promise her that I wouldn't let you out of my sight for even a minute," I confess.

Her smile doesn't reach her eyes, but honestly, I'm just thankful that she's finding the strength to smile at all.

"Let's go home, Ellis." She says it like it's our home, and I don't know if she even realizes it. My chest grows tight, and I don't know if she realizes that she's my home.

"Everyone has been made
for some particular work,
and the desire for that work
has been put in every heart."

— RUMI

CHAPTER

TWENTY-FIVE

A Life Less Beautiful

Ellis

My bag has been packed for perhaps a week now, sitting in the corner of my closet like a ticking bomb ready to detonate. Today is D-day. I left Harlow sleeping—I couldn't bear to say goodbye, that's what last night and this morning were. We've spent every night together since she was discharged. There wasn't any need for a conversation or talking things through, our hearts did all the talking our lips couldn't do. Once she'd fallen back to sleep I slipped out, knowing if I stayed a minute longer I'd lose my willpower and wouldn't be able to do this. I drove to my apartment and collected my stuff before calling Logan's hotel. He's on his way over to the motel where I've just now arrived.

I pull the strap of the duffle bag higher on my shoulder, using one arm to cradle it against my lower back so I can bend and fill out the information card for the room I've just rented. The receptionist's eyes feel like they're burning holes into the side of my face while she watches me. "That's fifty-dollars even," she says.

I nod and slide her a note under the glass screen, noticing now that she's come closer just how young she looks. She's a skinny little thing, wearing too much makeup and not enough clothes. I'm hoping like hell she's not going to need to be present to let the authorities into my room.

"Here's your key, there's an ice machine outside room seven and check-out is at eleven." She drops a key into the metal bin and slides the drawer back so I can take it.

"Enjoy your stay," she mumbles, before walking back over to the stool where she was reading when I arrived. She blows a huge pink bubble until it pops and the gum smacks on her lips. I pause watching her for second as she picks up her book. The cover is all worn and bent out of shape; I guess this isn't the first time she's read it. Jesus, it looks almost as old as she does.

I take the key and call out a "thank you" as I exit the reception area and walk across the parking lot that's still darkened by the shadow from the nearby hospital to find room number four. The stucco around the doorframe is chipped and peeling, and the key jams in the lock. I have to twist and hammer at the damn handle while shoulder barging it for it to finally open. I stumble through into the room that looks every bit how I imagined it would, given its fifty-dollar price tag. There's no way anything in here's been updated since at least 1983. I pull the door closed behind me and make my way over to the bed. The blankets are a saccharine mustard color with a dark green palm leaf print that makes my eyes sore just looking at it. I drop my duffle and perch on the end of the bed for a moment.

It's suddenly all too real.

I look around and see a small desk in the corner, so I pull over my bag stuffed full with documents and instructions for the poor bastard that finds me. I pull out the notepad, envelope and pen I'd pushed into the top of the bag and take them over to the desk. If everything goes to plan—and I have to believe that it will, otherwise what's all this for?—this will be all over inside of the next twelve hours.

I just pray Logan can make it happen.

My chest feels so tight it hurts. It would be a cruel twist of fate to drop dead of a heart attack at this point, but I absolutely believe it could happen. All of this would be for nothing, and Christ, that scares me. My hands are trembling so hard I need to place the pen back down onto the desk and take a long deep breath.

You can do this—you have to.

I press the heel of my hands into my eyes. I don't want to cry, so I push hard, so hard that for a moment it hurts more than the ache in my chest. I doubt what I'm about to do will take the sting out of the tears I'm trying to make disappear or loosen the vice wrapped around my heart. I can hope, though. The pen is an unexpected deadweight in my grip when I pick it up and press it to the paper once more.

This is it.

The beginning of the end...

Dear Harlow,

Being in love with you hurts. It's the sweetest form of torture, but it's torture all the same. You consume my every thought, every moment, and every breath. I can't recall a time when I didn't love you. What did I even think about before you took over my mind? What do you suppose I had done with my hands before they were able to pull you close? When I close my eyes, it's your face imprinted on my eyelids, and it's your voice I hear, even in silence. I'm an ordinary man, but I love you with a brilliance beyond anyone's understanding. It scares me.

I realized today, or maybe I've always known, I can't live without you, Harlow. I sustain myself with your affections, and that's why it needs to be you who must live without me. You'll hate me at first; I can accept that because I know that when enough time has passed, you'll realize it had to be this way. I can't see any other path, I've exhausted all avenues, and when I weigh the pros and cons, the answer is glaringly obvious: I have to be the one to do this for you.

You've had my heart since I was ten

years old—you have it still. I gave it freely without any agenda, only a fierce hope that you'd one day give me yours in return, and you did. I don't pretend to know why, but you did. I can't even begin to express how terrified it made me feel—and how powerful—that you loved me back. I know the extent of the love I've given you, but it worries me that I'll never truly know what **you** received—does that even make sense? I'm wracking my brain, trying to figure out if I told you enough what you mean to me, what you've always meant to me even when we were apart, because you deserve to be reminded every day.

Every.

Single.

Day.

And more than that, you deserve to be shown. I hope you saw it, I hope you felt it, but above anything else, I pray you never forget it.

Goodbye for now. I love you.

Ellis

I drop the pen and fold the letter, stuffing it deep into the envelope as quickly as possible— the weight of what I've written makes my throat burn.

I don't want to do this, but I have no choice.

My head feels too heavy for my neck to support; I rake my fingers wearily through my hair, lean back on the cheap plastic motel chair and let out a frustrated blood-curdling scream. It bounces around the room, echoing off one grubby laminate surface to another. Streams of light tear through the shadows as the ceiling pendant swings from the occupants next door banging loudly on the paper-thin walls. The din of their television rises as I hear it being turned up—no doubt to drown me out. I could be murdering someone in here for all they know, and they ignore it, annoyed by the interruption in whatever drivel they're watching. Pay-per-view porn, if this motel is anything to go by.

I have to laugh a little—not because any of this is funny, it's not. But the irony of the situation causes a strangled moan, half disguised as maniacal laughter, to hiccup out of my mouth. I am about to murder someone in this motel room.

Me.

I go back to the bed and take out the DNR order that I'd signed at Lo's practice the last time I was there. I lay it out neatly, along with the folder's contents: documentation from the NC Donate Life clinic, my living will, documents verifying Logan Smith as power of attorney, and the copy of my medical records attached to the *Living Donor Consent Evaluation*. I registered with them so that most of the relevant tests and procedures the hospital use to evaluate suitability are already done. A big part of it is that you're required to undergo a psychiatric evaluation to determine competency and sound mind to go through with donation. Logan thinks it will help him once I've done the deed and he has to argue my case for the hospital to agree to the transplantation.

I'm not an idiot; I know the risks are high. I'm about to go through with this to save Harlow's life, and all I might achieve is ending my own. The medical staff can refuse to perform the procedure on ethics alone, but it's a risk I'm willing to take. The alterative is to watch the woman I've loved my whole life die before my very eyes. I won't watch that. I can't. I refuse to live a life less beautiful in her absence, and if I have to go so that she won't have to, so be it. I've taken so much from her already; at least this way she gets a chance to live, and that brings me peace.

I've had a long time to contemplate what loving Harlow means, and I've come to understand that love isn't a commodity; it can't be traded or substituted. You can't imprison it because it's transcendent, and you can't ignore it because it's a force of nature. Loving her means putting her needs before my own, and wanting what's best for her, even if it costs me. The only way I can make any real difference in Harlow's life is to not be in it. I know that now.

My cell begins to ring and I look over to the desk where it rests, then back at the bed, making sure everything is sitting in place.

Harlow already has my heart; her name was written on it from the first moment I met her, and it's been hers ever since. This just makes it official.

"In all the world, there is no heart for me like yours. In all the world, there is no love for you like mine."

— MAYA ANGELOU

CHAPTER

TWENTY-SIX

A Long Kiss Goodbye

Harlow

I wake up sore in all the right places, sated and more comfortable than I can remember being in forever, and for a second—just one delicious instant—I forget. I forget to be sad, and that alone is something to rejoice.

In our haste to make it to bed last night, I never drew my curtains, and the early morning sunshine is making me pay for that mistake now. It's entirely too bright, and I can't quite open my eyes properly against the light. I take a minute to soak up the feeling of waking with Ellis pressed beside me. For so long, I struggled with falling asleep alone. I wasn't used to not sharing my bed, and the empty space beside me served as a painful reminder that my life was irrevocably different. I still sometimes fix the pillows to mimic his form.

It's not like I haven't been with other men since Ellis. I even managed a four-month relationship last year with a guy called Max, whom Molly's husband Ben had set me up with. He was smart and funny and sexy, but it still wasn't enough. He was perfect on paper, but I couldn't make it last. They all felt like a poor man's replacement. Then add to that the whole issue of not knowing if I could ever have a proper future, one that included a family. My heart isn't strong enough to withstand a pregnancy and who'd want to hitch their wagon to a prospect as damaged as me? I still dream of what it would be like to lace up my shoes and go for a run, or throw myself out of a plane skydiving, even go rock climbing, and know that my body would allow me to do it. That's all they'll ever be now, dreams.

The absurdity of my situation is that I was prepared to die. I'd finally managed to wrap my head around it until Ellis reminded me what it feels like to live. I want those things now, and I want them with him. And this isn't fair.

I turn in his arms, my nose brushing against the warm skin of his chest, and I'm completely surrounded by his smell. I inhale deeply letting my lungs fill up and bask in the comfort of it. When my eyes open, Ellis is watching me. His face is relaxed but pensive.

"Morning, you."

"Morning," I reply, my voice still raspy with sleep.

He lifts a hand and gently traces the back of it across my cheek. I can feel his stare in every nerve ending across my body. Slowly, he moves forward, never looking away, and presses his lips on top of mine. There's nothing hurried about his kiss, it's slow and deliberate as if he wants me to really feel it. I do; I feel it all the way down to my toes and back up again. The tip of his tongue runs against my bottom lip, and I let out a soft moan at how wanted he makes me feel. No one has ever been able to kiss me the way Ellis does.

He rolls me onto my back, leaning over me and bracing his weight on one arm as he drags his hand unhurriedly down the length of my side to my hip, and gently squeezes. He pushes himself closer and whispers against my lips, "Let me make love to you."

I grab a fistful of his hair, and soft sighs turn into needy moans. Our caresses grow into greedy hands, squeezing and touching. I struggle to drag in enough air between kisses, and my panting is dizzying but oh, so worth it. He's kissing every part of me he can reach as he settles himself where he needs to be and then completely steals my breath, claiming me in one swift thrust.

I gasp into his mouth as my whole body reacts, tensing entirely. His kisses become needier and his eyes are glazed. He almost looks tormented, like he can't get close enough, kiss me hard enough, and it spurs him on more fiercely. I'm so breathless and lightheaded that all I can do is surrender myself to him.

I curl my hands into his hips, pushing my fingers so deep into his skin that I'm sure it'll bruise.

"Ellis," I whimper. "Oh, God."

"I love you," he whispers back. "Always."

I bury my head deep into the crook of his neck and my reply is muffled against his hot damp skin. There are spots in my vision, and for a moment I think I might actually faint. I grip Ellis harder, trying to stop the spiraling, and he groans as his body trembles against mine. His back stiffens, and he stills for a second and then he's shuddering through his release as I sink deeper into the mattress, and fall a little more in love.

He slowly lifts himself from me and onto his back, one of his hands finding mine and lacing our fingers together while the other quickly swipes at the wetness under his eyes.

"I'm not going to be around today," he says softly, staring at the ceiling. "How come?"

His eyes fall shut when he answers. "I have some important business at work, I can't put it off." He opens his eyes and turns to look at me. "I'll be thinking of you the whole time, though."

I smile as he places a quick kiss on my forehead, and then sigh. I don't want him to go.

I must fall back to sleep after he leaves because I'm woken later to a shrill beeping and an empty bed. I lean over, blindly hitting the top of my alarm clock. The damn thing doesn't stop, so I sit up, rubbing the sleep from my eyes. I reach for the power cord and pull it from the socket, but the beeping doesn't relent. I pause in confusion, and it's then I realize what the noise is: the pager that Dr. Butcher gave me is flashing at the side of my bed. My heart jolts in my chest, and my pulse begins to hammer in my temple.

"Oh my God!" I whisper shout into the empty room.

I jump from the bed and immediately reach for my phone with a shaken smile on my face. There's only one person I want to call. One person who understands what this means through everything that's happened—from my past to the present—and what this means for the future.

I pick up my cell, and I dial Ellis.

"True love stories never have endings."

— RICHARD BACH.

ALSO BY ELLE BROOKS

Promises Hurt
Forgotten Promises
Empty Promises

Reveal

Elle is a little neurotic; she functions on a tiny amount of sleep
and a huge amount of caffeine. Elle loves old movies, green
skittles and has an irrational fear of stormy weather.
When she's not locked away writing down the crazy stories that
occupy her mind, she can be found in her home in
East Yorkshire with her husband and two children.
Elle can be persuaded to do just about anything with the promise
of new shoes, a good book or a bottle of bubbles.
Oh, and she also love to write.

Elle is the author of *Reveal* and the Promises Series, including
Promises Hurt, *Forgotten Promises*, and *Empty Promises*.